FRANKLIN PARK PUBLIC LIBRARY
FRANKLIN PARK, ILL.

Each borrower is held responsible for all library material drawn on his card and for fines accruing on the same. No material will be issued until such fine has been paid.

All injuries to library material beyond reasonable wear and all losses shall be made good to the satisfaction of the Librarian.

Replacement costs will be billed after 42 days overdue.

AFTER THE

SNOW

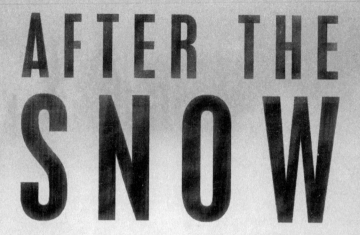

AFTER THE SNOW

S. D. CROCKETT

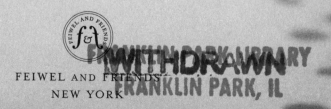

FEIWEL AND FRIENDS
NEW YORK

A FEIWEL AND FRIENDS BOOK
An Imprint of Macmillan

Library of Congress Cataloging-in-Publication Data

Crockett, S. D. (Sophie D.)
   After the snow / S. D. Crockett. — 1st ed.
      p. cm.
   Summary: Fifteen-year-old Willo Blake, born after the 2059 snows that ushered in a new ice age, encounters outlaws, halfmen, and an abandoned girl as he journeys in search of his family, who mysteriously disappeared from the freezing mountain that was their home.
   ISBN: 978-0-312-64169-6 (hardback)
  [1. Survival—Fiction.   2. Adventure and adventurers—Fiction.   3. Voyages and travels—Fiction. 4. Missing persons—Fiction. 5. Winter—Fiction. 6. Science fiction.] I. Title.
  PZ7.C8718Aft 2012
  [Fic]—dc23

2011036122

Book design by Barbara Grzeslo

Feiwel and Friends logo designed by Filomena Tuosto

First Edition: 2012

10 9 8 7 6 5 4 3 2 1

macteenbooks.com

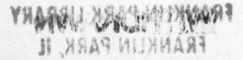

For Tim, Peter and Willow

In memory of:
J.E.B.S.
Margaret Heald

For they have sown the wind, and they shall reap the whirlwind.

—Hosea 8:7

PART I

SNOWDONIA

In the black season of deep winter a storm of waves is roused along the expanse of the world. Sad are the birds of every meadow plain, except the ravens that feed on the crimson blood, at the clamour of harsh winter; rough, black, dark, smoky. Dogs are viscious in cracking bones; the iron pot is put on the fire after the dark black day.

—*Irish, author unknown, eleventh century*

I

I'm gonna sit here in my place on the hill behind the house. Waiting. And watching.

Aint nothing moving down there.

The valley look pretty bare in the snow. Just the house, gray and lonely down by the river all frozen. I got to think what I'm gonna do now that everyone gone.

But I got my dog head on.

The dog gonna tell me what to do. The dog gonna help me.

The house look proper empty—don't it, dog.

You just sit quiet in these rocks, Willo.

The dog talking sense like he always do.

I reckon the fire in the house probably gone out by now with no one to feed it cos everyone gone and I been sitting on the hill all day finding that out. Everyone got taken away cos I seen tracks in the snow. They all gone.

Dad gone.

Magda gone.

The others gone.

But I don't know why.

Tell me, dog—what am I gonna do?

. . .

I find the dog in the heather one winter. Cold and dead. He been a big old black dog. Fur getting mangy. But one time he been leader of the Rhinogs pack cos I seen him enough times out on the hill. I bleach his bones out on a rock behind the house. Summer come and the skull just sitting there washed out and white, teeth still holding in his powerful jaw. Talking to me somehow.

That's when I know he been *my* dog. And I got him stitched up onto my hat with stones tied into his old eye sockets so he can see. I near beg Dad to help me cure the skin cos he say it *aint worth the effort*. But he do it anyway and I stitch that tattered hide on my coat. Dog gonna keep me warm and tell me what to do after that.

Sometimes before a hunt I get him up to my secret cave on the Farngod. Get the power of the dog strong inside me then. All his cunning. His sharp ears and cold eyes. The oldness of the mountain and all its knowing inside my secret place. And I need it inside me too. That's how I catch so many hares see.

Dad say, you're strong like a Spartan, Willo. Could have left you out in the snow and you still gonna keep screeching.

Dad say we're like Eskimos now. And when he tells me about Eskimos I got to believe him cos he been born before and knows what an Eskimo is.

See, Dad got this book in his box filled with stuff from before, and when he gets it out he lets me look in it, and there are pictures of Eskimos in that book but they got funny faces not like us.

Sometimes the grown-ups sit around the fire and give us a Tell about the old days—that's the days before everything got proper cold. Everyone got trucks and cars back then. And stuff like electricity and hotbaths and water coming out the wall.

That's *always* in the Tell.

But like I say, that was in the oldtime, before the sea stop working, before the snow start to fall and fall and fall and don't stop. Grown-ups like remembering all that old-time stuff—they make out it's so the kids aint gonna forget, but I think they talk about it so they aint gonna forget it themselves.

Sometimes I sit in the corner with my dog skull on. I know the stories roundside about, but the dog might like to hear them. Just like the little kids who sit at the front with their mouths all red and open like baby birds. They lap all that stuff up.

I only get interested when the grown-ups talk about real things—like what's been happening in the city and the stealer camps by the power lines. Cos that stuff is more exciting than listening to a bunch of weary thin graybeards talking about hotbaths and food. But I don't need to tell you that—you probably got your own bunch of boring grown-ups to listen to.

My dad though, he's all right. He's got enough boring old-time stuff inside him too, but he's my dad so I got a bit more time for him than all the rest mostly.

Sometimes he sticks his arms around me and spouts on about how much he loves me and stuff that makes me feel a bit different inside. I don't mind it when my dad spout all that soft stuff, except that I get this feeling sort of hot like a strong wind blowing into my head—and it makes me want to cry. And I don't like that so I tell him to *leave off* which he usually do.

But he's my dad like I said, and you got to respect your dad I reckon. My mum got dead when I been a baby still scrieking in my ass rags. That happen a lot up here when the snow been deep and your breath freeze in the air. But Magda live with Dad now, up in our end of the house. Magda's in charge of the little kids and I don't envy her that job. If it been me I'm gonna bash them all.

Bash. Bash. Bash.

But then I probably been just the same way annoying when I been small and Magda look after me too then, so she's all right, and she sometimes does that arm-hugging thing like my dad. But it's better cos she's careful to do it when no one's looking—she's clever like that, so I always keep my face and none of the other kids don't touch me for blubbing.

Cos if I catch one of *them* blubbing I'm gonna stick it to them. That's probably why I'm not the most popular. But I don't care. I catch a lot of hares. And no one sticks it to me.

But aint no point thinking on all that homespun stuff right now. The house gonna be cold but I got to sleep there or I'll freeze, even if the dog is scared. So I keep the wood on the sled and I tell the dog, *leave off worrying,* and I stick my head out from the rocks. But quietly all the same.

Dad let the trees grow just like they want and they near growing under the door so you can't see the house except from up here on the hill. Gray stones built up good and strong in the walls though. You can see it took a long time to put those stones together so neat and make them all square around the windows. Those old-time people been proper clever.

Magda get angry about once every month cos of those scrubby bare branches tapping on the walls but the grown-ups decide at the meeting that the trees are a good thing cos they keep the house hidden. Don't need anyone except farmer Geraint to know where we are and we been here near three years and no trouble, so Magda know to keep herself quiet now.

I hope none of the little kids got clever and hid in the attic or nothing cos I don't want no crying kid around my legs if I been the only one left.

That thought punch me right in the guts. Me being the only one left I mean.

But it aint no time for getting soft. Cos I seen some boys who gone soft. Usually with a girl at the Barmuth Meet. Then they start blubbering on to the girl and that aint gonna last long if you ask me cos the girl always talk about it afterward, and then I'm gonna find out.

But I aint too bothered about girls. Magda says I will get bothered. She says a girl is *what I need*. I don't know what she's talking about. It sound like I got something missing on me when Magda say stuff like that. I got all my arms and legs and even all my teeth still. So I aint got nothing missing so I don't see why I need anything—especially not a girl.

What I need, Magda, is a GUN. That's what I want to say. I mean I got a knife. My dad got it from Geraint last year. One to keep—just for me. I trapped a lot of hares for that knife.

But no gun.

Geraint can't get me a gun really. He's just a farmer. I mean, he knows deer and skins roundside about, but he aint gonna be any good getting a gun for a straggler without papers. Geraint's got a gun himself. He got papers for it. He let me and Alice hold it once. But if you got a license like he has I guess you can get anything you like.

Gun gonna make me feel pretty good right now. Being alone up here and everything. One day I'm gonna get one. I know where too. No one knows this but I been right over on the other side of the Farngod to the road where the power lines run. To a stealer camp. I reckon they got a gun and I'm gonna steal it if they come back next summer. I been there in the snow when they gone back to the city. I smelled it all roundside about and can get around in the dark, quiet like a fox. They aint never gonna know I been there. Until they can't find that gun.

I like the thought of that. Stealing from a stealer. I got a laugh inside me when I thought that up.

But I didn't tell no one about my plan cos Dad don't have no time for guns anyway. And he's gonna get angry if I tell him about the stealer camp cos he's as scared of stealers like they were starving dogs or something. But stealers don't move too far away from the power lines so all you need to do is hide somewhere quiet and far off if they come out. They aint gonna be wandering on the mountain long in their woollen rags.

But what does Dad know? He don't sit out in the freezing wind with his fingers working slower and slower tying the wire up on the trap runs. I'd rather sit with a gun and get a dog every now and then than sit up on the Farngod in the snow all winter for hares, even though I'm the best there is at trapping.

Somehow I got a knack for it from somewhere. Dad says it's cos I been born out on the mountain and don't know anything different. Maybe he's right. But I don't plan to spend my whole life on this mountain getting old and thin. My dad just waste his time dreaming of getting a license. When he aint dreaming he's getting angry about it. But they aint gonna give him a license. I know that. But he don't.

Geraint knows it too, and he should know cos he's got one. He's allowed to farm his deer and go down to the city and sell stuff and have a gun and everything. Government even give him juice from the power line sometimes and a big fence around his farm to keep stealers out.

My dad say it aint right that we don't get a license, we don't even get papers—so we can't sell our own animal skins. It make my dad angry. But Geraint don't come by too often and even I can see that we need him cos we aint never gonna get a license. That's for sure.

If my dad complain, Geraint—sitting up all smart on his pony and laughing—says, go down to the road and get a truck ride to the city if you don't like it, Robin. You can be legal as you like then.

Geraint find it funny when he say that to my dad. But my dad aint never gonna bring us all to some dirty cold tent in the shanties and not be able to move about or hunt or trap. No way. We aint gonna go down there to the government even if that mean we got no papers cos of it. When Geraint laugh like that at my dad he aint really being funny though.

• • •

"Let's have a look what you got for me then, Robin," Geraint gonna say, getting off his horse, all mean.

"We need oats and salt and more alum—and Willo wants a knife," says my dad handing over my hare skins and the snowshoes Magda make.

"And I need pencils for the children," says Magda. She always got her own list.

"I can give you a hundred yuan for these skins and ten for the shoes," says Geraint.

"A hundred ten? We need more than that."

"No papers, Robin—can't just sell them as easy as you think. A hundred ten's all I can do. But I'll get the boy a knife—a real Chinese one—and Magda her pencils on top. Because I'm trying to help. But nothing more."

Dad go back in the house then and come out with one of the dog skins he been keeping. I know he don't want to sell it cos we need it for making new boots.

"What about with this one?" says my dad, looking at Magda. She nod.

Well, there aint nothing Geraint don't know about fur and he see this dog skin is probably half wolf. He feel the skin with his short fingers.

"I'll give you two for the lot," says Geraint.

Dad aint happy with that. I see it on his face—but what can he do? He got to agree.

Geraint unroll his pack and give my dad a deer skin. "Hundred fifty for you when this is cured too." He got a bag of oats tied on his saddle and he give it to Magda along with a bar of soap. He say it's from Alice.

My dad's face goes a bit dark then, but he don't say nothing. We got the oats though so I guess Geraint aint *all* bad—cos he know he cheat us on the dog skin. After he got a baby with Alice and let her come up and live on his farm, he got softer with us like that.

"Don't forget the boy's knife," says Dad. "He nearly froze to death to get those extra skins."

• • •

And that's how I got my knife. But I earned it proper good sitting up on the Farngod in the wind tying snares.

When Geraint is gone my dad's dark face gets darker. Same as when he talks about me wearing my dog skull or when I don't speak to no one sometimes.

He don't understand that to trap a dog I got to wear the dog skull and not talk to no one. I got to get the power just like with the hares, only stronger cos the dog is cleverer than a hare in some ways.

But I think Dad got a dark face thinking about Alice, cos she was fourteen and they aint supposed to get a baby until they get older even though they can.

That's what all the grown-ups agree at the Meet.

But my sister Alice got a baby with Geraint when she was fourteen. And he's an old graybeard. But I don't know why it make Dad get that dark face. We got the oats. And the soap. I know Magda like the soap.

Magda puts her arm around my dad. "We got the oats, Robin," she say.

He push her arm away then. I think I see that Dad got wet eyes, but I can't be sure. My face gets all red when I see that and I go away from the house cos I got respect and he's my dad and I try and forget I ever saw it.

Maybe I'm gonna steal the gun from Geraint instead of the stealers. Be easier too cos Geraint's old and spends all winter getting thin on the mountain like his fathers before him. There aint much to steal in the middle of the winter see.

I don't know why I'm thinking of all this stuff though. There's more important things to think on now. Number One, I'm cold sitting here in the snow. Number Two, I got to have a plan. Don't know why I been talking in my head about the others.

You're thinking wrong.

Why?

But I'm pleased the dog is talking to me. This dog must be half wolf he's so clever.

You're thinking wrong because the others aren't in the house now. You're alone, boy. And gun or no gun, you've got to start thinking about things happening now. Like food and where you're going to sleep and what you're going to do if your pack has gone without you.

• • •

See, I know the dog gonna help me.

2

The dog telling me to be careful about going down to the house. But I aint got nowhere else to sleep so I creep out the rocks all stealthy.

I want to ask the dog about the tracks in the snow but I reckon the dog don't know nothing about them cos it's a dog and dogs don't know about those kind of things.

Must be something big come through here by the size of the tracks. I got a smell of it in the morning when I come back from breaking the ice on the water—which is why I gone and hid on the hill. That and Magda shouting out all angry.

I aint never smelt a snow truck up here before. I know it can't be stealers cos A it's the winter and B stealers don't have trucks. Only government have snow trucks. But what they're doing up here away from the power lines I don't know.

We aint doing nothing except sell our skins to Geraint without papers. Government need skins and people in the city need skins too. So where they think they're gonna get them if it aint stragglers like us freezing our fingers off in the mountains trapping hares for their warm gloves and boots? We aint stealers. We're just up here looking after ourselves.

Dad say we're beacons of hope. I never really know what he's got in his head when he talk like that. I don't know what he means. And I'm worrying about all that beacon-of-hope stuff and the government trucks, and my sled bash me in the leg cos I'm not concentrating on getting down the hill proper and I'm dragging it behind me. I got the firewood on it that I got this morning so it's good and heavy and running away if I let it.

. . .

The barn been open. I sniff inside. The goats gone. I close the doors. Shut them tight. Got to go and look in the house.

I'm right about the fire. It musta gone right out cos the house is cold as stone. And dark.

The door scrape across the stones. I stand inside still as I can, but my breathing sound really loud so I try to make it quiet, but that don't help much. I wait about half an hour just standing on the stones with my breath on the air, ready like a hare that heard an eagle.

"Anybody here?"

It's dark as dark inside.

I got to listen good, cos if someone been upstairs waiting for me I want to hear them creaking on the floor above.

But the only creaking is just the old house moving in the cold.

And there aint no answer.

I put my hand against the wall and feel my way down the passage. I can feel every lump under the cold plaster and I know my palm's gonna be dusty white if I can see it. I come to the coats still hanging on the pegs, the fur all soft. But no one go out without their coat in this weather? I don't understand why the coats still here and the people aint.

I got a funny feeling being all alone in the house cos my back's to the door and it's dark and I don't like it with no one here.

But like the dog say, can't stop to think about that now.

I get to the kitchen, the same roundside smells seeping out of the dark. I tap along the beam to find the box of tinder cos I got none in my pouch—but the box fall to the floor with a bang. It really make me jump and I got to stay still for a while more. But no one come leaping out the shadows so I reckon the house is safe for now.

The dog worrying me too much. Thing is, dogs can't make fire and stuff so they got to be more careful than us. That's the only trouble with wearing the dog skull. The spirit of that dog get right inside me sometimes and I forget who I am. That's what my dad say when he make me stay in the house with the others and do my reading with Magda.

I say, "Dad, I can read enough."

Cos I had to sit around with Magda all day when I was little, doing reading, and what do I need it for when I got to catch hares and get wood and stuff as soon as I got old enough?

Dad say it's cos I'm human that I got to learn reading and not spend all day out on the mountain thinking like a dog. I don't think Dad know about my secret place where I keep the animal skulls and get my power from, but I think he got a bit suspicious. I mean he just about let me wear the dog skull but he aint happy about it. I know.

Dad hit me once cos of it—the skull go flying across the room. *You're not a bloody dog, Willo!* He been good and angry. But the skull aint broken. I got a strong feeling that I hate him when he do it but it pass by the next day. Can't hate your dad. Cos he's your dad. And sooner or later you're gonna want to show him something clever you done, like catching a big hare or stitching a neat pair of gloves. Don't matter if your dad hit you or not—you're gonna want him to know what you been doing.

My dad got funny ideas about things. He always think things gonna change, things gonna get better like they were before. He says man thinks he caused all this cold and snow, but he didn't. Dad say the snow gonna come anyway after the sea stop working—he say the planet's stronger than all the people on it and gonna do what it wants. He say we just got to learn. Like in the days long ago. That's usually when he start talking about beacons of hope.

He got this picture see. He keep it in his book. I really like this picture. It got painted a long time ago by a man called Broogle. It's called *Hunters in the Snow*. What I like about it are the hunters walking through the village with all their dogs, I mean you can tell it's proper cold cos down below the lake is frozen over and the sky is all green like it gets. Raven sitting up in a tree.

The thing I like best though is just the dogs. The hunters got loads of dogs. Thin kind of ones with long noses and all of them sniffing along behind the men. But the hunters only caught a fox. Not much to eat on a fox. Maybe they catch it for its fur. But Dad say no, he say the hunters only got a fox cos it's a hard long winter. He says all the things in the picture were put there to say something like telling a story. So the dead fox supposed to tell us that the people aint be too successful on their hunt cos times been hard and there aint no hares. He say the picture got painted a long time ago when it been cold like now. He say it snowed for more than a hundred years and everyone got proper hungry and lots of people died. Aint no different to now, just less people and they know how to get on better then. They didn't have to go and live in the city then. They didn't have a government telling them it gonna get hot when really it aint—it gonna get cold. Dad say we're like those hunters, and people call us stragglers, but we got to be beacons of hope til things get better.

But if everything in the picture got a reason behind it then what I see is that raven black and hungry. Raven just sitting in the tree looking down on all those people in the snow. I reckon that raven looking at the dead fox the man got slung over his shoulder, and the raven probably thinking, *I could do with that dead fox, man.* The raven aint looking at the people in the village skating on the ice or the frozen mill on the lake or the woman making a big fire by the house. He's just thinking about food.

But I don't say nothing to Dad about that cos he thinks that picture telling us everything gonna be all right again one day, that the snow gonna melt and everyone gonna get on like before. I don't know about that, but I know the picture roundside about and I really like it.

. . .

Soon I got the fire lit good, and it make a soft dance on the walls that gets the whole room friendly just like it used to be. And warm too, which is good cos I got proper cold by now and everything shaking. My teeth shaking. My hands shaking. My legs shaking. All from sitting out on the hill all day in the snow.

Only thing is there aint no people here.

I aint gonna mind if the place been filled with kids shouting and scampering. No I aint gonna mind that whatever I say before. In fact, I almost wish a little one been clinging around my leg right now. Someone who's gonna tell me what happened, just keep me company.

It get to me in a moment.

I go to the door and shout out to the valley but my voice get eaten in the dark. Outside the snow's falling heavy. There aint no wind so the flakes are all big and round and soft and they just keep dropping down from the sky one after another straight down like they aint never gonna stop. Falling soft and silent, covering my footprints down the hill, covering the track marks from the truck. That kind of snow gets deep real quick. I aint never gonna know which way that truck went now.

Looking out at the snow falling down from the big black sky brings that panic bubbling up in my throat and I feel like I'm gonna choke if I don't stop it. I got a feeling terrifying inside me in the darkness. Dark and nothing all around me.

But the dog saying, *I think everything gonna be all right inside the house tonight, everything all right for now. The storm coming in and you just got to make the best of it.*

So I get some coats and lie down by the fire.

You can't do much except sleep or talk in front of a fire and I aint been tireder for a good long time. Sometimes sleep been the best thing. Maybe tomorrow gonna be better.

Yes, tomorrow gonna be better.

That's for sure.

3

I wake up wrapped inside the coats. It feel proper warm and good.

Then I remember what happen the day before.

I never hear Magda shouting like that before. And no one here. No one come back to the house.

Thinking that make me sit up pretty quick and heavy I tell you. I never got awake that heavy in my heart before, not even when my sister Alice gone to live on Geraint's farm.

This is ten times worse than that.

The fire nearly out now. I just sit there on the floor wrapped in all those coats. I guess my mouth been hanging open cos I'm staring at the fire but not really at it, sort of past it, and I can see my breath in the air and a thin line of light between the boards at the window cos a new day begun.

A picture of Geraint come into my head. It's a picture of Geraint up on his pony laughing at my dad. For some reason I can see his short dirty fingers like they're too big. They got to be the biggest thing about him in my headpicture.

Maybe I'm gonna go across the mountain to Geraint's place. Sell some skins.

You're dreaming, boy.

It's the dog again.

But I don't feel right about Geraint with that picture of him in my head. I'm not sure Geraint's gonna welcome me with open arms if I turn up at his place either. A dark thought cross my mind. Maybe it all got something to do with him? Everyone being taken away I mean. Maybe he tell the government about my dad living up here without papers, or something proper bad, something bad that got a bit of truth mixed in with it.

My dad say he aint causing no harm. He says, *if you're gonna be a beacon of hope you got to be positive and not think negative thoughts.*

He usually talk that kind of talk with Patrick when they're curing the skins. Sometimes I think he's talking to me with all that stuff but I act like I aint listening. That way he thinks I just been concentrating on scraping the skins cos if he thinks I been listening he's gonna ask me a lot of stupid questions I aint gonna answer.

Patrick never say nothing much back. But he listen pretty good all the same. I reckon he know my dad's head roundside about the amount of time they been spending together curing skins and my dad spouting on all the time like he do.

Patrick aint been with us for too long. He just turn up one spring day and say he want to stay. He virtually beg on his knees cos he been proper thin then and no warm clothes on his back. He just come right off the mountain. He say he been in the power plant at Wylfa. But he run away and then he find us all hidden up here. Which is lucky for Patrick cos I reckon a couple more days out on the Rhinog like that, and he's gonna wake up dead.

But Patrick's lucky in other ways too. Number one, he got here in the spring. Cos if he try running from Wylfa in the winter he's gonna freeze for sure, and if he come here in the snow we aint gonna let him stay anyway.

No way.

Not after that family from the city come up here one winter mewling and begging.

You can't afford to lose even one potato in a bad winter. That family, they just eat our food and then die anyway. When they die I think Magda put the baby out on the hillside cos I seen footsteps in the snow the next morning but I didn't say nothing cos the baby been near starved and covered in sores and crying all the time after the woman died and we got no milk or nothing for it. Specially not in the winter. Sick baby you can't do nothing for's gonna drive you mad with its crying, I tell you that for a fact.

Anyway, after that the grown-ups decide there aint gonna be no charity no more. Not in the winter. You got to work for your share all summer if you want to stay. But Patrick, he come in the spring and everyone see he got big strong arms on him even though he got no fat left on his bones.

At first my dad want to know everything about the power plant and trouble stirring in the shanties. But Patrick don't talk much about his life before. That's the first thing you got to know about Patrick. Cos you're gonna see from his frostbitten hands and the lines on his face that he want to forget all that kind of stuff. Patrick's just gonna get on with hauling wood and trapping and curing and that's that.

But he listen to my dad talking. My dad say the government

keep everyone blind by making them live in cold little boxes and not move anywhere without papers and send them off to work in the power plants or coal mines even if they don't want to, just cos they manage to get an extra pair of gloves or a stick of wood. I guess he's talking about Patrick then.

One time I hear Patrick say that after all the troubles, when lots of people die—government got even more control then and people start getting angry and my dad say yes, it's cos the people got scared which make them angry, and they got guilty they made all the bad weather happen—and while they been scared and guilty and angry and busy digging themselves out of the snow, government been planning. And the government got all the money and the food and the medicine and the keys to the trucks and power lines and the juice just like it always was.

Dad says it was gonna happen anyway and we just got to learn to live different, and it don't matter about all the oil and stuff especially now there aint so many of us. People just got to forget the government and learn to live different, and we're all gonna be all right in the end when the snows stop.

That's why he keep that picture, the one I told you about. I guess that's the kind of thinking he read about in his book—but it's just his thoughts so I don't see no harm in that. Patrick say it aint gonna be long before they're gonna come looking for people thinking like that. If we make it on our own up here, Patrick say, then more people gonna come from the shanties, and the government aint gonna like that one bit. Not one little bit.

We aint doing nothing wrong, but if someone like Geraint tell

the government that my dad thinking like he do, I reckon they defi-
nitely gonna send up big trucks to find us. And like Patrick point out,
it don't matter how many trees growing in front of the house then.

I been getting cold sitting here on the floor. That dark thought
about Geraint ratting on us don't get any better with thinking it
roundside about you see. A picture of his short dirty fingers pop
back into my head. And then I start remembering about how Alice
got a baby with him. And she only been fourteen.

Maybe this been how my dad feel all the time?

But if I get to Geraint's farm maybe I can sneak in all quiet and
stick it to him for ratting on us. Get him to tell me where Dad is. I sit
up on my knees and stir up the fire. Soon it start to get going again
and I put on my clothes. I left them hanging from a nail so they aint
all freezing and damp but good and warm. Part of me wants to
crawl back inside my nest on the floor, but I know I can't do that
today. The others are all gone and it's the first day of me being
number one. I aint never been number one.

I light a candle on the mantel. The kitchen look like it always do.
The stones on the floor all worn by the pantry door, scrubbed so
clean they almost shine. Big wooden table running along the wall
and the benches pushed out like someone just got up. They even
left the bowls and cups lying there like they been halfway through
breakfast. One of the little spoons that Dad carve when the twins
been born lying broken on the floor. I guess that been exactly what
happen. The government trucks come and pull everyone out the
house before they even finish eating.

I open the door to the pantry. Aint no one here to scold

me: *Get your hungry fingers out of there, Willo.* The pantry got that smell it always got from the onions strung up from the ceiling and the barrel of salted butter and the herbs and potatoes—and if you been lucky a couple of hare.

Government people didn't take none of our food by the look of it. Just the goats in the barn. Aint touched the big sack of oats and salt. They didn't take nothing except goats and people. People without their coats.

Maybe that's what Magda been shouting about so angry yesterday. Being taken away with no coat on this time of year. But she got quiet real quick. I didn't see nothing cos I was still down by the river then. I just hear her shouting out.

• • •

Maybe the trucks gonna bring everyone back sometime when they see we aint doing nothing wrong?

• • •

A scary thing happen then. I just been standing in the pantry, thinking about my dad and everyone without their coats. I can see the light coming through cracks in the boards at the window.

And something pass by. I see a shadow block out the crack of light for a second. It just go past the window. All quiet and quick.

I blow out the candle.

Stop breathing.

Someone out there.

My heart beat so fast. I hear the blood rushing in my head.

Hide. Somewhere dark and safe. And make it quick. Whoever is out there, soon they're going to be in here.

Dog always know what to do.

There's a door that go up to the workroom above the kitchen. I get in quick cos I know it's dark up there. And I don't know if that shadow I seen at the window gonna be coming inside the house or not.

And I don't know what that shadow gonna be like.

Hungry stealer with a heavy stick in his hand creeping about the house maybe. Sniffing me out. That's why my dad got all the boards on the windows.

My head been drowning in a bucket of fear. I feel like I'm falling— legs just aint got nothing below them no more. Falling down forever into a dark icy sea.

Get up those stairs, boy.

The dog's here to help me cos I'm tumbling in the freezing black and no arm to pull me out.

And I hear it now. At the door.

4

I stop breathing to listen and there it is—the front door open.

Footsteps in the passage.

I can see right in the room through the cracks in the door. I can see the glowing embers of the fire where I stir it up—anyone coming in gonna know someone been there. Maybe they're gonna smell me and come sniffing right up to this door.

And me only two steps up the stairs.

My guts feel like they gonna empty out of me but I got to keep quiet.

I hear footsteps going away to the other end of the house. Scraping and banging. Crashing around in there.

I creep backward up the steps a bit more with a taste, salty like blood, in the back of my throat.

That's right, aint it, dog?

Yes. Fast as fast can be on your long man legs. Fast as fast can be.

Upstairs, the workroom got tables along one side. And two big metal tubs for soaking skins in. I can see it all roundside in the dimness. But I aint looking at all that cos I realize pretty fast this room gonna trap me and I got to get up in the attic but my heart beating so fast and loud I can barely move.

Quiet I get up on the bench. I hope I'm gonna reach cos I aint the tallest after having no mum and the rest, but I reach up and I know I'm gonna make it then cos I feel that the ceiling aint as high as I think and I push the hatch up and over and hang on.

My arms feel like they gonna fall out hanging up there and that's when I hear it downstairs in the room under me. It been in the kitchen underneath and I been hanging in the air with my arms exploding and my breath catching so hard.

I hear the stranger downstairs breathing too.

In my head I see him look about the room. Head turning one way then another. Smelling me. Looking at the fire and the coats on the floor.

That gruesome thought work good on my arms I tell you, and pretty quick I pull myself up through that hatch like a rat's tail slipping in a hole. Pull the cover over quiet as I can. Face down above the ceiling, feeling my breath on the wattle. Whoever it is still pacing around down there. Then the pacing stop. I hear it.

The door been rattled.

I can hear the handle on the door shaking. And it open.

But the person coming up those steps aint worrying about creaking. In two seconds flat they come up those stairs. Now they been right underneath me. So close I can hear breathing—in and out—right under the hatch. Sniffing me out.

I hear a tinder strike.

Coc!

A dim glow seep through a crack in the hatch. I reckon they lit a candle down there.

And I got to tell you.

That voice?

27

I reckon I know that voice.

Sound a lot like Geraint.

Looking for stuff. Just like a stealer.

But he aint looking for me cos I hear him breathing loud and crashing about gathering stuff up. He's huffin and puffin down there stealing stuff. Stealing my dad's stuff. It take my dad nearly his whole life to get all that stuff. Tools like he got aint easy to get and Geraint's just stealing it all.

Well I aint gone, Geraint. I'm still here. I'm right up above you and I hear your dirty short fingers poking around in my dad's stuff.

You're putting your dirty fingers in a clean bowl of milk. And if you do that, you're gonna get it. You know it. You learn that pretty quick as a kid.

Don't go putting your dirty fingers in the milk, Willo. Twins gonna get sick, and you're gonna get a whipping.

Everyone know that right off.

So, Geraint. I'm gonna give you a whipping. I'm gonna get you. I squeeze my eyes closed, try not to think about what he's doing. Cos now I aint scared—I'm about to JUMP DOWN THERE all angry.

The farmer's got a gun and he's twice as big as you. You just stay put in your dark hiding place. You can get him later. We can think about that later when he's gone.

Dog come back. Just in time.

So I say my words to myself. In my head. Not like when I'm in my secret place on the Farngod. Got to say the words quiet now, just quiet in my head.

28

Big hares little hares
come into the circle
cos the dog gonna talk and tell you a story
bout the hill and the rock
and you scratch at the snow—

. . .

Coc! (Down below Geraint drop the candle—cos the light go out.)

. . .

—and dig yourself deep
when the wind and the eagle come.
But you aint gonna see me
with my trap and the wire—

. . .

Geraint ripping the boards off the window now.

. . .

—Big hares little hares
come into the circle
cos the dog gonna talk—

. . .

Something fall. I hear stubby hands scrabbling on the floor.

Geraint down there sticking his fingers in the milk.

But I know my words roundside about see, and saying them in my head stop me going mad and jumping right down there.

They really do.

5

There been little pricks of light under the eaves and my guts screaming out for food and water. It must be morning. Hands so cold I can't
feel them. Lucky I been wearing my coat else I'm gonna be frozen
near to death up here.

I got to come down sometime, dog. Cos I been waiting up
here since I hear Geraint leaving the house yesterday.

I push the hatch over slowly, inch by inch. Stick my head down
to see. It look like a whirlwind come in through the window and tip
everything about. But it aint no wind done it. On the floor I see my
dad's box spilled out under the bench. Pages from his book lying
on the boards. His writing all spidery on the paper. I drop down from
the hatch to the floor. Very slow I creak down the stair. The door at
the bottom is open. I stand and wait. Listening. Down to the empty
kitchen. Out into the hall.

The house been quiet. He been gone for sure.

I open the front door.

A pile of snow fall in across the step. It been snowing hard all
night by the look of it. Soggy gray light coming through the clouds.
No tracks left in the snow.

I guess I got a Plan B in my head. Cos I got to leave this place. I
didn't stop and think it through or nothing but I know in my heart

I need a Plan B. I don't need no dog telling me it's just a dream staying in the house all winter on my own. Not now.

I been thinking about Plan B all the time—but without knowing it. It sounds strange to say, cos every plan need thinking on. I mean I don't just kneel down and put a trap wire any old where when I'm gonna catch a hare. I got to think on where the hare gonna be running and look out for the tracks.

I'm gonna go to Geraint's farm. Make that old graybeard tell me what happen to my dad and the others. I'm gonna sneak in at night and tie him up in his bed. Tell Alice what a rat he is.

I got a racing feeling inside me. I got to get away before the freezing dark come down. While the snow still gonna cover my tracks and I got time to make a shelter out on the mountain. I reckon I got to be careful like the dog say. Cos Geraint got a gun aint he?

I eat what I can from the pantry and throw a pitcher of water down my neck, I been so thirsty. After that I get the firebox and the tent. I get them from the barn and tie them onto my sled. I aint never been allowed to take the firebox before. That firebox come with us on every journey. The men make it from the metal on the old truck they found. It's gonna be strange taking it without Dad saying yes or no or giving me some kind of lesson about how precious it is. But I reckon he's gonna understand all the same.

I go upstairs to my dad's room. To Magda's cupboard—to get the bag of tinder. You aint gonna believe what a fuss it been making those little charred sheets of tinder. Magda know everything about making stuff and looking out for herself though. She tell me she learn it all from her grandma in a place called Poland back in the old days. Her grandma plant a great big field of potatoes every year even though she been about a hundred years old, and every year she haul those potatoes up out of the ground and hang them in sacks in the cellar. Magda say her mum always writing letters saying, *Please tell Babula to stop lifting potatoes. We'll send you money.* But Grandma tells Magda, *I know what it's like to be hungry and I'll plant my potatoes til the day I die.* And she was right, wasn't she? Magda say.

Magda got her books in that cupboard. Some of them are proper interesting—like the one about every kind of disease a sheep gonna get if you just let it alone and don't go checking under its tail for maggots and under its wool for maggots and behind its ears for maggots. I tell you, sheep must be like a big pile of shit to flies, cos they sure gonna get a maggoty disease just by standing still. Or be falling off a cliff or giving birth in a snowy ditch or some other trouble if you're gonna believe what that book tell you.

The sheep book aint as good as *Robin Hood and the Silver Arrow* though. I get that out the cupboard along with the tinder. We all learn to read on that book.

A lowdown feeling creep up on me then kneeling on the floor. It come up from the smells on my dad's bed and the strip of light that fall across the boards and up on the wall just how it do every morning, but now my dad aint there breathing heavy under the covers with Magda opening her eye and smiling at me. She always hear you sneaking in when you want to creep under the covers.

I look at that homesome room pretty sad I tell you.

• • •

I finish loading the sled. I got my tent and the firebox, my trap wires, two fur coats from the passage, a goatskin rug, a few tools, and some firewood, got it all loaded and covered with a big leather hide tied down hard for when the snow start blowing wild and thick. I got all the food I can carry from the pantry in a pack. I step back into the passageway.

Dog telling me to leave quick.

It's still inside the passageway. That old house got a smell. It's the smell of wood and smoke and people. I aint never really thought about it before.

Aint no one to say goodbye to. It's a big lonely feeling closing the door. Stepping out under the scrubby trees. Walking away from the house with that deep winter snow blowing about. I feel like every step just gonna swallow me up. I really do. But I put my feet one in front of the other. Trudge, trudge, trudge. Cos the dog talking the truth. He say I'm gonna have to fight to stop the ground swallow me up.

I look back from the end of the pass but the wind blow a cloud of snow so thick I can't see the place no more. Just got to lean into the rope pulling the heavy sled and soon the river and the house and everything I call home been behind me and my eyes aint wet no more and I stop thinking I wish my mother aint dead in the snow when I was just a baby and gonna be here to put her arms around me.

• • •

I tell you, the wind soon dry that kind of thinking right out of your
eyes.

• • •

Bide your time, say the dog.
   An eye for an eye, say the dog.

6

That sled never been so heavy. It feel like dragging a dead goat over the hill. Really. All the time things sliding over and I got to keep stopping and tying it all in place.

The snow been outrageous and the howling wind whip up mean and nasty from over the peaks of the Rhinogs and pretty soon anything standing still gonna be buried forever. I got to remember that I aint got no home now. This stuff's all I got. Never know when I'm gonna need it.

But I feel like Scott of the Antarctic all the same. If you don't know, he been a great explorer from before. I read about him in my dad's book. Scott go out on a long walk in the snow to find the South Pole with a great big sled full of stuff too. But he never come back.

The only way anyone know about it cos he been pretty mad and write about himself in a book every day—even when he got stuck in the snow and know he's gonna die he write in that book. He know he's gonna die so he write *Last Entry*. Just like that. I mean you got to be some strange kind of person to write *Last Entry* down cos you know you're gonna die.

Funny thing is he don't need to go on that long walk in the snow with a great big heavy sled. He do it just cos he want to. Why don't he just stay at home in front of the fire? That's what get me.

Thinking all this stuff make me forget that on the mountain weather gonna come down on you quick as an eagle. Just swoop right down with real sharp claws. And if you aint got yourself ready for it you're gonna be in big trouble pretty fast. But I know that which is why I got myself prepared. I aint no stealer caught out in a storm. And I aint planning to write Last Entry in any book either. Dad always scribbling in his book, and I don't see no point in it.

The wind blowing up hard. Picking up the fresh snow and whipping it across the hillside in great sheets. Ripping at my coat seams. The shapes of the gullies and crags fading into the snowmist, storming far off on the flat hilltops. Got to get the tent up quick I reckon, or I'm gonna freeze to death in this storm. Got to do it now.

When I take my gloves off to get the tent out that wind near cut my hands off. The cover on the sled slapping about in the gale. Got to use all my strength to hold it down, get up the poles, and haul the sled round. But in the end I got it done and struggle under the canvas with the firebox and an armful of wood.

There been a stillness inside a tent when you leave the wind outside. If I got any advice to you it's gonna be A don't forget your tinder and a strike and B keep it nice and dry. Without that you aint never gonna start a fire in the wet and cold. Believe me. You're gonna freeze to death pretty quick.

That's one thing the dog never gonna think of cos a dog just turn his tail into the weather and make himself a hollow in the snow for the night. He don't make no fire cos like I said earlier, a dog's a dog.

It come to me that Geraint's gonna be out in this snow too.

And I hope he aint got no tinder in his pouch. Or no firebox neither.

I reckon this storm gonna be sitting on top of me for a few days yet. I just got that feeling. But I got the sled downwind of the tent and I got enough fuel if I let it burn real slow, got some food, got a warm goatskin rug to get under.

But I find out that my tent aint as strong as I think—and every time the wind gust up hard and push it over at the front I got to go out and fix it. It sound pretty easy when I say it like that but it aint easy when you been shivering under the rugs and you got to fight your way out the tent and get near blown off the hillside and covered in snow. You know you only been a breath away from getting eaten by the cold even if you aint thinking it out loud.

The snow blast at me in great sweeping drafts—it sting in my eyes and get down my coat and the whole thing get to be a proper fight. I shout pretty hard at the wind and the snow and myself too for not making that tent good and strong. If you don't get angry sometimes you're gonna get trodden on or swallowed up or just plain washed over.

But after a while, the snow got blown up around the tent in drifts. Kind of peace reign then with just the ringing of the wind in my ears. So I eat a bit and got down under the furs and a laugh got up inside me real strong. I don't know why but I been thinking about that man Scott again, thinking on him and his friends on their mad walk to the South Pole. I mean it's pretty funny, aint it? It aint no wonder they never come back from their journey being so mad as they all been.

But I'm gonna be all right for a few days I reckon if I still got a laugh like that inside me. Ground aint yet gonna swallow me up. Few days tucked safe in my tent gonna give me plenty of time to think what to do after the storm too. Where I'm going and the rest of it.

7

After the storm stop raging I sleep good and proper. When I wake up and stick my head outside I see that the storm clear the sky. New snow sparkling and crispy white.

You can see Trawsfinnid Lake from up on the other side of the Farngod and over the valley where Geraint got his farm. That's where I'm headed. But first I got to go to my secret place on the Farngod to get the power and say my words. Get the dog inside me strong.

The way to the Farngod gonna take me low down through the pass. If the weather turn bad again it aint gonna catch me out so quick there. I pack up the sled and pull the rope across my chest. Hunger starting to grow deep in my guts. I strap on the snowshoes, lean into the weight of the rope and drag my load down through the crags, rutting the fresh deep snow.

Thing is the freezing wind gonna eat you up if you just let it. So I guess I know I been good and lucky that I aint frozen to death like a stone up on the hilltop. It bring me a lowdown feeling though— thinking on my good safe home I left behind.

• • •

It been thinking like that, and along that side of the pass, that I come on an old house buried in the snow.

Aint a good house, just a couple of boarded up windows and a small stone shed on one end. I shout out like I always do.

If you just jump up in front of a house without shouting out then maybe you're gonna get a surprise you aint been looking for.

I guess she hear me shouting. The girl I mean. She come out in the crack of the door. She got red lips. That's the biggest thing I notice cos the rest of her's so thin and washed out. I mean she got the same color in her skin like a greening winter sky. Staring at me with her red lips like blood on the snow.

I aint expecting no one to be in the house cos it's got to be the sorriest place I ever seen on a cold winter's day. Aint expecting no one to come out of such a place with no smoke coming out the chimney or nothing. The girl got bits of stuff all tied around her feet and just rags hanging off her.

After she stare at me a bit I come closer and she got a look on her face proper scared then. I forget I got my dog skull on, so maybe she just see the teeth and think I'm some sort of dog man come to get her in the snow. That's the kind of thing people always thinking. They always got to see some sort of scary thing in everything. I know I been like that too so I aint saying it's strange. And she duck back inside that house real quick and shut the door.

"Where's your dad?" I shout it out not too scary or nothing, but there aint no reply so I say it again.

"Or your mum. It don't matter. Mum or dad."

Still no answer. I go right up to the door.

"I aint a dog," I say. "It's just a dog skull—aint gonna do you no harm. Just on my way somewhere but I got stuff your mum or dad gonna want on my sled if they got something for me to eat."

I don't know why I say that, cos if the girl is anything to look at, then her mum and dad aint gonna have nothing to give me. I look around me. The dog tell me I been a bit stupid shouting out all the nice things I got on my sled. I pull back a little from the house which aint too easy with my heavy sled which don't want to turn around in a hurry.

"He isn't here." It's the girl. She's saying something through the door. "He isn't here."

I drop the rope on the sled and look around again. "What, your dad aint here?"

"He went outside."

"Well I'm gonna be on my way cos it's too cold to stand around waiting aint it?"

"Have you got any food for us?"

I don't know what to say cos I don't know who's listening now and I got a bit jittery about this strange place. I start thinking that thin girl in rags look fresh out the city. I never heard of no one living out this side of the Farngod and the graybeards are gonna know about anyone so close to us, I'm sure of it.

I take my knife out my belt then, real slow and steady. The wind blow up eddies of snow and whip them around the front of the house. I'm gonna talk to the girl like I don't know nothing.

"I aint got no food," I say. Then I step along the front of the house to where the shed is. It's all broken down but I can see that one time it probably been a good strong little barn. But that was a long time ago and now the walls are all pitted where the stones fallen out and the roof aint been fixed up too good either.

At the front is a low opening musta been a window. The ledge is deep in snow. I got my back to the wall and the knife in my hand. That knife that Geraint got me, it got a good long blade that go right up in the handle and it's made of proper Chinese metal so I can sharpen it easy. Which I done a lot, which make me feel better standing here like this, not knowing what gonna be in that shed. Maybe that girl aint really on her own and her dad or someone waiting to get me. Cos hungry cold people aint the nicest. That's true for sure cos I seen it with my own eyes.

But I got to look inside now and my mind racing all over the place, and I feel like I got myself in a Broogle picture where everything got a reason to be in it.

"Have you got any food for me and our kid?"

I can hear the girl's voice shouting through the cracks in the door back there but I don't say nothing, just lean around into the shed and look through the window. It's dark inside, and the floor is covered in ridges of snow that blown through the open door at the end. Cold and dark.

Then I see something. In the corner. And I see it's a person. A pair of bony feet sticking out from under a pile of rags, the toes all black.

And the feet aint alone. They been attached to a body covered in rags.

On the floor of the shed.

All twisted.

There's an arm upright, the fingers sticking out from under the rags too. Dead body just thrown down on the floor by the looks of it.

I pull my head back and lean against the wall.

I tell you my heart beating like a drum now.

The girl's voice come from the house. "Have you got any food? Just a tiny bit of food."

I'm still leaning against the wall. "Where's your dad?"

"He went out after the woman to get some wood, but that was two days ago. I'm waiting for him to come back and make it warm and get some food. Have you got a bit of food? It's just me and our kid Tommy who wants a tiny bit of food. Please."

I hear the door open, and her head peek out, staring along the front of the house at me leaning back against the wall. And hanging around her legs is a little kid. A boy. He aint no more than about five and he got the same white face and green under his eyes and he got his little bony hand sticking out the door at me as the snow blow up around the girl's legs.

"Want food." He say it all quiet.

And I know then they alone, and they got the same color skin like the dead body behind me in the end of the house and I know their dad aint coming back.

These two kids just gonna die out here.

"Want food," say the little boy.

But I can't stand it no more. This place is wrong. I know it.

You may as well throw your food to the storm. You don't want someone else's sickly pups suckling at your dugs. You've got to get up to your place on the Farngod before nighttime.

The dog talking to me good and slow. And the dog talking sense.

"Want food," say the little kid.

"I'm gonna come back later," I say.

"Don't go," say the girl.

"I'm gonna come back later." I pick up the rope from the sled.

Those starving kids calling after me with their hollow eyes and thin voices, but I don't look cos I know I aint coming back, and I just got to go away from this place.

· · ·

An eye for an eye.

· · ·

Just pull myself away from that rotten body lying in the snow and those starving kids begging for food and lean forward into the rope and pull my sled out of there as quick as it gonna go.

8

I got proper angry with that sled bashing my ankles—the sweat starting to soak right through me which aint good out on the side of the mountain like this. Once the sweat wet you through, you're gonna end up like an icicle.

I shout at the snow quite a bit. The shouting aint helping me I know. It probably make me sweat more and my face got red I can feel it. But sometimes when you're gonna be that angry it aint something you can stop just by saying *it gonna be a good thing to stop.*

It's like a mad dog got inside me, just jumping around under my skin like he's walking on a fire and frothing at the mouth and barking, and nothing gonna stop him except going back for those kids.

But I don't reckon it's *my* dog making me feel like that cos my dog's a clever dog and he don't get the frothing-mouth disease and go all mad on the mountain. No, he's the sort of dog who gonna curl up tight with his back into the weather like a sensible dog.

And my dog been good and sensible. He told me right when he make me go quick away from those kids just standing all frozen and starving with their dark eyes begging me. They're just gonna be *deadweights.*

It got to be a mad dog inside me now telling me to go back. The mad dog that go dancing around making me shout at the sky and the ground and the sled and get that hot wild feeling.

I got to get to my place up on the Farngod but I can hear a telling beating through my skull. The telling spit at me with every snowflake stinging in my eyes. The telling dancing about on hot coals shouting like a lunatic but I don't want to hear it.

• • •

My sled heavy enough. I been hungry enough. But all the mad dog see is that little girl and her red lips.

You don't want sickly pups suckling at your dugs. Might as well throw your food to the storm.

I been proper pleased to hear my good clever dog talking all calm to me. I aint gonna hear him if I shout all angry at the sky like that. Good clever dog gonna make it all right. He gonna tell me what to do. Maybe he gonna bite that mad dog on the tail and make him roll over on his back all cowering like dogs do when a bigger stronger dog jump on them. Dogs sensible like that.

If you been wondering how I know so much about the dogs—well I got it mostly from watching them. Cos sometimes in the summer after the melt, I just lie down behind a rise on the hill and watch if a pack of dogs make a summer camp up there. I got to be upwind of them and quiet and still and the rest of it. But once I got myself all tight behind some rock, I'm gonna watch those dogs all day if I can. You got to know about dogs cos trapping one gonna be proper difficult if you don't know how they move about and how they do their being-a-dog stuff.

46

Sometimes when I been watching them I wish I been a dog. But in a pack there's always one dog who get bitten and scuffed and only get the worst bits of the kill to eat and I wouldn't want to be that runty dog unless he turn around one day and grow big and strong and clever and stick it to the other dogs. Then I'm not gonna mind being the runty dog. Cos sometimes the runty dog got a pretty interesting character. Runty dog looking out for mean tricks all the time so he's gonna be pretty clever too.

I never try and trap a runty dog, not just cos he probably got dog-bitten fur—that aint the reason even though it's a good reason. No, I aint gonna try and trap the runty dog cos I reckon he need every chance he can get if he want to jump up big and show the pack what to do one day.

I say I want a gun so I can get a dog real easy. When Geraint let me and Alice hold his gun I got a big strong feeling that I'm gonna shoot at anything that move if it been mine. I'm gonna be able to shoot all of them if I want. Just like that. Bam. Bam. Bam. Get plenty of dog fur then.

I ask my dad about that feeling and he laugh pretty loud and tell Patrick what I been saying. Patrick laugh good and proper too so it's obviously a pretty funny thing I say even though I can't see it.

My dad tell me a story then about the old days. He say, *Let this be a lesson.* But it was quite a good story not like a lesson at all. The story was from the time long before the sea stop working. Back then you're gonna be able to sail across the sea to America cos the cold aint come then. Now near half America got snow like us but no one don't care much about America anymore, Patrick say, everyone just looking east these days.

Anyway, back in the days before all that, lots of people sail across the sea to America, cos America got lots of beautiful hills and rivers and forests and hardly any people living there. And they got all these grassy plains covered in big animals with thick warm fur, and these animals been called bison. Anyway, the people who live in America before everyone come across the sea—they called the Indians—they gonna be sitting up behind a rock with a spear or bow and arrow, watching the bison. The Indians got funny names like Chief Touch the Clouds and Chief He Dog, so I got pretty interested in that. And those Indians follow the bison cos they got tent houses they can move called teepees. And they follow the bison across the plains and kill one every now and then. And that bison make all the clothes and tents and food their family gonna need, which is pretty lucky for the Indians being surrounded by so many of them.

But then the people come from across the sea and they got guns. And when the men with the guns see the bison all standing around eating grass in the sun, they got proper excited. They don't need to sit behind a rock and live in a teepee to catch one. They just shoot them. They shoot and shoot and shoot, and the shooting got to be just a game my dad say.

And then one day, everyone wake up and the plains just covered in dead bison rotting in the sun. And that been the end of that. No more meat and fur and leather. No more bison.

Bet the Americans wish they had all those bison now, Patrick say.

Anyway, that was the story my dad tell me. And my dad tell me, *That's the truth about guns.*

I guess that been the lesson cos lessons are always about things you want to do that been wrong things in the end. But I still want a gun. Just now I know you got to watch out and not go mad if you got one.

I reckon if that mad dog in my head got a gun he gonna shoot just about anything. Even the snow and the wind, maybe even himself. But I think the mad dog sleeping now.

• • •

I got to be quite close to the Farngod. I come up on the west side of the mountain and I reckon soon enough I'm gonna find the ring of stones. Magda say the ring of stones look like a crown of thorns. But no one gonna make a crown out of thorns. Girls especially. They gonna make a crown of flowers in the summer maybe. That's the kind of thing they do at the Barmuth Meet anyway. Magda say some funny things sometimes.

My dad tell me the stones been as old as old can be. Older than writing and books—and crowns. Big stones all sticking out of the ground like teeth. All in a circle. He said it been made so long ago the people who did it probably didn't even have names back then.

The sky grow pretty dark in the east. I got to find some place to bed down and get a fire going. Got to get a brew on or my sweat gonna be ice before I know it. Gonna be colder than those kids down in the pass.

I always been lucky though. Cos right now when I reckon I

been proper lost and night coming down and the rest of it, I see a shape on the slope above me.

Arcing off the ridge—a broken wincone with half a blade still on. I stop and pull the rope off my shoulder and stand up straight. The snow pelting down around and it been hard to see for sure but I reckon I turned up right in the middle of the winfarm without even knowing it. I can see the busted towers over to the north and up on the ridge that broken wincone lying on the ground.

A wincone, especially one with a blade still on, is a pretty impressive looking thing I tell you. Big and smooth and lying on the ridge like a great broken bird just fall out of the sky.

The last haul up to the ridge been the hardest part of the day. The hill so steep and the snow got proper deep here.

The wincone aint got nothing left inside it—stealers probably got that right off a long time ago. But that been a good thing for me cos I'm gonna be able to get inside. That's what I mean about lucky. The wincone big enough even for my sled, and I use the last light of the day to fix up a good entrance tunnel in the snow and get the firebox going. Nearly as good as a house in here.

I feel good and snug. I aint got to worry about the wincone blowing down or dogs getting in or nothing. Tonight gonna be a good night for thinking about Plan B a bit more. I make myself a warm bed and get myself tucked in tight. I can just about make out the writing on the inside of the wincone above my head. I been studying it as the fire go out. It say NEW VISTA ENERGY in black letters.

It gets me thinking of the old-time stuff my dad and the other grown-ups always talk about. They say the winfarm been made to make power back in the old days, but the old-time people find they don't work too good in the cold cos the blades can't turn. Everyone been thinking the government done a good thing building the winfarms, but it aint worked, and now they all broken on the hilltops. Patrick say the government shoulda been making more nuclear plants like the one at Wylfa, which is strange cos he run away from there. *Maybe you're right,* says my dad, *cos then it wouldn't be ANPEC who got all the money and power.* But my dad don't hold too much with any of it really. Say we got to look after ourselves. I really wish my dad been here so I can ask him more about all that stuff. My dad usually got an answer for everything.

I got a nasty feeling then like I been a stone just tossed into the middle of Trawsfinnid Lake sinking slowly down into the black water and no one aint gonna know I'm there cos once that stone go under the surface it's gone forever.

I tell you I got a big panicky feeling lying in the dark in that wincone all alone thinking I been a stone sinking in the lake.

9

The mad dog slip right back inside my head.

It must be about four o'clock in the morning. That time when everything look worse the more you think on it.

I stir up the fire. I got to talk to the dog, but the stones in his gray eyes staring at me flat and cold. I stroke his bony skull. Why aint you biting that mad dog on the tail? I ask him. Why aint you getting him quiet?

I'm tired, boy. Let me rest.

But I need you dog.

I said, let me rest.

The mad dog been proper excited finding me awake at this bad time of day. He's practically dancing for joy.

Tell me dog, what am I gonna do?

But my good dog just close his eyes and sleep.

The mad dog gonna kill me I know.

He got me thinking about those two starving kids again. He's standing there barking cos he don't want to leave them all cold and starving with no mum or dad or nothing. Mad dog live like he permanently in summertime with plenty of food, and he won't stop barking and tugging on my sleeve with his telling. He just won't stop. He say, *Remember the leveret.*

Once I come back to a snare I set and found a leveret under the hare. It was young but it got its eyes open and everything. Just sitting there helpless with its ears pinned back all soft and silky and a bit pink. Sitting there and its mother all strangled in the noose. Just a bit of blood dropping out her nose onto the snow. That's what that little girl with her red lips remind me of. The blood on the snow and the young hare lying all scared and flat when I go to pick it up.

I never lay my snares so early again after that.

Course I put the leveret up in my place on the Farngod but it been too small so it die anyway. I didn't keep that tiny skull on a stick. I just bury it up there. I didn't tell no one. I been sorry about it—I really am.

Maybe the mad dog aint been a mad dog at all. Maybe it been that mother hare. I got to go back for the kids see, cos if I don't then the hare and the mad dog gonna come back to me night after night til it been too late and I'm gonna go mad if it do that.

Reckon I just get those two kids and take them down to the power lines soon as the weather clears. Leave them on the road. A government truck gonna come by cos they keep the roads pretty clear underneath the pylons, even this time of year. Then I reckon the government truck gonna take the kids to the city—that's where I reckon they come from—cos they're only kids after all, aint done nothing wrong. And it aint far off my way.

• • •

First light come up. My dad aint gonna be too pleased knowing I left the tent and the firebox and all the stuff up in the wincone

53

but I aint hauling my sled up and down the mountain heavy like a boulder. I reckon I'm gonna need to take the sled cos those kids aint ready for a long walk in the snow. No way. It been a dangerous tactic I know cos you never know when the weather gonna come down. But really I aint got no choice. And Dad, you aint here now.

I put some oatcakes in my pocket. Got my tinder and strike too.

Outside the wind look manageable but I got to tread careful over that deep snow, even in snowshoes. Back down the mountain, back down into the pass, back to that house stinking of death and the thin girl with the red lips. And I got to be quick so I can drag those hopeless kids back up to my camp in the wincone before night come again or I'm gonna be as starved and frozen as they been. Another thing I got to be careful of is losing my way cos snow's like a blanket that make everything look the same.

You see what I mean about the mad dog trying to kill me.

But my feet just fall down the ridge in the deep snow and it aint too hard to see. The wind stop bluffing around my ears when I get down off the hill. It really tire you out when the wind don't know what it's doing, cos one minute it gonna take your hood off and the next it lie so still there aint gonna be a ripple on water.

All across the hills the snow fold down into the crags and glens. The gray sky touch the hilltops so you can't see where the hills stop and the sky starts. But that gray sky take the sting out of the cold which is one good thing.

I struggle and heave and make my way back down into the pass best I can. I got a feeling pretty tired and washed out. Aint really been too warm or full in my stomach these last few days. And something jittering about inside me. I aint used to being Number One; that's the truth.

The peaks of the Rhinogs just grow out of the valleys, rising up from the sea. One minute you been lost in the snow-covered heather in the lee of a crag and the next you get up on high and see the sea stretching away, far off from Harlech to Barmuth. It's a mighty big place.

So it's good when I tuck down among the craggy rocks at the bottom of the pass and follow the hill. I stop when I round the bluff.

There it is. That ragged little house. I pick my way a bit careful down toward it, remembering those black toes sticking up out of the rags. I wonder how that body got there and who put it there and all that gruesome kind of stuff that make me want to turn back. But everything good and quiet. I go down through the pass and stand out in front.

I got a funny feeling. I don't like this place. Really. I'm glad I aint those two kids been left here all on my own. They sure gonna be pleased to see me.

I bang on the door.

"It's me," I shout. "I come back with some food."

I wait there for what feel like a pretty long time but nothing happen. No sound come from in the house or nothing.

I bang again. Feel like someone watching me which don't feel good.

"It's me who came with the sled," I say. "Said I gonna come

back with some food for you and your brother. I aint lying see. I aint gonna just leave you."

Right by the door is a small boarded window and I step up to it. Maybe I'm gonna be able to get a look inside cos I still don't hear nothing.

But right when I lean forward to look through a crack in the boards something catch my eye. Down in the snow. I stare down and my eyes follow the footprints. Down to the end of the house. Down where the shed is.

And as I follow those tracks, I raise my head up and I see him.

His head coming out from round the end of the house. Like he just heard me. He aint pleased to see me here cos I can see he's been busy. His mouth all dirty and red.

That hungry dog will kill you, boy!

Good dog calling me loud.

"Let me in!" I shout at the door.

The blooded dog aint moving yet but he's gonna. He's growling low down in his throat. He's big and thick in the shoulders—black turning to brindle gray.

He come right out from around the end of the house and stand foursquare straight at me, head and shoulders flat and low. He aint scared of me—I see it then.

. . .

Big hungry dog with manblood on his mouth.

. . .

"Hey, girl. It's me. Let me in or the dog gonna get me!"

. . .

The growling dog step forward. Our eyes meet. For that moment everything been hanging in a dark tunnel between us. His spit splatter out across the snow as he rage deep down in his hungry guts. His jaws snap. Mouth open. Teeth bared. Eyes full of fearsome anger.

• • •

He's gonna get me down in two seconds.

• • •

There's a crunch in the snow—she-dog slinking along the front of the house behind me—

"Let me in!"

Her shackles are high. Growl make my blood turn cold. Those two dogs kind of talking to each other now about how they gonna bring me down and the fear burst open inside me flooding down my legs.

Then, like a miracle, the door of that house open.

I don't think nothing. Just fall inside. And big dog bound forward angry and dump down in the snow where I been standing.

But the door bang shut at my back.

The dog jump up—his heavy feet shudder against the door— and I can hear his slobbering rasps of anger behind the wood. My chest heave up and down so fast with breathing I think I'm gonna fall.

• • •

"You aren't going to hurt us, are you?"

It's so dark I can't even see the girl.

There's a nasty smell in here.

The girl witter on. My heart been beating so fast I think I'm gonna faint in this cold dank dark place, and I been mighty pleased I can't see that thin pale face for a minute or two. But pretty soon she stop talking.

I kind of pull myself together then cos I got to think this thing out good, what with that mean dog slathering just a board's width behind me with the taste of manflesh on his lips cos he been feeding on that dead body in the barn for sure.

"Here I am," say the girl, all quiet now, and I feel a light hand clamp on the arm of my coat. "The dogs are outside, aren't they?"

"You got a candle in here?" I ask.

"I don't know how to light it. Only me da know how to do that." The girl pulling my arm and I stumble after her. It feel like I got under a frozen rock in this house it's so cold and dark.

"Where's your brother?"

"Sleeping."

She's fumbling in the dark. "Here." I feel her hand running down my sleeve, and she put something in my hand. It's a candle. I kneel down on that cold floor and pull my strike out from my pack. I light a bit of tinder and get the candle lit.

The light from the candle draw out the room slow and flickery around me. It's a small room, and the window been stuffed with grass and branches behind the boards to keep the cold out. But it aint a good job and there's sticks and stuff fallen all over the floor. I been kneeling in front of a small chimney. The stones all black where there been a fire sometime, but it aint been recent cos the soot's all damp. There's a leather saddle on the floor and an old wooden chair in the corner facing the wall.

My breath mist the cold air.

Beside the chimney been some mean shelves with nothing on them except a big book. Underneath the shelf I see a pile of rags and old grass and under a blanket a small shape. It's the brother, for sure.

But he aint moving. I see that right away. His head face the wall. It been thrown back like a dead fish floating on the water all stiff and aint the right way up somehow.

The girl still looking at me. She can't see her brother dead and stiff behind her cos she's blinking in the glow of the candle.

"Food. You said you had food for me and our kid." That's when she turn to the shape under the blanket on the floor. "Tommy. He's come back. Tommy."

She move all funny like you do when you been so cold you can't hardly walk. She go down on her knees and slowly she reach out to shake him, but I see her stop then.

She sit staring like that with her fingers resting on his body for quite a bit but I can't see her face.

Then she turn to me, her hair long and tangled, thin hand sticking out from her ragged sleeve and there aint nothing much in her eyes.

"You said you've brought some food," she say.

And she put open her palm.

I got a bit of oatcake in my pocket and I give it to her just to see what she's gonna do, and she take it and shuffle back to her dead brother under the shelf and then she just get under the blanket with him, her face to the wall.

"What's your name?" I say.

But she don't say nothing back.

Right then there been a great noise outside, snarling and shrieking and growling like the dogs been fighting over that dead body in the end of the house. That's what hungry dogs do. I reckon there been a runty dog just got a good cuffing.

But I aint a runty dog and I got a problem good and proper, cos I got to get out of this place of death and cold so I can get back to my camp but I been surrounded by a pack of hungry dogs who got a taste for manflesh and I got a girl too. A girl curled up next to her dead-smelling brother eating my food and not talking. I wish I know what Magda gonna do cos she been good with the kids and know what to say and all that kind of thing. I reckon my charity drying up pretty quick.

I got a feeling—kind of angry and sad at the same time. It aint my fault her brother's dead. I aint gonna be able to take him with me yesterday cos I near didn't get the sled up the hill on my own. Couple of kids aint gonna make it easier. All the same, that feeling been a bit like when the baby hare got dead in my place on the Farngod and I don't like it.

10

The dog pack musta smell out that rotten body in the end of the house cos they been hungry dogs. One thing I know about dogs, they aint gonna eat something that been dead awhile unless they been proper hungry. What they want is something that start off alive, weak and ill maybe cos that's gonna be easy to bring down, but alive.

And the dogs seen me now and smelt the girl and most likely her brother too, so they aint gonna leave this place in a hurry. Dogs pretty patient if they get hungry. I mean one dog gonna be easy cos one dog on its own gonna remember something about a man and behave. But more than one, and the dog got its own pack and you just gonna be the same as any bit of meat if you let the dog get wind of it.

They just gonna wait.

But waiting aint gonna be any good for me. I got to think a way out of this. Beside the door been that little boarded window. Aint big enough for no dog to get in and high up. I stretch up to take a look out.

There been two dogs I can see in front of the house. One lying down all curled up; the other cleaning itself. And they got a hand. It's just lying in the snow.

I drop down from my toes all cold. You see half a person's hand all bloody in the snow and you gonna get cold right down in the bottom of your stomach too.

I reckon this pack been half wolf by the look of the Number One dog who try to get me earlier. The wolf-dog aint so fond of people as the dog is. If they get hungry or got a taste for manflesh you got to hope you don't meet a pack of them on the mountain.

Well I aint got no choice about that now but I aint gonna sit in here blubbing about it either. That's the kind of thing Alice do when she got pregnant. Just sit upstairs blubbing like she got to think the whole thing roundside about or something.

Aint nothing to think out, Alice, I shout through the door. *You only fourteen.* But she don't come out even though Magda say she gonna brew up a tea and see what she can do to *sort it out.* But Alice don't want to think on that—she don't want to sort it out—so now she got the baby and gone to live with Geraint.

Well I got to sort this out. I got to think hard and fast and good. Longer the dogs sit there, sharper and faster and hungrier they gonna be, that's for sure.

I look out the hole. It aint a big pack, just a dog and a bitch and last summer's pups grown-up I reckon. The only thing I can do to keep those dogs off my back is make a bit of fire. Dogs pretty scared of fire.

"We got to get out of here," I say to the girl.

She don't move or say nothing but she can hear me I know. I break up that old chair, and with all that brushwood and grass be-hind the boarding on the windows, I make some torches by tying the brushwood bundles on the end of the chair legs. It warm me up and stop me thinking about the girl and her brother.

I go to the door and look out the window again. Big dog hear me this time and he bound over and I hear his feet thump against the wall outside which make me pull back proper fast. I hear him snarling. The others got a bit interested too I can hear.

My sled. It's sitting out in front of the house. I aint gonna get my sled when I got to fight for my life with a whole pack of dogs and get that girl and me out of the pass. No way.

That get me down.

What am I gonna do with no sled? I kind of slump down by the door then. The whole thing gone wrong. Dog tell me. He say, *Don't need no one else's sickly pups suckling at your dugs.* He tell me enough times, but I didn't listen cos the mad dog or the mother hare or whatever it was got me in the night and make me come down here thinking about the girl and her brother all cold and hungry on their own.

The girl say something.

"Tom," she say. "Tommy? The boy's come back. We've got to go wi' him."

It been good and useful she's acting alive again cos she's gonna have to help me. But she's gone a bit funny in her head talking to the brother cos she know he been dead.

"Tom aint gonna go nowhere. Tom got dead the same as you and me gonna be if we don't think sharp and get out of here. But I got a plan—so we can get out of here. You're the only one left, and I come a long way to get you against what the dog in my head tell me. I done it, so you got to get up and help me too. Or you gonna be just as cold and dead as your brother."

I reckon I said that pretty kind. Patrick say I talk good and straight. He tell me stuff like that when we been out together on the mountain. He talk a bit more when you got him on his own but most people just don't give him a quiet space to start. But he say he can trust me cos I can't lie too good.

Anyway I reckon I told the girl straight all the stuff she need to know. Just want her to get up from under that blanket.

But the girl aint moving. Even after my little talk she's still lying there. So I grab her up by her arm—feel like it gonna snap if I pull too hard. But now I got her standing up she gone all stiff with those dark eyes all screwed up so tight I got to push her eyelids open with my thumbs.

"If you aint gonna come now, then you can stay with your dead brother," I tell her. "I aint gonna stop you."

I got fire in my belly growing ready for the fight we gonna have with the dogs, so I aint got much charity in me if she aint gonna hurry up. Stupid girl still aint realizing what I got to do to get her out of here.

"I'm gonna lose my sled cos of you!" I shout that out pretty loud and angry in her face.

Outside the dogs hear me, and they scuffle about a bit. It aint bad they hear me angry.

"I'M GONNA LOSE MY SLED COS OF YOU!"

I shake her hard.

The girl open her eyes proper then.

"What about Tommy?"

But I aint gonna answer stupid questions like that.

"You gonna have to get on my back. There's a big pack of hungry dogs out there and they aint friendly either so we got to scare them with fire to get out of the pass."

She look at me good and proper now.

"You got to be on my back nice and tight and looking behind us too. You see a dog come up mean behind me you wave this at him."

I show her the torch I make and wave it about a bit so she know what I mean.

"Mary."

"What?"

"Mary. My name."

"Well we got to go, Mary. You hear all that stuff I tell you about clinging on my back and keeping the dogs off with fire?"

"Yes."

"Good."

I get down by the chimney, get that big book down off the shelf, and tear the pages out of it to start a fire. The pages all thin and crinkly.

This is the book of the generations of Adam.

That's what it say on the first one I tear out—it sound like a good story coming up. Magda aint gonna like me tearing pages out of a book cos she get pretty angry at anything like that and you gonna have to watch it if she get angry with you, I tell you.

But I reckon this been different cos I got to make a bit of fire,

Magda. I aint got no choice. I reckon if it gonna be STAYING ALIVE against BURNING A BOOK TO STAY ALIVE, then anyone gonna burn the book. Cos the book's just an idea—Patrick tell me that. An idea's fine but it aint the same as staying alive. I mean Dad go on about doing my reading and stuff cos it make me more human than talking to the dog skull and he say I got to choose sometime—but choose what though? We all got to keep living aint we?

Patrick say some people *die* for their ideas and he tell me, he say, "Willo, I'm not one of those people who gonna die for an idea, and the reason why is because men are bad and all their ideas too. You never know what they're really thinking—give them an inch of rope and they'll be making a noose for your neck with it before you turn your back."

That's exactly what he tell me cos I remember it pretty good. Patrick aint gonna mind me tearing up this book. It's me or the dogs. And it aint gonna be me, I tell you that right off. Dogs do dog things and man do man things, and they aint supposed to get muddled up cos when they do it aint gonna be good for no one. Each got to respect the other. Same way with books and ideas and all that kind of thing the grown-ups talk about—aint good if it all get muddled up with staying alive I reckon.

"How many dogs are there?" It's the girl asking me.

"Bout six."

She stand all quiet, but she lean down and pick up one of my torches.

"That's right," I say. "Hold it tight like that and if a dog come near poke it in his face. Don't get too scared. They only dogs after all—you got to think like that cos they can smell fear and that makes them really good and hungry."

She give a small nod.

The little fire of paper blaze up for a second and it give out a warm glow that make a good feeling in that dingy dread room. Girl sense that too I reckon and she stand near it to soak up some heat like it been the first warm day or something. Probably one day long ago people sit in front of that fire reading that big book about Adam, all happy and calm, and the house aint got boarded windows or dogs outside then either. It kind of make you sad knowing that.

I got to light the torches quick though before that little fire go out. Time like this you just got to go, aint no good thinking on it too long and letting all that fear in your stomach get your legs weak and useless.

"Get on my back," I tell the girl.

I bend over and she climb on light as a feather. She's coughing cos the room near filled with smoke by now.

Got to face the pack.

"Are you ready?" I say.

"Yes."

The light outside blind me for a second.

Big dog jump up from the snow. He been mighty surprised cos I start shouting to the sky and waving those torches around. I got to get really big and loud and mean cos dogs sense it. The just-grown pups turn and hide their tails at the god of fire and anger I become right then, so the Number One dog got to show them why he been Number One, and he curl his lip real nasty.

I know that. I know he gonna come at me straight with his dirty red mouth all angry. His lip pull back and I see the bloody teeth and spittle for the second time today.

He come fast and straight across the snow.

I flail my torch at him, the girl shrieking on my back.

"Keep on tight, Mary!"

The big dog bounding through the snow loud and nasty. My heart screaming to run but I got to stand. Number Two bitch coming from behind clever and sneaky again.

The girl scream and sway, hang on with her legs and near take the breath out of me.

Big dog circling and snapping for a weak spot. I strike out. He sway to the left but lunge at my arm. Snap. The bitch get real close and hungry seeing that scrawny girl on my back. She-dog gonna bring down my flank if I aint clever.

I lash out, the blazing arc of fire rushing in the air. The torch crash down on her shoulder blade. I smell the singed fur. She-dog stumble and scream. Big dog leap to her side and come in at me. But I got that bitch hurt and I strike out again.

"Down there!" Mary scream again. Young runt full of teeth come in low and fast like a spear. He grab that bony Mary on the leg but he just get rags and he's pulling and she's screaming and I thrash out with the other torch but the weight of the girl and the dog tugging on her pull me down to my knees in the snow.

Down on my knees surrounded by the pack.

Aint today though. Aint gonna get me today.

I beat at the runt with my stick. I been so close I can look right in those eyes. There aint nothing there.

The she-dog take a lunge but this time I got angry inside from somewhere—and the anger make me strong, and I rise up from the ground as the slathering bitch leap up and when she do I hold the torch high and bring it down.

This is the book of the generations of Adam.

The chair leg been sharp under the flame.

She been soft between her shoulders.

I bring the point down and she fall at once—legs just crumple—and she wimper loud and high.

The big dog stop when he see her down. Cos now it been dog blood on the snow—

I shout out the words my good dog taught me. The pack fall in on that dead bitch. Tearing at her. That hungry pack so hungry they gonna eat their own. The young dogs fighting over the carcass.

It been our chance.

Number One dog aint too sure what's gonna happen if he try me so he's staying back a step but it won't last long I don't reckon.

"Keep looking behind," I say to the whimpering girl clinging on my back like a squirrel.

The snow pretty deep but I been on top of it cos of the snow-shoes. I look back. Big dog bounding toward us up to his chest in the snow.

"Run," scream the girl.

I come to a narrow pass between two rocks, and I stick down one of the torches. KEEP BACK DOG COS I GOT FIRE.

But it aint gonna keep him back for long.

"Run! They're all coming!" It's the girl screeching. She's hammering on my back like mad now and screaming *run* at me like I can't hear her.

If I run I'm gonna be quarry.

I got to front him again cos I been a man.

And the dog got to understand I aint dead so he got to do what I want, not the other way round. He got to have a bit of dog left in him. He aint all wolf yet.

When I turn around in the pass, I see him come—brave in the deep snow, the others with hungry bloody mouths at his back. Girl still screaming like mad but I push her off behind. I get down then, low like a hare. But I got my knife out my pocket and I got my eyes looking right at that big dog. He still got a bit of brindle on his back from his mother. He aint bad. I don't want to kill him but he don't listen too good to what I been telling him.

· · ·

I got fire, dog. I got fire and hands and snowshoes, and I kill your mate like I can kill you so keep back and let me pass. Let me pass.

• • •

But he just keep coming. The hunger in his guts shouting loud in his head. That's when I stand on my two man legs and I hold my torch up cos it still just about alight and I step right toward him. And I tell him again—

And that big Number One dog stop then.

Maybe his hungry guts hear me now.

Cos I been a man.

He get scared and drop his eyes for just a second and then I know that I won so I tell him pretty loud.

"Let me pass."

Big dog remember what his mother taught him then and get proper frightened and stick his brindled tail between his legs.

He been a dog, not a wolf.

I get the girl on my back and run.

I run and run and run. My legs feel like stones wading through the snow but I aint safe, not til I get up to the winfarm. The breath inside me coming out hard and painful, but I got to keep running.

I look up on the ridge above us for a pair of dog eyes looking down. Aint no sign though and I get a full heart then. I feel Mary's cold bony hands clinging to my neck. We been up high above the pass. I stop and get a breath. I stand on the hillside. Shout at the sky.

This shout been full of something.

It been full of me and my winning.

She whisper, "Are we going to be all right?"

"Yes," I tell her.

Cos I aint worried now—the fire inside gonna get me up the hill before nightfall. I know it.

I shout out loud to the dogs and the hills and anyone out there who listen.

"Tommy isn't with us, is he?"

"No," I say. "No he aint."

12

The Rhinogs turn red and orange behind me as the mossy dark of evening spread across the sky from the east.

Up ahead I see the Farngod rising, the towers of the winfarm all about at last. I drag myself up to the eastern ridge—toward the broken wincone. The sun drop fast this time of year and night gonna come up on us any second now.

The girl been moaning a bit. I get her off my back. I got to un-pick her hands from around my neck cos they got so cold and stiff clinging on. She don't move. Her lips got blue and her skin look like wax. With the last bit of strength I drag her inside the wincone and near collapse beside her.

I know I got to stay awake but the warmth of sleep been wash-ing over me and I don't care about nothing no more, just sleep and no more running. Just sink into the quiet dark. Floating in the black-ness of the night with the stars all around. I try to open my eyes and get up, but the tiredness pulling me down. Pictures floating in my head. I start thinking about the never-ending stars and the sky going on forever with nothing outside it. That thought go round and round in a circle in my head cos it got no outside, no beginning and no end.

Once last summer when we been hunting up on the Farngod,

Dad and Magda lie close under the blankets in the heather and all of us just staring up at the sky. Big black sky and all those pricks of light up there just like now and I remember I tell them about that thought of the stars in the never-ending sky and they laugh and Magda say *the force is strong in this one, obi-wan* in a funny voice, and we all laugh together, even though I don't know why it's funny. But it been good when they been laughing together and not arguing about the trees growing under the door or Alice or God. Magda say maybe the world just been a speck of dust in a giant man's pocket and outside been a whole other world of giants we know nothing about. *Think on that, Willo,* she say. And I do.

• • •

You can't sleep.

• • •

But I don't want to open my eyes. Just lie here dreaming in the dark with my heart pounding in my chest and the sweat drying and my shoulders aching from carrying the girl up the hill. I don't know if it been the good dog or the mad dog, but something in my head been tugging on my sleeve, saying I got to wake up. Got to get the firebox going cos the girl dying of cold right next to me.

And it feel like Magda's there shaking me to get up. *"Think on that, Willo."*

She's trying to say something but I can't hear her.

"Wake up, Willo. No time for sleeping yet."

I sit up. Just like that. But it aint been Magda talking, just the girl moaning. I look down at her bony shape, shivering and breathing shallow. I got to warm the girl up before she forget I aint carried her from that house just so she can die. No way. Her clothes are all wet with the snow so I got to get them off slow and easy and get her dry.

Without those rags she look like a worm do when it fall in a puddle. Scrawny and white. And when I pull her body under the rug she feel like a lump of ice sucking my warm blood up and that feel good cos I don't want her to die like the leveret.

"Mary. It aint good to sleep and dream of the stars—you got to wake up a bit and have a brew. You just cold, Mary."

I feel a bit of a movement in her legs, just a twitch, and her eyes flickering a bit. Got to warm her blood good and slow and get some brew inside her.

"Mary. You all right now. Aint no dogs here. Don't go to sleep again cos it aint good."

"Da," she mumble all quiet.

"I aint your dad. I been the one who got you out the house, remember?"

"Tommy?"

"No, I aint Tommy."

I aint got much to say to a girl really. I just aint, and I been sick with tiredness. But I got to keep her from going back to sleep.

So I tell her the rhyme my dad always tell me when I been small. He got it written in his book. I know all the words.

"'I went out to the hazel wood, because a fire was in my head, and cut and peeled a hazel wand, and hooked a berry to a thread. And when white moths were on the wing, and moth-like stars were flickering out, I dropped the berry in a stream and caught a little silver trout.'

"You like that Mary? You gonna like it when you wake up proper. Cos I'll tell it again if you like. Mary, you hear me? I say you gonna like it when you wake up."

"Are the moths on the wing, Da?"

She still got her eyes closed, but I know she gonna be all right when she start talking.

"I aint your da but you gonna be all right, Mary. Ask me some more questions if you like."

"I'm cold."

"You gonna be all right though."

"What's your name if you aren't Tommy?"

"My name's Willo."

"Willo," she repeat it soft. "My name is Mary."

"I know that," I say. "You got to keep talking, Mary, cos it's good, and then I'm gonna make you a brew and it gonna get right inside you and melt the ice in your stomach."

"I've got ice in me stomach?"

"No it aint real ice just cold that feel like ice but the brew gonna make you good again and after that you gonna sleep warm and safe."

"What about me da? Our kid Tommy?"

"We're gonna talk about them tomorrow," I say. "You just look at the fire and talk to me, and maybe I'm gonna tell you the story about the silver trout again."

Well, I aint gonna bore you with all the stupid kid stuff she talk about. I near fall asleep with it cos I been tired and done in after that kind of day. It been hard to think only a few days ago I been at home with Dad and Magda and the others and now they

76

all gone. Just gone—and I aint got no clue where they are, and they aint got no clue about me either.

Except now I got the girl Mary. Even though she's just a pesky starving girl who gonna eat my food and get heavy on my back, she still gonna know where I am and what I been so I aint quite alone. That's it—I aint alone now I got the girl here and it feel better than before even though I don't know her or nothing.

I close my eyes easier thinking that.

• • •

When I wake at dawn, she's still asleep. But alive. Curled up tight. I'm gonna make up some warm clothes for her out of an old coat. She's gonna freeze otherwise.

But I aint gonna stick my nose in and ask a thousand questions. She's gonna see that. She's gonna be fine with me. Magda gonna be proper pleased with me if she see how good and kind I been with this kid.

Tomorrow we're gonna have a good walk to my place on the Farngod, and then I got to take her down to the road under the power lines. Power lines run from Wylfa all the way into the city. Trucks always coming by. I reckon Mary can get a ride back that way.

After working on her clothes a bit I go outside on the ridge. The sun shine out. My eyes blink it shine so bright out here. I can see the whole of the Rhinogs behind me and the craggy white mass of the Farngod up in front. Can't believe there been such a snow in the night.

"Are you there?" come the girl's voice from inside. "Where are you, Willo?"

"I been outside on the ridge."

"Are there any dogs out there?" she ask.

"No, there aint no dogs. Just you and me."

"No dogs?"

"No, you been safe here from dogs I reckon. But I'm gonna come in—I make you some gloves and things. You want to see?"

"Yes."

I crawl back inside and she's sitting up, eating from my pan of yewd.

"I make you a warm pair of gloves and fix up Magda's coat so you aint gonna be cold again. Look. I done it all myself while you been asleep."

She reach out and I show her the gloves. They aint no work of art and only an old cut-up rabbit, I know, but they're warm gloves all the same.

"They're magic," the girl say. She just stroking those shoddy old rabbit-skin gloves.

"And I fix up the coat, see. All the same, nice and warm. Do you like it?"

She put the coat on, her cheeks a bit rosy now. It been a pretty good thing to see after her being so waxy white and near dead yesterday. I pull the coat over her head and she got to put her skinny arms up in the air and she laugh quite a bit and so do I. She's all swamped in it and she look like a big rabbit. It really got a laugh up inside me good and proper. It been the first fun I had in a fair while really.

"Thanks," she say, and it make me feel clever and useful even though she only been a stick-thin girl.

"I can make them much better—if I got more time," I tell her.

"Well, I think they're magic. I've never had fur gloves before, never had nothing made wi' fur." She look at me all sad. "Is me da coming back?"

It's all she been thinking on I reckon.

I shrug.

"Me da—" She stop a bit. "He came out to the hills wi' us on the pony. Da's a ponyman, and he said we were going to grow some oats and trap some animals til the spring. We camped down by the water north of here, by the power lines."

"So you're stealers," I say.

But she aint listening.

"Tommy was happy there. Da found the little house then. It was cold, but we had the fire to start wi' when we had wood. The woman wanted to go back. 'Callum, I want to go home,' she was always saying. She always wanted to go back."

"Where?"

"To the city—where d'you think? And the food ran out, and we ate the pony, and me da only talking about the boat that's going across the sea. And Tommy started to get sick."

"Why didn't you get to the power lines and wait for a truck—I seen them go along under the pylons there. Government trucks."

Mary look at me serious. "But they're going to want to see Da's papers and know then he took the pony. And if we go back to the city . . . how are we going to find the boat back in the city?"

She scrape the bowl with the spoon now, but she gone a bit quiet-looking all of a sudden, thinking bout her dad again, I guess.

"What boat?" I say.

"The boat that's going to take us away."

"There aint no boats on the mountain."

"I can't eat wi' all this on," she say, and she take the gloves off. "But thanks for making them."

"It aint nothing."

"Wish our kid Tom had a coat like this. He wouldn't have died from the cold then, would he?"

"I don't know," I say.

Maybe he's dead cos he got no food and no dad, I think to myself. Or maybe it just been sick bugs inside him, who knows?

"Do you think the dogs got him by now?" she say, eyes open all wide.

I want to say yes, cos it's true—they gonna snuffle in that old house and tear his dead flesh apart pretty quick—but I look away and tend the fire a bit cos it seem better like that.

"They will, won't they?"

I shrug my shoulders again.

Mary lie down and pull the coat over her head all quiet—I reckon she knows. I see her from the corner of my eye. I got a bit to think on though cos half my plan is taking the girl to the road and leaving her there, but if she's right about needing papers and everything I aint so sure.

I mean I can spot a hare run and tie up a good snare—I can do that in my sleep—and there been plenty of things I can do good better than that, but I aint really got no clue about papers and trucks and city people.

"Mary? . . . Mary?"

"I want me da."

Mary been crying again.

I go outside, cos that's another thing I aint got no clue about. Crying kids who lost their da and Tommy.

I reckon the world been a scary place full with gruesome things, but I aint seen much of it. I aint even been to the city. I mean even that girl inside the wincone been there. My dad live in London before, and he say that's the biggest place—but I aint seen that either, just what he tell me cos London been a proper long way under the power lines, and I been born on the mountain, but he come up here around about the time of the troubles, before the snow got so deep only government trucks gonna make it.

He come up here long before that, cos he say he can see how London look after a few long winters and no food, and he aint never going back, and I say, *How it gonna look, Dad?* cos I really want to know.

He say *it gonna look bad, Willo,* with people all mean and angry on the streets cos they been pretty mean and angry before the food stop coming in big trucks. They been pretty mean and angry when they got hot water and power coming out the wall, he tell me.

It sound like London aint been too great even before the snow and the troubles come, but Dad say no it aint been that bad. Just all the bad things been waiting, kind of hiding under the ground like the grass wait under the snow for summer to come. Except they aint been good things like grass but bad things—all the angry things and hungry things, and my dad say *the animal bit* inside people's heads.

I mean, I reckon he got to be a bit right cos I seen hungry people, and like I said they aint been the nicest thing you gonna meet if you got food and they aint. Dad find this wild place up here cos he say no one gonna want a bit of these mountains, even though people been living here forever so there musta been something good here.

You can see he been right about that cos there been all the old-time houses just sitting up on the hills empty. He say, *People in the city got to learn,* but Patrick aint so sure. He say people in the city aint gonna want to be up here in the snow alone, they just looking to get to China, and what we gonna do if they all got the same idea anyway, cos there aint gonna be enough mountain to go around— gonna be what he call anarchy if all the people come, which is a good point. I mean I don't know who been right except I see that Patrick stay here with us so that say something, don't it?

Me though, I reckon I been itching to go to the city since Geraint tell me that's where he got his gun. One day I'm gonna get along the power lines to Manchester, maybe even London. After I find Dad.

But right now I just got to get through another night with this sad girl and get her off to the Farngod in the morning. Maybe take her to my secret place before I take her down to the power lines. Ask her some more about the trucks and papers too. I don't want her getting in trouble or nothing after what she been through. I really don't.

13

"You the first person been to my secret place. I aint never show no one before."

Mary don't look too comfortable with the pack on her back and that coat hanging round her but I tie it round the middle so the wind aint gonna get under it.

"You got the pack on good? Cos I aint gonna keep stopping."

"It's all right," she say, lifting her foot to see her snowshoe.

"Just put your feet down easy and flat. You soon gonna get the hang of it."

"D'you make them?" she ask.

"Magda make that pair, but I can too if I want—it aint hard."

"How far have we got to go?"

"It's a good way in this deep snow, so you got to do what I say and keep easy or you gonna get proper tired. You understand?"

"Where are we going?"

"I'm gonna take you down to the power lines. You can get a truck ride back to the city then."

She get quiet all of a sudden.

"But I don't want to go back to the city," she say after a bit.

"Well you aint got much choice cos that's where I'm taking you."

I don't know why girls always got to be talking. But I aint paying much attention, just looking over the ridge now. I aint told her but I been keen to get going cos I hear that wolf-dog howl far off in the night. With the sun putting a crust on the snow it aint gonna be long before they dance on top of it up the ridge.

I make a pack up for the girl with the food and light stuff and a poor type of sled with a piece of metal from the wincone for me cos you know how I lost my proper sled down at that house but aint no use getting angry about it now. I got the tent and fire-box and heavy stuff on the bit of metal and I can drag it behind quite easy. The rest I been hauling on my back.

All around, the towers from the old winfarm rise up tall from the snow. They been so big they look like broken giants striding around on top of the mountain. I can see them sharp as a pin cos the sky's blue like the blue never gonna stop it been so clear and light and just going on back into the forever.

Big raven wheel and scriek overhead. It make me think of those two bodies down in Mary's house and I get sick thinking it near been our bloody bodies torn up by the pack in the snow with that big dog and his red mouth standing over our guts.

That raven probably wheeling around just waiting for the dogs to leave. Either that or he been looking down at me and Mary, waiting for us to drop. Something about a scrieking raven and him all lonely up in the cold sky always make me think some bad thing gonna happen.

I never spend much time on this side of the Farngod. Mary been a good kid tramping behind me without a word for now. The shadows on the snow all blue and the whiteness burn my eyes cos the snow sparkle in the sun like a million stars. The snow creak underfoot and the sound of my breath been trapped inside my hood and the warm heat of my body rise up through the neck of my coat.

I got to get east. That's where my secret place is. I got a thrill thinking about showing it to someone, I really do, which is funny cos I aint never wanted to show it to no one before.

The little valley open up between rocks cresting a rise, and I see the ring of stones rise out the ground far ahead. The crown of thorns.

"It aint too far now, Mary."

She stop a bit and look over the valley.

"I don't want to go back to the city," she say.

I don't pay no attention. The raven still circling overhead. He aint following us which been good, but I aint so sure about the dogs. When that raven dip down into the pass down there I'm gonna know the dogs on the move again and he just picking over guts and bones. It's a gruesome thought for sure—the raven being some sort of sign I mean.

I let her take a rest. I reckon it been about the middle of the day. Mary chewing on a bit of food quiet. I reckon she's just about okay for walking still. It been lucky the sun got out and no wind either else she gonna struggle cos she's thin as a branch with no leaves.

"How far is it?" she ask.

"Three hours maybe. Til the sun go close to that ridge over there."

"Dogs aren't following us yet, are they?"

"Don't reckon," I say.

"But I heard them in the night. They aren't following us, are they, Willo?"

I look at that little stick girl a bit different for a while then knowing she been listening to the dogs in the night same as me.

"No, they aint following us yet." I point to the raven. "When you can't see him, then we got to start running."

She look up matter-of-fact. I reckon she's pretty scared, but she aint showing it too bad.

I shoulder my pack and pick up the rope from the sled. "Slow and steady, Mary, though. Aint no point to get scared and sweaty," I tell her, "that raven still in the air for now. He still been waiting, so we been all right."

14

Soon we get over to the steep side of the glen. It look like there aint no way out but I know the way and I won't get mired down at the bottom on the marshy ground under the ice. We been close to my secret place.

We come out of the pass. Down to the north been the Afon Eden Valley clad in snow, and Trawsfinnid Lake all ice and silver and orange in the evening sun, birch trees like shadows along its edge and the dark green of the conifer plantation far off.

"It look pretty good, don't it?" I say.

Girl nearly falling over with tiredness, but she look all the same. We look at that lake a bit, breathing into our hoods with the climb.

Behind us a wall of rock rise up out the side of the hill. Up in the crags been my cave. I block up the entrance at the end of the summer.

"Come on, Mary, you got to climb up here and get inside or you gonna get cold," I say, hauling my stuff up onto the rocks.

"You're going to take me to the road anyway, so why do you care?"

She sulk just like the little kids at home. I mean, I got to remember she's just a girl.

"How old you been, Mary?" I shout down.

"I'm not telling."

"How old?"

"Thirteen."

"Well, you acting like you been about six, cos if you don't stop sulking and get inside, you gonna freeze to death down there."

I know she gonna come up, just need a bit of time to look like it been her idea. Anyway, I got heavy stuff to clamber up and down the rocks with.

"Aint never show no one this place, Mary. You gonna be the first."

That make her head turn a bit and I see she getting ready to make it her idea and get up.

"Come on, Mary, you can climb up here easy."

I move the rocks still piled at the entrance and squeeze inside. The smell of damp and earth and goat hit my nose. There aint no wind inside the cave. And I got my feeling all special and magic like I always do when I get in here.

The floor been thick with goat droppings cos this been a goat cave when they been wild up here, and the cave a lot bigger than you gonna think from that slit in the rocks. Aint no goats now though.

Mary clamber up the icy ledges of the rock face. She aint talking to me, but later I'm gonna show her the tunnels. And the spirit deep inside the mountain. She's gonna like that I reckon.

"I'm cold," she say.

"Just wait. I got to get the other stuff."

I got to scramble up the crags with all the things I been dragging up the hill. She stand out on the ledge, watching.

"Just wait, Mary, we soon gonna get the fire going, plenty of goat droppings to burn."

She squeeze through the slit in the rocks, pressing her hands against the slabs of cold gray stone sheering up above us. The snow drifted across the floor of the narrow passageway in hard crusted ridges. It's so dark it take a while to see when you get inside. The roof way above us in the darkness. The floor deep in goat droppings rolling underfoot.

"Halloooo—" My voice echo back into the depths of the cave.

"Why do you do that?"

"It's my cave. Gonna do what I like."

She really start to annoy me.

I get down and get a fire going. Mary creep close. The light bounce off the jags and ruts of the stones. Far back the ledges rise up into the back of the cave. Back into the tunnels.

"I don't like it," she say.

She aint the only one cold and tired.

Aint the only one alone on the mountain.

"We can rest a bit," I say.

"But you're going to leave me down by the road tomorrow, aren't you?"

"Sleep, Mary."

"But you are, aren't you?"

"Just get some rest now. We got a long walk tomorrow."

"You are, aren't you?"

I just close my eyes.

15

When I wake up it been dark outside. I can see it through the slit in the rocks. A bit of light come off the fire and dance about the walls of the cave though. The roof echoing high up above us and I shout into it again.

"Helloooo!"

"What? . . ." She jump up.

"Hear that, Mary?"

I reckon this cave been here since the beginning of time cos its cold black walls of rock aint going nowhere. Just like an old man sitting in a chair who know he been all right and aint got no worries. Just a long pipe of baccy in his hand, watching the kids scampering and the grown-ups arguing and the snow falling outside the window. That's what I think of.

It wrap me up pretty good and homesome to be back up here. I know every corner of this place.

The smoke from the chimney curl away in the black, whisping now and then in a twist of air. Mary sit up looking at the fire. She's tired and pesky as a baby, but I got something I'm gonna show her.

"Come on, Mary," I say. "I'm gonna show you my secret."

"I don't want to come."

She really sulk pretty good.

"Well, I aint gonna make you come cos it been a bit scary. You just stay here."

Don't know why I want her to see my secret place. But I do. I really want to show it to her. I don't reckon she's gonna laugh when I say my words either, most people gonna laugh at me then, cos I got to say my words in my secret place, aint really a choice no more. It gonna be bad luck if I don't. That's why it's secret.

I got a candle. I hide it up here in the summer. I aint proud that I steal it from the house but I need it to find my way through the tunnels—it's just a smoky tallow candle but if I ask, Magda's gonna want to know why and all that kind of thing.

"Where are you going?" say Mary.

"Up there." I point to the blackness at the back of the cave.

"All right, I'm going to come wi' you."

"I thought you been too scared."

"No, I'm not scared." She's up now, but I reckon she is scared cos this cave's big and dark and she really is just a kid and don't want to be left on her own.

"Come on then, follow me." I got the candle lit and I head into the shadows. Up onto the ledges, Mary scrambling behind me. The hard rocks catch at my knees and we slide on the shale. We clamber high up to the back of the cave. The cold stone walls seem to close around the tiny candle flame like a sleeve.

Aint a sound deep in the earth here. Just our breathing. We sit for a bit on the flat ledge of rock in the blackness. The fire glowing down below us.

"Come on, back here." I lift the candle.

Behind us the tunnels look like open black mouths. I crawl into the darkness.

"I'm scared," Mary say.

But she follow me cos she aint got no choice. The floor been dry and gritty, the tunnels low—sometimes wide enough, sometimes tight.

The tunnels twist and turn. Other openings appear in the rocks. I see them in the guttering candlelight dancing up around us.

"I'm scared." She reach out a hand all eager in the darkness.

"We been pretty close, don't worry."

I aint gonna be holding someone's hand just cos it got a bit dark.

She whimper a bit, but I aint lying—we're nearly there. A bit further and she's gonna see my secret place. The spirit of the hare gonna jump up inside her and she aint gonna be scared of nothing.

But Mary scuffle up beside me right then and grab at my arm, which aint been a good idea cos when she do she knock the candle from my hand, and it fall on the ground and snuff out. Just like that.

She get silent like she been dead then.

"Well, that aint too clever," I say.

The dark screaming out it's so dark.

She cling on me like a bur.

Aint nothing left in this kind of darkness you want to think on too hard if you aint used to it.

"Don't cry, Mary. We aint lost."

I strike my flint, and I tell you, the flame that come off a little thing like a smoky old tallow candle after that kind of blackness been like a great fire burning in the hearth.

"I thought we were going to be lost in here forever," she say.

I shuffle forward in the little pool of light.

"I know."

"Wait. Please." She reach out a trembling hand.

"But look—we're here."

I crawl through a gap in the rocks and come up on my haunches—right in the middle of my secret place. Mary's eyes blinking like she just been born.

All around us been the spirit of the hare. The dogs dancing along the wall of the chamber where I draw them out with a charred stick. That big hare skull on a stick right in the middle looking down at us, his hollow eye sockets filled with stones. I got all the hare skulls on sticks—I know every one and where I caught it. The big hare I caught last summer—he got the stones in his eyes like the dog, cos I want to catch the biggest hares, so I got to give more respect to him than the tiddlers.

At first I been very excited when I come up with the idea of putting them all up here but now I don't go dancing about screeching. Dog teach me to talk all quiet and put my offerings down. Say my words. I got an order to it now.

The whole thing got like it aint even my idea anymore. It's like I got to do it or I won't get the magic.

Mary put her cold hand in mine. I don't say nothing this time, just reach up and put the candle on a ledge in the rock. Then I get

ready to say my words. Touch big hare first like always. Close my
eyes.

• • •

Eat the leaf,
Eat the grass,
The sun got warm
in the spring.
High up on the hill
I didn't catch you then,
big hare,
with my trap and the wire.
I didn't catch you then.
Come into the circle,
And through him and to him,
All things gonna see.
Come into the circle,
And through him and to him,
All things gonna see—

• • •

It been a proper good moment of calm.

"You get the spirit of the hare in you when you tell them the
words," I tell Mary. "We aint been the first I don't reckon. Look."

I point up to the ceiling. She tilt her head back, still holding my
hand.

"You got to get on my shoulder with the candle, Mary."

"But I don't want to—I'm scared to."

"You got to."

I give her the candle—wrap her fingers around it. Lift her up on my shoulders.

"See. Hold up the light and you gonna see them."

"Oh. I can see them now."

"You see them all?"

"Go back a bit. Yes, that's it. There are hares—two hares standing up next to each other. That's a goat, like it's been carved in the rock. And a deer—it's got antlers—and a beast with big hairy shoulders."

She's looking at the sweep of the ceiling opening up in lines and smudges like it been a grassy plain alive with animals. I aint the first person been in here. It gonna fill you up with magic deep in this cave, I tell you.

"Can you see the hands?"

"Hands?"

"On the wall. Look like someone hold up their hand and paint round it, don't it?" I say. "Reckon it been the person's hands who done the picture. Like it been their name kind of."

"It's magic."

"I got other things I find here too."

"Like what?"

She get down from my shoulders. I show her the little comb that been made of bone and the bracelet made of stone beads. I got them placed up on a ledge.

"See, we aint the first people been here."

Mary look proper frightened.

"There aint no one here now, Mary."

"How d'you know that?" she say, scared.

"I been here on my own enough time, and I know there aint nothing here gonna get you except the things in your head. The people who been here gone a long time ago. This place filled with spirits of animals and the mountain that's all. They aint gonna hurt you, not if you treat them good and say your words proper. See. Just got to say your words proper."

And kneeling there with our cold hands together brings a feeling that wash over me like a warm wind. I forgot I been hungry and tired and alone with this pesky girl.

I reckon that feeling gonna stay written on my heart forever, I really do.

16

"Let me come wi' you."

The girl Mary crying.

It's a shame cos she been a good kid really. After I show her my place, we come back down to the fire and eat a bit of food—we sit about pretty happy til we fall asleep. I reckon it been the first night she gone to sleep without crying.

But like every day, the morning come around like clockwork. I tell you, aint nothing stay the same for long.

Today I got to head on east, where the sun comes up, leave the heavy stuff in the cave for now.

I take the dog skull and put it up high on a ledge. He aint gonna want to go down to the road. I'm gonna come back for him and get all my stuff later.

I got to get to Geraint's farm but not with this girl. I know she want to stay with me and I got to like her enough. But I aint got no choice. I'm pretty near washed out and aint got much food left.

I mean, it aint like I'm planning to leave her out on the hillside for the dogs and ravens to pick over. No way. Just leave her under the power lines, down by the road. She can get a truck ride—make it back to the city. It been her home after all.

Right now though she's sitting on the ground crying cos she

keep saying she *aint going down there, and you can't make me.* She really been a pesky kid at heart, and I aint never had to stand by someone blubbing as much as she do and not stick it to them.

"You're right," I tell her. "I can't make you, but you aint so stupid to stay here on your own for the dogs to fight over."

"You're going to leave me because you think I'm a stealer, don't you?" She look at me hard with that question.

"Number One that aint the reason but I do reckon you been a stealer cos you come up here from the city and steal stuff, and like a scared dog with its tail between its legs, stealers run off back home when it gets too cold," I say.

"But we didn't run off."

No, but it been better if you did, I think—but I don't need to say that cos I know she's thinking on her dead brother and her dad gone and maybe the woman, and her eyes gonna swell up and I aint got too many more soft words to tell her about it all. I mean it aint her fault cos she been a kid. But her dad's just a stealer who got too big in his boots to admit he got to run back home, I reckon. I mean aint he never heard the story about the ant and the grasshopper? Everyone know how the ant work hard all summer getting food for the winter while that lazy grasshopper just singing all day til he die of hunger when the snow start to fall.

"Me da weren't a stealer," say Mary.

"Well it look that way to me cos if you aint been stealers then what are you?"

"I don't know. But me da weren't a stealer. He was a ponyman."

"I aint gonna fight over it. Really, I aint. Don't matter to me what you been. I come back to get you, aint I? I been sorry about Tommy and your dad I really am—"

"But you're going to take me down to the road?" She point down in the valley, over the lake where the lines run east. "You're going to leave me there, aren't you?"

I reckon I am, Mary. The snow aint getting thinner nor the wind aint getting softer yet. Got dogs and ravens and storms and I got somewhere I got to be. Don't know if I'm gonna make it. Aint gonna be no journey for a thin little girl.

But all I say is, "I thought you want to go back."

"I don't want you to leave me, that's all. Maybe Da's going to come back?"

"He aint coming back, Mary, and where I got to go aint no place for a kid like you," I say—which remind me I'm Number One again.

"I'm not scared," she say. But she's nearly begging she's so scared—I hear it in her voice.

"I'm not scared. Please don't leave me down there."

"It aint no point to talk on it."

"I don't want you to leave me on the road."

"I don't care. I aint no good with kids, and I got things to do."

"I don't want to go back to the city."

"It aint so bad. City aint gonna be worse than a pack of gruesome dogs on your tail, is it?" I say it as soft as I can but her eyes so wet it make me want to turn away. "It aint far. Big trucks come down the road every day."

But all the patience in me been draining out like I'm an

upturned bottle and I got a pretty strong feeling I just got to kick her up off the ground or maybe just leave her after all. She aint the only one got no dad. Or no mum. I aint got no one either. Aint got no clue where they all gone. And I'm tired and hungry like I aint never been before.

"You aint the only one been lost." I shout it at her. "And if you sit there I'm gonna just leave you for the dogs."

I really mean it too.

She hear that in my voice I reckon and get up without a word.

We shoulder our packs and set off at last. But it aint a good feeling, not like when we been in the cave last night.

Outside a hard, cold wind cut across the hillside. The sky been fighting a battle with black clouds scudding across from the north and it aint gonna be so easy getting down in the valley with the wind picking up again. I can feel it now. Bad weather about to jump down on us. It been that time of year.

A whirlwind of snow dance up in front of me right then—like a sign to be wary. I can still see the lake and wide-open plain below and far off the great metal pylons marching across the snow from Wylfa in the west. A gust of freezing wind catch my mouth—it take away my breath for a second. I pull my hood over.

"Keep close," I shout.

She stumble forward. Trip in the snow. I got to pick her up. I look into her face and I see she been begging me in her eyes. She been so thin and hungry and tired, and I don't know if she's gonna make it down to the valley if the weather get bad this quick.

"Don't try to go too fast."

The wind roar about us all of a sudden, whipping up her hair, lashing it about her face. I got to lean in close so she can hear me.

"Keep close. Storm's coming up quick. But it's better down there."

I point down below the bluff, the hillside gray in the snowmist and morning light. I think about climbing back up into the cave. Out of the wind. But we got to keep going. We aint got food enough for stopping.

Mary nod. Wipe the hair from her mouth. Aint no use in talking now the blizzard come in, just got to get off the hillside. If we make it off the Farngod, we can get under cover in the conifer plantation right alongside the lake. The wind aint gonna fight its way inside the trees so easy.

I tell you, I aint got too much strength in me after so many cold nights and bad food and worrying about the girl just sinking down in the drifts.

"Keep near," I shout as we bend against the wind in the flailing snow. It's all I can say.

Like I told you, the weather gonna swoop down on you like an eagle up here. We half fall, floundering down the icy slope on the north side of the Farngod. Plantation's gonna be the only way. I don't like it but aint no choice if this weather keep up. Maybe trap a hare in there. That's one good thing maybe. Thinking that make me proper hungry and forget worrying about that ragged sulking girl for a bit.

I aint been down to the plantation for a long while. It been close to the power lines and stealer camps. The trees so tall and dark and green in the plantation. Don't see much green up on the hills in winter. There been something shadowy though when you get right inside. I been a stranger down in the valley and I aint used to it and don't like it cos I can't see what been around and about. Just those dark trees—there's something dead under those always green trees. Like poison in the ground.

The snow got so mean and the wind so strong, it been hard to see even a few paces in front of me. And even though it give me a bad feeling, it don't take long before that sheltering forest of fir trees far off down by the lake guiding every thought in my head.

17

"Keep away from the edge," I tell her. "The ice get thin there."

Mary struggle to keep up along the edge of the frozen lake. We been close to the forest. The trail through the rushes lead up into the scrubby trees. The low birches brush against us and clumps of snow fall down from their spindly bare branches. I see a fox track heading toward the plantation. It's a good sign. If there been foxes then there's gonna be hares for sure.

"Can't we rest for a while?" say Mary. She sit down on a stump under the low trees and I put a little snow in her mouth.

"We got to get deeper inside the forest," I say. "Gonna be stiller there and we can rest good and proper, get a fire going, get something warm inside. Hares get inside the trees in the winter to eat the fir needles—I'll lay a snare."

"I'm so tired."

She pull herself off the ground. I take her pack for a bit.

Soon we get to the edge of the plantation. The fir trees stand up like a dark wall in front of us. I can hear myself thinking at last without that wind on the hillside torturing every move I make.

"Is it safe?" she say.

"Well it don't look too bright but it's sheltered enough and like I say, we'll get a hare maybe. Get to the pylons easier out of the weather. They cut right through the trees somewhere."

She hang her head but don't start spouting on like before.

We push into the green boughs hanging low like hands reaching out of the gloom. Into the shadows of the fir trees. You hear some pretty bad things about the forest when the kids been telling stories to scare each other at the Barmuth Meet. Some of those stories coming right back to me now, but I don't say nothing to the girl cos she looking around like she heard the stories too.

On through the close rows of trees. Stubby low branches catching our coats. The snow aint too thick under the flat green boughs above, but here and there where a tree blown over the snow fallen through the canopy in deep piles.

"I don't like it, Willo," she whisper.

"You aint alone."

We been deep inside. Tree trunks standing up like soldiers all about.

"Shh."

I stop cos I reckon I hear something. Maybe I just smell something instead.

"What?"

"Come on, but quiet."

In my head I been trying to think what that funny smell is. I got a bad feeling—like we aint alone, like eyes been on us. But I can't see nothing, everywhere just been trees stretching out in the gloom—far as the eye can see. Just thoughts in my head. I got myself proper spooked. Mary sure is keeping close and quiet. Every now and then I turn around. Glance about behind us.

"Please can we rest?" she say.

"Not yet. Let's get deeper inside."

"Where are we going?"

"The road cuts through somewhere further north."

"I want to rest."

"It aint far now, Mary, aint far to the pylons, just can't see them til you been right underneath almost."

But she's falling behind.

I stop near a fallen bough.

"Sit here then. Have an oatcake if you want."

"Where are you going?"

"Look for hare runs."

"Please don't go."

"I'm just gonna have a look about. Lay a snare."

"Don't leave me. I'm scared."

"I aint going far, just keep your eyes open and shout if you want me."

She sit down on the fallen branch.

The snow's pretty deep here, the trees bigger. Away in front of us I seen a fallen trunk. I reckon there's gonna be a few hare runs right under the branches. Where they been feeding. It aint gonna take me long to set a snare.

Coming in among trees always make me think of Robin Hood, cos he live in a great big forest. I pretty near learn to read on that book about Robin Hood that Magda got, so I know the story roundside about. It been a proper old-time story, and the book been so ratty Magda got to sew it all back together about twenty times. All the kids like it. *Robin Hood and the Silver Arrow*, it's called—I reckon I'm gonna remember the words in that book til I die. But Robin Hood aint been that easy to trick, Sheriff of Nottingham, cos he got a green coat and won a silver arrow. But mostly he been stealing from the greedy and giving to the poor and getting away with it.

I always want to know if Robin Hood been an ant or a grasshopper. My dad say it aint so simple, Willo. The poor had nothing cos the greedy got it all. And I say, you mean like the ant—he got it all cos he work hard like us. But Dad say no, not exactly like the ant, and he say he's gonna explain when I get older—but he never do. He just say, *You remember that story*. Reckon these days Robin Hood gonna have a gun instead of a silver arrow though.

The fir tree been pretty big when I get up to it. There been fresh hare runs sure enough. I got my pack off to get the trap wire and then I see up ahead there must be a new planting cos there been a thick low wall of green. Young trees with their branches almost touching the ground.

That gonna be the best place for hares for certain. Good cover and plenty to eat. Sure enough there been a good set of tracks where a hare been lolloping through here.

I sling my pack over my shoulder and crawl toward the bushy trees. Just gonna take me a few minutes and I'm gonna be able to set a snare right in the trees. Reckon it aint gonna be a long wait before I get one.

I push my way under the low branches. It been black as night here and the ground pretty bare from snow. Just sharp fir needles like a carpet under my knees, and then I lose the tracks. It look like there been a bit of a gap in the trees up ahead. If I get in there I can look about.

I check behind me but the tall trees been hidden by the young branches weighed down with snow above me. Can't see Mary.

I creep along on my front toward the light. Creep forward right to the edge of the low cover.

I wonder why there been a planting of young trees right in the middle of the forest? Maybe we come right through to the other side already. But we aint come to the road under the pylons, so I can't work it out. Maybe we been going around in circles.

I edge up careful on my elbows. I push the branches apart to see what been inside the clearing.

But it aint no clearing.

I near fall over the edge when I crawl through the tree line.

My guts come right up inside me.

A great big pit. Stretching out in front of me.

Deep pit dug right in the middle of the forest.

And the pit been full up. Full up like a gruesome nightmare. Pit full of arms and legs. Dead bodies. Limbs sticking up like twisted frozen branches out the snow.

A pit full of dead people.

My heart thump hard. My head trying to work it all out.

And drifting across from the thick trees on the other side is the smell.

The smell I picked up further back in the plantation.

That smell just hanging under the trees.

It been a smell of smoke.

All the stories, the bad stories flooding through my head. Stories graybeards tell to stop you coming down in the plantation. About the dead from the cities. About hungry stealers left on the mountain in winter.

And over on the other side, an icy path slide into the pit from a gap in the trees. An icy track where something been scrabbling in and out of that pit of dead bodies.

Something that been feeding in there.

Then I see it. Dark shape moving under the trees. My heart pounding. *Bang bang bang.*

I slip back inside the low trees. *Bang bang bang.* The smell of burning fat and smoke in the air. I got to get back to Mary. But I can't see nothing. Just low branches all around. And the panic get me. Hands reaching out in the darkness pulling at my legs. Pulling me down into that pit. Into that grave of frozen bodies.

Got to listen to the dog in me. Dog aint gonna panic.

Quiet as a mouse, Willo.

Every move I make sound like a storm. I slide out of the young fir on my belly. Back away from the pit. Away from where men been feeding on men. My hands are shaking. All I see is the tall trunks marching off in every direction.

Panic pounding behind my eyes.

I see Mary now, far off between the rows of trees. Hunched over her pack.

And she aint alone.

Flitting in the flat green shadows. Something moving.

Between the rows of trees. Just a quick flash to the left and another off to her right.

She look up.

A man step out of the trees behind her.

"Mary!" I shout it out from the bottom of my heart. "Mary!"

He come out from behind the trees far behind her. I see him good and proper now. Thin and raggy like a starving beast. Face cracked in a grin. Moving his hands. Saying something I can't hear.

Mary turn her head cos I been shouting and pointing. And then her mouth get like a hole. That stealer got a stick in his hand. More figures come out of the trees either side of him, under the trees like shadows. Like wolves. They just stand up out of nowhere somehow.

My dad always tell me, *Hungry stealers in the winter aint men, and you just got to run if you see them.*

"Run, Mary!" I shout.

She drop everything and scrabble up on her knees.

"Willo!" Her scream cracking under the trees.

"Run, Mary!"

They're coming through the snow.

All the things the graybeards say about stealer packs in the plantation. Gruesome thoughts. And now I seen it. Where they been sliding down into that pit of dead bodies.

The noise of my breath and fear banging in my head. I crash through the drifts between the trees with my heavy pack. I nearly been blind with it.

"Willo!" she scream out behind.

"Just run, Mary!"

We flee through the forest. Not looking back. Running for our lives. Dog spirit bounding ahead of me. Showing me the path. His flat back rising and falling as he gallop and leap through the snow.

"Willo!"

I *got* to turn back. I can hear it in her voice. But the dog running off between the trees. Aint stopping.

Mary fallen down on her knees in the snow. Thin mean Number One stealer with the heavy stick in his hand coming up behind her. Bounding at her with his legs plucking high through the snow, the others close by. Snow spray up around them as they push through the drifts knee-deep.

The leader make a strange noise, sucking and whistling. The other three fan out, out in the trees in the thick heavy snow.

"Mary! You got snowshoes, they aint, get up."

"Willo!"

"Get up and run," I scream into the forest.

Mary scramble to her feet. Up again and coming toward me, but I aint looking now, got to outrun the pack. The branches snag me but I aint gonna stop. Breath loud and painful in my chest. My legs thumping down. Just concentrating on putting my feet down good.

Keep running cos they're like wolves.

Branches slash at my face. *Thump. Thump. Thump.* The sweat rising up like a hot mist.

"Willo!" She got pleading in her shouts.

Then suddenly it feel like the ground open up underneath me. My feet fall away, down, down. I tumble forward on my face. Head over heels down a steep bank. Everything hard and white.

From the dark into the light.

KAMAZ. That's what it say on the front of the truck.

KAMAZ.

I fall straight down on the road. Right through the trees down the bank onto the icy hardpack snow on the road under the pylons. Trees dark all about.

Big dirty green truck high up off the ground on great wheels roaring and sliding toward me.

KAMAZ. High up above my head on the great curve of its front. The letters stamped out and shining like Robin Hood's silver arrow.

Mary crash through the trees and tumble down the bank ahead of me. Behind her a ragged man leap out and roll down the bank on top of her.

In front of KAMAZ.

The pylons above us march on through the trees, shielding the road with their gentle humming, so tall it seem they almost touch the sky.

18

She got a gun. I see her hold it up between her hands. Aim at that man struggling to his feet. Pull the trigger. The shot explode in the icy air.

Crack!

A lump of snow fall down from a nearby tree. The man stumble. I see the rags tied around his feet trailing in the snow. The remains of canvas hang off him, his hands bound in rags. Deep-set eyes aint got nothing left in them. He drop his stick.

Crack! The second shot fell him. He collapse forward on his knees and fall onto the snow, the blood spilling out his mouth. He make a gurgling noise deep down inside.

The woman from the truck look about either side of the road into the trees. She got the gun steady in her hand still.

"How many of them?" she shout at me.

I still been sprawled out on the road just getting myself up.

"Three."

"You all right?" she shout to Mary. But Mary all right.

The man aint dead yet but he's gonna be cos the blood's spitting out of him, staining his matted beard like a feeding dog. The noises aint human. He's still on all fours on the road, his cudgel lying useless on the ground.

The woman aint scared of this bleeding man and she stride

toward him. She got on a thick felt coat come down to her ankles. I see it tight across her shoulders as she walk.

The man put one hand up, like he's saying *please don't kill me*. His breath misting the freezing air like he's breathing out smoke. The woman with the gun still coming though.

The man aint got strength for holding himself up and roll onto his back. It aint words he been trying to say no more.

And the woman with the gun take that last step and hold the gun right up to his head, and she pull the trigger.

CRACK.

And the blood and the brains and all the things that were inside the man's head make a red puddle under him now, but I seen the woman do it and I see her eyes at the last second cos I been watching pretty good and Mary scream and slip on the ice and come running toward me.

It been the first time I seen someone shot with a gun.

That woman in the big coat turn to us now.

"Are you on your own?"

"Yes," Mary say, staring at the blood on the road.

"Well, in a few minutes the rest of our convoy is going to come by."

"What about . . ." I point to the dead body.

She look about in the trees and sweep her arm around into the dark forest. "They didn't get you, so they'll have to eat their own instead."

A voice come from around the other side of the truck. "Moira, we've got to move."

113

The woman sling the gun in her belt and climb up to the door of the cab.

Mary grab onto the woman's leg as she climb up.

The woman look down.

"Please."

"Come on, Moira, it isn't safe," say the voice from the truck.

The woman look back at Mary, and then out into the dark trees. I see her thinking.

"Please don't leave us," say Mary.

The woman jump back down onto the road. She got big flat boots, hard and shiny.

"Don't take them." It's the other voice in the cab.

But the woman aint taking much notice, cos I seen her close her eyes in the last moment when she shoot that stealer, so I know she aint as mean as she look.

"Come on," she say. "Get in the back."

She pull me up by the arm and Mary too. The back of the truck got a heavy green flap hanging down, faded yellow letters painted on the back:

ANPEC

The woman lift up the canvas, and we got to climb up inside.

Like my dad say, I been lucky cos the one bad thing happen and then this good thing happen. But I got a bit worried now how this good thing gonna end cos the truck got the girl, but it also got me. I aint never been in a truck. I aint never been this close to a truck before even. Bad-smelling smoke come pouring out a pipe in the back but the woman push us up and inside it. No time to think.

Either side are benches and a crowd of faces all turn toward us. In the middle a small stove, the chimney going up through the roof.

"Get them out before the checkpoint," say the woman to the people. That's all she say. And then she close down the flap. I hear the door of the cab slamming shut. We move off.

There aint been one sound made by those people, just eyes staring at us.

Old graybeard sitting close lean forward with thin dry lips. He been wearing a stiff canvas coat come right up around his ears. Thick gloves all stiff on his hands. He put a hand out. Nasty-looking smile on his face.

"Nice coat you got, kid, where d'you steal that?"

He been so close to my face, I can feel his breath and see in his eyes that he aint too friendly.

"Let him be, Reuben." It's a woman sitting further back.

All those people sort of swaying together as the truck bump and swerve along the road. Like trees swaying in the wind.

"They aren't stealers."

"How d'you know?" someone else say.

"Stealers don't have fur coats like that—look at the stitching. They got fur gloves." The woman lean forward when she speak. "If they're stealers, Moira's would have them too."

"I'll give you some bread for your gloves." It's the old gray-beard again and he lean close and reach out touching my coat.

"I said let him be."

The old graybeard laugh a bit chesty and sit back. "Just offering the poor kid a bit of bread."

"Come and sit up here at the front," say the woman.

Mary the first to get up, and I follow her. I'm just gonna look and listen, watching this pack of dogs.

"You've got to get out before the checkpoint, like the driver said," the woman telling Mary.

"When's the checkpoint?" ask Mary.

"I'll tell you when—you just sit up here."

"Why don't we just throw them out here? What happens if we get stopped? We all get it then."

"How do we know they aren't stealers?"

The people talking about us like we aint there.

"They must be stealers. I say throw them out."

"It's only Rose saying they're not. They must be stragglers."

"And Moira aint shot them. . . ."

"Didn't know there were any stragglers left up here?"

"Well, you don't see leather packs and coats stitched like that these days."

"You don't see much at all these days except snow."

Everyone laugh at that, a few coughing too.

"Hey, kid, are you a real straggler then?" It's a big square-headed man asking. He lean over and grab at me, turning me so I got to face him.

"We aint stragglers—we're beacons of hope," I say.

That get a bigger laugh than before. But I wish my dad been here cos he gonna say it better, and they aint gonna laugh then.

116

"I said let them be. They're not going to hurt anyone—they're just kids," say the woman.

Some of the people at the front of the truck move along and I sit tight on the bench opposite Mary. I can hear the engine juddering underneath the bench. Mary look at me with her scared eyes but we don't say nothing.

"Hey, Rose, it's Saturday—why don't you come out with me tonight instead of going home to that lump of a man you got?" someone shout above the engine.

"He's a better lump than you are."

"I've only got one lump, Rose, and that's cos I haven't been home for a month."

"Me neither—I'm itching down here, how about it?"

Some of the men start laughing and jeering like they been a bit mad, and I get scared then. It all smell strange, and they act strange, and I don't know where we been going and how I'm gonna get away. I got to get out of here. I don't know how quick the truck move along but I reckon I been far off by now and no food in my pack an all my stuff up in the cave.

"I said, d'you really live up in the hills?" The man got his face right up close all of a sudden. I aint heard him in the din. He been leaning over and grabbing onto my coat. "Hey, kid, I said, d'you live up in the hills?"

But right then the truck slow down and everyone lurch forward.

"Get under the bench." The woman pulling at Mary and a few people move their legs. I feel a strong arm on my shoulder and someone push me down underneath the bench too—don't know why. There's three bangs on the wall from the front of the truck.

"What the hell now?"

"Road police," someone whisper.

"What are they doing out here?"

The boards on the floor of the truck are all damp, and I'm trapped behind a wall of boots, all look the same—dirty and thick—and I push myself as far back as I can.

"What if they find those kids?"

But the canvas lift up, and a blast of cold air blow into the truck. A rough voice bark out.

"We need four of you. There's a drift needs shoveling off the road, and you aint got no plow, so get a move on. You four, not the old man, we haven't got all week."

There's a shuffling and I see some of the boots move and there been murmuring from the men.

"This aint a party so less talking, ladies."

There's a bit of laughing from the rough voices, but like Geraint when he laugh at my dad it aint funny, just mean.

"I said we aint got all week!"

Everyone gone pretty quiet now. I look across at Mary behind the legs under the bench opposite. She put her finger to her lips.

"All right. You. And you. Come on, get a move on." The policeman bang a metal stick on the back of the truck, *clang clang clang* like he been in a hurry.

Some of the men get out then and we can't hear too much just the police laughing and shouting—

"Don't need gloves, feel the radiation coming off 'em."

"I said shovel, aint got til summer—"

After a bit the men get back in the truck.

"Move on, driver," shout the police.

The engine start again and we move off.

"Fucking police," someone say.

"They're as bad out here as in the settlements."

"Leave it now. We'll all be home in a few hours."

"Without us, there wouldn't even be half an hour's power a day."

There been an angry muttering.

A strong arm pull me up. "You sit close, boy. You won't get out before the checkpoint now. No chance."

"What do you mean?" Mary say.

"We got stuck in that drift on the road, and the rest of the convoy caught up with us. The driver's going to see you if you get out. And I don't think that would be a good idea."

He's right cos I can hear the other trucks behind us.

"If I was you"—he turn and look at me; his face is as black as coal—"if I was you I'd get back under the bench when we get to the checkpoint. That's what I'd do."

"Then what?"

"Then if you're lucky you'll get through. It's Saturday night and everyone wants to get home, even the police, and you'll be safe inside."

"Inside where?"

"The settlement."

"What if we don't get past the checkpoint?" Mary ask.

The truck swing to the left and half the people fall forward in their places.

"Can't say, girl. Can't say."

"Why are you helping us?"

"Why not?"

He fall silent then.

Mary look across at me. "There isn't any way back now, Willo—" she whisper.

The truck travel on under the pylons for a long time, swerving and bumping, sometimes fast, sometimes slow, but I can't see nothing. Just got to sit on that hard bench, wondering how we're gonna get out of here. Fear pumping in my stomach so hard I can't think straight.

It seem the people aint interested in much now though. Silently pushing a foot-warming pan filled with coals along the floor. Some of them with chins nodding down on their chests. A shovel of coal been thrown in the stove now and then but that drafty truck still been cold and dark.

It seem a long time I sit there. Aint no way to get out. Mary falling asleep against the woman on the other bench. I see her head drop forward. The truck slow down. People sit up. I kick Mary's foot. There's a bang on the wall from the front.

I can hear shouting outside.

"Get down, Willo," she say, dragging me under the bench. I hope the people in this truck gonna let us be. Cos I don't know who been good and who been bad and everything happen so fast and I aint got no choice.

"Don't do anything. Just keep quiet—"

120

. . .

Wylfa Convoy.

"How many in the back?"

"Fourteen."

"Any incidents?"

"Had to shoot a stealer back at Trawsfinnid."

"You'll have to come in Monday and do the report, you know that. I suppose you've got a witness?"

"Yes, my co-driver."

"What about the body?"

"Left it on the road. It was dangerous."

"Why did you stop? Where was the rest of the convoy?"

The woman pause.

"We got ahead. Stealer jumped out and came at the truck. He wasn't alone."

There's the sound of boots walking round the truck.

"We'll all get it if they find the children," says that old man Reuben.

The man with the black face sitting above me speak low.

"If you say anything about the children, I'll find you slumped in a corner sometime full of drink, and I'll make sure you can't talk again. Do you understand?"

"I'm not frightened of you, Max."

"Do you understand me?"

The black man's voice got a chill in it pretty cold and mean.

Then there's a blast of cold air—the canvas been lifted up.

"I hear a stealer got shot out on the road. Any of you got anything to say about that?"

121

There's a bit of murmuring.

The policeman bang his baton on the metal, a bit impatient.

"We didn't see it," say Rose.

"All right, papers. Pass them down. I'm not getting up."

Behind us there's a truck blowing its horn.

"Just wait!" Policeman shout it like he know the other truck gonna wait for sure. "Come on, hurry up and pass your papers down," he say.

There's a shuffling of papers. I can see Mary's eyes wide and scared. She just been staring at me from under the bench.

My heart been thumping *boom boom boom* in my chest, right up into my throat. Maybe that old man gonna rat on us. Seem like Mary been right about not wanting to get a truck ride back to the city. I aint got nowhere to run now and I don't know the smells and the sounds and my ears just ringing with everything so strange, cowering like a dog with its tail between its legs. Don't want that policeman to drag me up from under this bench and send me off down a coal mine or lock me up in some cold box and I can't even say my words in my head my heart beating so loud.

"All right. Move on!"

The canvas come down. Policeman bang on the truck. The engine roar up and we move off.

Just like that.

"Don't you bloody talk to me like that"—the old man cough—"you gonna get his coat yourself, that's what I reckon. DON'T YOU TRUST THAT BLACK DOG, BOY! He's going to have the skin off your back."

"Shut up, Reuben," say Rose.

"He'll have the skin off your back"—but the old man break up with coughing again.

The black man don't say nothing. I can't see him, just his boots in front of me on the floor of the truck.

And his big strong hand reach down and get me up.

"You're inside the settlement," he say. "Better look out for yourself."

PART II

THE CITY

This is the place: these narrow ways, diverging to the right and left, and reeking everywhere with dirt and filth. See how the rotten beams are tumbling down, and how the patched and broken windows seem to scowl dimly ... Narrow ways, diverging to the right and left ... where neither ray of light nor breath of air appears to come.

—*Charles Dickens,* American Notes

19

The flap come up on the back of the truck and the driver shout, *Everyone get out!*

I got to jump down with the others. My feet land hard on the ice. Mary tight behind me. I see the shacks and tents stretching out all around. Choking smog hanging over it all. The smog just drape itself over everything. And the smell of smoke and the stench of animals and shit and rubbish knock right back in my throat.

Wooden poles lean every which way along the edge of the street, power lines sag between them. A few dim lights swing in the wind above the trucks. The snow been heaped up into great banks along each side of the roadway. Above us the blank inky sky never ending.

We been in a great line of trucks smoking and rumbling along the side of the road. Out the back come a tired stream of people with deep canvas hoods pulled over their heads. The breath rising up from those people in the thin smoggy light been like terrible steam drifting about their heads. Their boots tramping down on the cold dirty snow, no one talking much, and I been one of them—cold and tired from sitting for hours on that hard wooden bench.

"Hey!" An old man pulling a wheelbarrow piled high with boots push past, shouting, waving his arm. "Hey, out of the way!"

Tramping right beside us is a thickset black and white horse pulling a creaking cart. The horse snorting in the cold air. On the cart people sit up under a canvas roof wrapped in heavy woolen cloaks and capes. The driver shout out at the stream of men and women all about. A little girl clinging on to the rail at the back stare at me. Her mother pull her back under the cover. All around us been a thousand huts and tents built up from scraps of canvas and wood and old bricks and doors and metal sheets piled higgledy-piggledy like leaves when they fall. Bits of loose wood and sheets of metal hanging from makeshift shacks flap about as a cold wind gust down the street. It lift the cloak of an old woman leading a cow. The cow got a sacking blanket covering its back—cow just plodding slow in the gutter like it been blind.

A truck come pushing out through all those carts and waggons and people, horn blasting. The cow scare and slip on the ice with a scared moaning sound. All those horses and wagons and carts got to move over quick then, and everyone been squashed up still further against the banks—aint no choice as the truck push through.

We get off the road, jostled by the crowd through a gap in the snow into some kind of market alongside the street. A few lights swing wild overhead. Someone with a goat, shouting, *Fresh milk, fresh milk,* and chickens squawk in cages and rabbits held up by their ears and people stitching leather with big machines they turn by hand and women stirring steaming vats of soup over glowing barrels of coals and all about people pushing and shoving and grabbing and shouting and everywhere rubbish gray and filthy in the snowy night. And the smell of people and animals and smoke in my head like it just gonna burst open, cos I aint never seen so many people and things and heard so many noises or smelled so many strange and awful smells in all my life.

Just feel like I'm a leaf that fall in the river, and the river gonna sweep me out to sea any way it want as that tide of men and women wash out among the tents and streets of the shanties like the waters at Barmuth flooding into the estuary.

"Willo!"

Mary nearly swept out with the crowd, but I grab her shoulder, and she find me crouching flat against the bank of snow. The biggest place I ever been before is the Barmuth summer market. But Barmuth gonna fit in the pocket of this place.

The street been strewn with cinders, gray and dirty underfoot. All along it tables and boxes and wagons are piled high with boots, rags, potatoes, bundles of hay, sacks of oats and salt, battered tins and glass bottles, bits of wood, piles of coal. Everything you can think of. Someone ride by on a stout pony with just a pack on their saddle—they been so close I can smell them. There's a clanking and a shouting and the sound of too many people. A new gust of wind howl along the street and everyone dig themselves deeper inside their coats.

Mary cling on at my side, whisper in my ear, "We've got to get away from here. Follow me."

• • •

When I been little, my dad take me down to a pool in the river. It been a really good summer cos the sun been shining warm and everyone got their coats off all month—I remember that cos Magda got them laid out on the table all week, unpicking the seams and smoking out the lice. The melt been and gone so the water in the pool aint been too freezing.

My dad say, *Willo, you got to learn to swim.* I reckon I think he been mad cos people can't swim. I mean, they can walk and jump and run, but *Aint they gonna sink in the water, Dad?* My dad say, *No, they aint gonna sink, silly child. Cos you got lungs filled with air.* Then I remember it pretty good cos he take all his clothes off.

I can see the skin on his neck and hands all dark against his thin white body, with the grass poking up around his bare feet. He go to the pool and dip his foot in. I can see it been pretty cold cos he pull it out quick. Then he do something I aint never forget. He just hold his nose and take a breath and jump straight in.

I tell you I been screaming out then cos I think my dad gone forever and been drowned in the river but no—he come up all of a sudden. His head pop up, and he been gasping for breath and making funny noises like, *Ooh, ooh, ooh,* but after a bit his breathing calm down and he been moving his arms about and start swimming around that pool like a goose. And I got a laugh up inside me then, maybe cos I been a bit scared to start with, but he look proper funny all white and making strange noises and laughing sometimes and ducking down under the water to frighten me. But then he say, *You got to come in, Willo. Get your clothes off and jump in. You'll be all right.*

I aint never been so scared. Aint no way I'm gonna throw myself into that freezing dark pool like my graybeard dad. Cos I know I'm just gonna sink right down to the bottom, and my heart been beating and I run away onto the hill and my dad come out all dripping wet and shouting after me but I aint gonna come down til he forget about teaching me to swim.

And now I got the same feeling when Mary say, *Follow me.* I been frozen with fear. Stuck against the side of the street. Those crowds of people terrify me like that freezing pool—I just know they gonna suck me under. I think on what my dad say about all the dark bad things just waiting in the shadows of the city after the troubles come. Dad say, *You lucky you aint been alive then, Willo.*

· · ·

Mary reach for my hand, and I look at her proper scared. This girl got something soft in her eyes.

"Come on, Willo, we've got to get away."

"I don't want to," I say.

But there aint no hills to run and hide in here.

"Come on." She pull on my arm.

I got to do it. Take a deep breath. Close my eyes and jump. Throw myself out into the stream of bodies.

"Come on," say Mary again.

And I do it. The swirling river of people swallow me up, crashing about me and bashing against me. A sea of people—and Mary leading me along, off and away between the tents. Between the piles of rubbish and dirty snow. I follow her, hurrying along dark pathways. Away from the crowds.

"Keep close." Mary pull me into the shadows. Now and then we pass someone slipping between the lanes like us but no one say a word. Two men fall bawling and angry through a doorway, and we dodge down a pathway away from them.

"Where we gonna go?" I ask.

Mary turn and stop for a second. "I'm not quite sure yet."

Far off on the dark horizon I see a craggy tower rising up from the smoky tents, black against the dingy sky. Dogs barking all about. Mary still trotting on.

· · ·

Cos the dog, he's a wolf-dog
He got cunning and clever
Knows your hills and your valleys
All roundside about.

· · ·

So this been the city.

I aint swimming, Dad, but I aint drowned either.

No I aint drowned yet.

20

The lights from the market been far behind us now. Mary hurry along the icy tracks and pathways between the shacks and tents. She's just a small shadow in front of me in the dark. When she stop I see a flash from her eyes and she put a finger to her mouth. Listening.

Far off a baby start to cry.

I hear something else. Rising all around the settlement. Shouting. Muffled in the cold air. Far off—the banging of sticks. Now and then a wail rise up in the sky. There's something animal in it that scare me right down to my guts.

"Beetham gangs," she say. "We've got to get away."

People in the shacks start coming alive around us, grunts and whispers—the noise of awakening—cos they hear the angry noises too. A sound like baying dogs.

Far off a girl screech. But it aint a long screech—kind of cut short.

"Down here." Mary crouch beside a broken wall. The noise rear up now and then to the west—shouting and chanting and the beating of sticks on metal. Ahead of us something flare up above the tents. Someone padding quick down the path. They near stumble on top of us—woman with a child in her arms running like she been crazy. She don't see us, and I hear her hard breathing as she run, fleet-footed, like a hare from a stoat, past us into some unknown darkness.

It's so dark you can't see where you step. Mary pull me up.

"Quick!"

She been quicker than I think, ducking low here and there, swinging off away from the noise of the gangs. I pad behind her, jumping piles of rubbish between the broken huts, following the dirty warren of paths, fast as we can go.

Soon the pathways widen out onto a snowy track. A scared dog come running up from behind, his scrawny haunches down and his tail between his legs. He give us a quick look and skitter past. Mary stop.

"Rest a minute," she say breathlessly.

All around us great mounds of horse dung steam in the snow. Ahead there been a line of low wooden buildings along the edge of the track. A warm smell rise up from them.

"Look." She point over, and in the night air I see the breath curl around a pair of horses, their heads hanging over a rail across the open front of the shed. Other creatures rustle quiet in the stalls and a pair of goats jump up against the gate all curious. The smell of animal been sweet and rich on the air.

"Me da was a ponyman," she say.

"What are the Beetham gangs?"

"People you don't want to meet."

"What are they?"

"Just gangs on the grog. But shh." Mary point into the dark.

At the end of the row of animal pens a fire burning in a metal drum and a couple of people standing round, shapeless in their coats, holding hands out to the warmth, ragged tents sprawled around and about. A dog on a chain start to bark in our direction. Way off another dog reply and then another and another.

"This way—"

She slip away around the dung heaps and over a broken fence and we been out on another field deep in snow. There aint no shacks here, just a tall metal fence cutting across the ground and behind it plastic tunnels stretching out as far as the eye can see. The snow falling all around, but there's a kind of steamy mist in the air like those tunnels been breathing. Along the fence been signs tied on with wire every so often.

ANPEC
PATROLLED
KEEP OUT

Mary skirt along the fence.

"The 'lotments," she say. "For growing food."

I stare. "How they gonna grow food in the winter?"

"Wires in the ground, I reckon. Just potatoes and things, but you won't get in. They got dogs and guards going to shoot if they see you."

"Where we going?"

"Over there's the city." She point way off over the field.

Mary seem to know this place roundside about, and I wonder if she been living in one of those sorry smoking tents hunted by

135

the bad people before her dad take a pony and get her up on the Rhinogs. I look up and the freezing wind catch my breath and coil around my neck. Ahead of us on the northern side of the 'lotments been a darkness in the night sky, solid shapes against the horizon.

"Hurry up, Willo, this way."

I aint got time to stop and think if it been a good idea just following this girl cos we got behind a lonely row of houses now, cold and dark, a great row of houses like the trees in the plantation. Some of the houses got a bit of light behind the boarded windows. The snow been thick on every roof and piled up high in great banks. A woman pass by down between the buildings. No one gonna say a word though and we shrink away from any strangers passing in the night like they been ravens scrieking and quartering over the Farngod.

Mary stop walking, look about, beckon with her arm, and I follow her, scrambling down a steep bank thick with snow beside the track. At the bottom the ground level off to a tolerable path alongside a great empty trench twenty feet across. Steep walls fall down into the dark. The ditch disappear off in both directions, deep and wide, almost like a river.

"What is it?" I ask Mary.

"The old ship canal. Goes west all the way to the sea. Empty now."

Ahead of us a bridge arch up among some trees, and far off on the edge of the path, a lantern hang down from the front of a house lighting a sign. It say, THE KING WILLIAM.

"Come on," Mary say. She point at the building.

"What is it?"

"The King Will. Beerhouse. Me da used to go down the rat pit there. If Vince is there, we'll get some food."

"Who's Vince?"

"You'll see, come on."

I been proper hungry it's true. But I wish my dog gonna tell me what to do. I call out to him quiet in my head. *Good clever dog, where you been, what you gonna do?*

But the dog keep quiet. Reckon he run off quick and clever before he get stuck under the stinking fog of the city.

"Come on, Willo, it's safe, I promise. And there's a storm coming."

Mary been right, I can taste it on the wind.

And I step down the path in the shadows behind the beerhouse to a dark wooden door. Mary put her hand on my arm. "It's all right."

She push open the door.

In the corner is a woman dealing out cards. She turn and look at us. She's old, wearing a long thick dress, tatty at the hem. The room aint bright, just candles burning here and there and a small fire in the corner. Along the back wall been a bar with a door behind it. On the left a bench and a scarred old wooden table like at home. On the wall behind the woman, there's a picture of a dog standing all brave, and underneath it say, THE KENTISH BITCH.

Mary say, "We want soup," to anyone and no one.

"Vince!" the woman sitting in the corner shout.

A shutter in the door behind the bar slide open. A man's face appear. He got a beaky nose and small dark eyes, glinting through a grille.

"What?"

"Children. They want soup."

The man look at me suspicious. Then he see Mary.

"Mary. I aint see your da," he says. "He hasn't been here for months. You got a message?"

"It's not me da I'm looking for. Just want something to eat," say Mary. "Me and me friend."

The grille slide shut, but pretty soon the door open and the beaky face come out with two pails of hot soup in his hands. He clatter them down on the bar.

"Two quid."

"Haven't got any money," say Mary.

The beady-eyed man look me up and down. I see he been looking at my coat.

"Your da should be at home looking after you kids. I aint seen him for a long while though. When you see him tell him, 'The moths are on the wing.' Tell him to come and see me. Where's he been?"

"Don't know. Haven't eaten in a few days."

Vince crease his forehead up. "All right. But give him the message, you hear. And watch out roaming about this time of night. Curfew won't stop the gangs. Sit in the corner," he say, scratching his ear with long fingernails.

"What's that about moths on the wing?" I ask Mary, but right then an old man get up from the bench where he been sitting in the shadows. He stumble up beside us and put some money down.

"Another drink," he say.

This old man smell pretty bad. His shoes wrapped in rags. His face lined with wrinkles under his dirty graying beard and his eyes been dark holes under a slab of hair hanging down over his pocked forehead. He aint too steady on his feet either.

"Another drink," he say again, mumbling into his coat and banging a mug down on the bar. Vince don't look too pleased but he fill the dirty mug with some sort of grog and the old man dilly-dally pulling imaginary things from his pockets then shuffle off back to the corner with his mug.

"Don't mind Piper," say Vince. "He brought the rats down the pit for the dogs tonight. You two just sit quiet in the corner til you've finished your soup. Then—" He make a gesture with his thumb toward the door.

Vince scrape the drunk man's money off the bar and without another word he slink back to wherever it is he go behind that little door and the woman go back to pulling cards out her hand.

But I don't care cos that soup in the pail steaming hot and smell like the most delicious thing I ever smelled I been so hungry. Mary already busy spooning hers into her mouth, and I do the same. Good big lumps of cabbage and potato at the bottom gonna fill you up good and I aint looking up got my mouth so close to the pail and I don't notice that old drunk man slide along the bench and sit up real close now.

"Hungry little children, aren't we?" he say. Sound like Geraint.

It make me jump. He's so close I can see the dirt under his fingernails. His dark knobbly hands clutching at the mug.

"Want to see a rat, boyo?"

I wipe my mouth on my sleeve and stare at him.

Mary kick me under the table.

"Do you want to see a rat, look you?"

"I seen plenty of rats," I say.

"Bet you won't have seen one like Ruby though?"

The man reach down into his pocket and pull out a big black and white rat that sit all quiet on his hand as he stroke it—

"Out of the houses, the rats came tumbling, great rats, small rats, lean rats, brawny rats, brown rats, black rats, gray rats, tawny rats—" The man's lips get all wet as he speak.

Then he put the rat back in his pocket, looking like he gonna say something more but forget what. He take a deep gulp from his mug.

"I aint never seen a rat like that," I say.

Looking up, he twitch his mouth into a brief smile—laugh to himself. The laugh break into a cough, his head shaking on his neck.

The rat start climbing up the sleeve of his coat. Mary and me just sitting quiet. This drunk man aint gonna stop. I can see it. Just gonna swivel his watery brown eyes on us again any minute.

"Shall I tell you about trapping the rats?"

His arms slide forward on the table. He aint holding his mug too steady, just staring at nothing behind our heads.

"When you're trapping you never, never, never put bait on the traps. Always put traps in their runs.... You'll find rats are cunning after a few have been caught—oh, aye, they'll jump over the traps, so you've got to try another night—"

The man's elbow slip off the table, and he cough, and I can see his spit spray in little bloody spots on the table. But he aint finished.

He hold up the rat in front of him. "More precious than rubies is wisdom . . . and she's got riches and honor in her hands." His voice get all quiet and sticky-sounding. "Her ways are ways of pleasantness. Don't forget that, children." His drunken face got real close now. "Yes, children, her ways are ways of pleasantness, and all her paths are peace."

His eyes close. The rat drop down onto the bench.

The old man slump forward against the table, his head slowly falling til his forehead's resting on the scarred planks. Snores flapping out from his hairy old mouth right in front of us.

With a gust of cold air, the door open. Two men come in from outside, snow on their shoulders, big coats pulled so high can't see their faces in the candlelight. One of them got a short thick dog pulling on a rope, but those men don't look at us, they just bash on the door behind the bar shouting, *Vince!*

But the dog look over. I watch him give a quick turn of the snout.

The rat man snoring on the table and his rat still sniffing about on the bench. That rat aint got too much sense what with that stocky dog straining on its leash so close, cos the rat hang down by her back legs and plop onto the floor, and now she been sniffing along toward the door.

I seen it. And the dog seen it.

Dog start whimpering and barking and scrabbling against its leash.

"Oy, Billy! Get back, will ya!" shout the man, rough.

But the man's too late cos the dog aint stopping.

The dog break free.

There been a great big commotion then: The dog shoot under the table, the rat catcher wake up from his dark sleep like a bolt of lightning cracking open a tree.

But it been too late cos the dog quick as a dart got the rat by the neck. The rat scream. *Eeeeek.* But with a flick of that dog's neck the rat been got and tossed against the wall.

The old rat catcher crash against the table and fumble drunk across the room, fall down on his knees. But he been too late. His rat all dead and broken. It take him a few seconds to see it.

"Ruby!" he moan.

And he's holding that rat in his hands like it been a baby or something and he got tears in his eyes running down his old cheeks and he's looking up at the men in their coats, and they just been laughing at him blubbing on the dirty cold floor of this room in his raggy coat—almost look as broken as that limp rat he been holding in his hands.

Vince come out at all the noise. And he see what happen—putting the bits together like a puzzle. Vince put this sorry story together quick, and he start shouting at those men with big hands reaching out and getting their dog under control. The men soon stop laughing pretty quick, cos Vince got something inside him make him seem stronger when he been shouting, even though he's beaky and got small little eyes and dirty long fingernails. *Can't you see that's all he's got? That rat? It aint funny,* he shout.

The big men look at each other like kids.

"Sorry, Piper," says one to the blubbering old man. "You'll get another one."

But he don't mean sorry, you can tell.

The rat man aint listening though, just sobbing and blubbering with his cheek right close to the dead rat. The men with the dog shrug their shoulders a bit. Vince help the old man up.

"Come on, Piper, they're right, you'll get another one."

"Not like Ruby. Not like Ruby."

He keep repeating that even after Vince pour him out another drink.

"Not like Ruby."

The rat lying dead in front of him on the table.

"Not like Ruby," he blub like a little girl.

The whole thing make me feel proper sad inside I tell you, seeing him crying like a baby over his black and white rat, even though he been a big old-time graybeard and drunk too.

He look up from his mug.

"Yes. Yes, it's time to leave, Ruby. Got to go now."

"We'll help you get home," say Mary.

I look at her hard.

"Yes, yes, little girl." The old man pick up the dead rat, pull on a large shapeless hat and make for the door.

"We've got to follow him," say Mary.

"You really want to go with him?"

"You've got a better idea, have you? We'll freeze out on the street. Vince'll kick us out soon, and the curfew's coming down. Don't want to be wandering about then. He's so drunk he won't do us any harm. Trust me."

The woman's still dealing her cards out in the corner. Staring down at them. She don't say a word.

21

Outside a fearsome wind blowing up. That old rat man stagger away from the beerhouse along the path by the canal. He stop and piss in the snow. Swaying. Mary and me stand back.

"Why do you want to follow him?" I say.

"We got to sleep somewhere. And he's not going to hurt us. Look."

The old man got the dead rat out his pocket, and he's blubbing on to it quietly, his coat flapping up around him in the wind.

Mary come up soft behind him. "Come on, Piper, got to get home before the storm, before the curfew."

The old man look at Mary. Then back along the snowy path.

"Got to get home, Ruby. That's right."

He put the rat back in his coat and stagger forward in the snow.

After a while he lurch toward the empty canal. I reckon he's gonna fall in it and break his neck, but there's a ladder. The old man lower his leg unsteady over the edge and pull his coat around in the wind. Clinging on and grunting, he disappear over the edge, down into the darkness below.

"Come on, Willo, we got to follow him."

"Down there?"

"Yes."

Mary already getting down the ladder, so I got to follow.

The ladder go down and down. Got to be tall as a house, the walls seem to fall in over me. Towering up in the night. The light from the beerhouse far behind us up on the path, the stony walls of the canal glint here and there with water, frozen in icy riverlets seeping from the brickwork, with just the night sky reflecting off the piles of rubbish and snow far down below.

At the bottom, the old man steady himself against the wall. He breathe heavy and rest his hands on his knees. Then he move off, his feet following an icy trail along the side of the drifts.

A group of scrubby trees sprout out from the wall. The bare branches just dark shadows against the snow. He push his way into the trees, following a well-worn path, fighting the twigs that catch at his coat.

Far off above us a loud siren blast out across the dark settlement, echoing in the night air.

"What is it?" I whisper.

"Curfew."

We push in among the bare branches. The old man coughing in front of us. Behind the trees, built into the wall of the canal, been an archway covered in boards. A doorway. He struggle to get it open.

"You want help wi' it?" say Mary.

The rat man turn and look at Mary then like he seen her for the first time. He gasp, scared. His wet lips moving soundlessly in the tangle of his beard.

"It's all right, we're not going to rob you, just need somewhere to sleep," she say.

The man cower against the door. Hands over his head.

"Baba's children. Are you come to rob me?"

"No, we aren't going to rob you. You said we could sleep here."

"Ruby's dead."

"I know, but we'll stay wi' you tonight. All right?"

Mary look at me with raised eyebrows.

"Just tonight," I say. "We're only gonna help you, old man. You can get up. We aint gonna hurt you."

I help him up. I aint scared no more, just thinking I been pleased I got that soup down my neck. Best thing about the city so far that soup. I don't care no more where we going or who he is we been with cos my eyes so tired I just want to sleep.

The old man seem happy that we aint gonna rob him. He mumble to himself and heave the door open. We step inside. Pulling the door shut behind us, he shuffle forward, his steps echoing in the dampness.

I hear something strike and his bearded face been lit up as he bend over a stubby candle trying to push his wobbling match onto the wick.

We been in some kind of tunnel arching up over us back into the dark. The tunnel pretty low and that old man got to stoop at the side where he been standing. It smell of damp and smoke and earth. Hanging off nails in the walls been wire cages and traps.

Stumbling, he take the candle to a small stove made from a

147

metal drum, the crooked chimney pipe stuck in the wall. He kneel down and fiddle about with sticks and a match but he done this before I reckon or he gonna be dead from the cold. That fire soon been spitting into life and he lay a couple of sticks on it.

"Nice warm fire for the hungry children, Ruby."

He take the dead rat from his coat and lay it in a small cage sitting on a shelf.

"You can use that—" he say, pointing to a pan by his bed. "But otherwise"—he gesture to the door—"outside."

He grab a dirty bottle off the shelf and stagger to a great pile of blankets heaped up on a bed against the wall. Without another word, he pull off his boots and fall down onto it. His head aint hit the pillow before he's snoring again.

Mary go over to the bed, she pull one of the blankets over the old man's chest. Girls always thinking of things like that. I see her hands in the candlelight, little finger just a bit crooked but the others long and delicate, tugging on the heavy blanket. She take her hood down, and her hair been in a proper mess, kind of hiding her face—it's the color of hay. I wonder if it smell good like hay too. She turn and look at me.

"What?" she say.

I look away.

"We can sleep here safe." She unpick a couple of rugs from the bed and carry them over. I drag some old planks to the fire and make up somewhere dry to lie down. We been so tired we just get down on the floor in front of the fire and pull the rugs over us.

"You really reckon we been safe here?" I say.

"Yes," say Mary. "No one's going to bother wi' us down here. Rat catcher's going to sleep til the morning. Curfew now anyway. Everyone's got to stay inside."

"Curfew?"

"Yes, you can't go out after curfew."

"What happens if you do?"

"If you get caught, you mean?"

"Yes. If you get caught."

"I don't know. Got to show your papers? Maybe they take you away?"

"Who takes you away?"

"Soldiers, police—whoever catches you. Worse if it's some gang."

"Then what?" I ask.

Mary wriggling close under the blankets. "I don't know, Willo. I've never been out after the curfew. Why do you want to know?"

"I want to know where my dad is. Where he's been taken. And the others. Magda. The little ones ..."

"Your da got papers?" she say, turning her head over her shoulder.

"Course not. We're stragglers. We aint got papers."

"No, 'spose not. So why did they take your da away?"

"I don't know. Geraint rat us out. But I'm gonna get him."

"Who's Geraint?"

"Just a farmer. He rat us out I reckon, cos he come back to our house after the government trucks been and taken everyone away. But I'm gonna go back to the mountains, to his farm, and get him. Find out where they take my dad."

She turn back to the fading fire.

"How are you going to get to Geraint now?" She yawn.

"I'm thinking on it," I say.

We been quiet for a bit. "What was all that about 'moths on the wing'?" I ask her. "Vince say it in the beerhouse. Sound like the poem my dad always telling me."

"I don't know. Vince is always giving me da messages like that."

I hope she aint gonna start blubbing, thinking on her dead dad. But she don't.

"Really. How are you going to get back to the mountains now, Willo?"

She's right. It aint gonna be easy. Feel like this one day stretched on for a week already. All those thousand people in the city. Stink and dirt and trucks and everyone cold and hungry.

"You think it's gonna be hard, Mary?"

There aint no answer.

"Mary?"

But Mary fall asleep. I can feel her little stick-thin body rising and falling. I aint gonna blow out the candle; I'm just gonna lie here looking at the side of her face a bit. Reckon if she got a bit of fat on her bones she's gonna be quite pretty.

"Whaa—!"

The old man sit up in his bed with a shout. But he fall back down again straight off.

Mary don't wake up. Just breathe on deep and heavy. Trusting. She shift in her sleep and I move the blanket back over her shoulder.

Outside I hear the loudness of men and women high up on the path. But the sound move along. Mary's right. I reckon we been safe down here tonight.

It aint gonna be easy.

I got to do it before morning.

Cos she's gonna make a fuss big and loud if I try and tell her. She's gonna want to come.

But I got to leave her. She's gonna slow me down.

She's gonna be all right here though. Got this place for a start. Got the old man. He aint gonna hurt no one. And Mary knows people. Knows how to get by I reckon.

I got things to do.

I got to get back where I belong.

I been thinking on those horses with their heads hanging over the gate. Horse gonna be what you need to get along quick.

Mary move again, making little noises in her sleep. Her arm fall against my face. Her cold hand resting on my cheek. I move it away real gentle.

I'm gonna leave her the gloves I make her. She's gonna need them. It don't seem the city people got much idea bout keeping warm.

Something sweet as honey about her hand somehow, just falling on my face like that. And she been proper smart and clever getting us the soup and finding this place to sleep. She aint the stupid little girl I think she been. Not when she been here in the city.

But really, I aint got room for no one else. Got to get Geraint, find out where my dad been. See Alice. Aint seen Alice for a year. Not since she went to Geraint's farm.

I got a tight knot in my guts thinking about that snake Geraint with his dirty fingers poking about my dad's stuff and ratting us out. Thinking about where my dad been, if I'm gonna see him again. I got a bad feeling about it.

Maybe I got a bit of a tight knot thinking about leaving Mary too.

She stir in her sleep.

"Willo?" she say all sleepy.

"I been here, Mary. Go back to sleep."

"You won't leave me, Willo. Will you?"

"You got to sleep, Mary."

The candle gutter, and it's out. Just smell its last breath of smoke in the dark. And Mary's hair. Smell that too. She reach out under the blanket.

"You won't, will you?"

I aint gonna say nothing. Just hold her still under my arm til her breath get deep again.

I wish we been up on the Farngod right now.

Up on the Farngod, quiet in the snow.

22

That old rat catcher snore in his bed.

Mary breathing deep.

Good and quiet I get up. A slip of light slide in through a crack in the door. I take the stubby candle and put it in my pouch. Take the gloves and lay them on the floor next to Mary. She's gonna know I left them for her cos I lay them down nice and neat. I reckon she's gonna understand.

• • •

I crack open the door with a lowdown feeling inside. Outside the light just getting up in the sky. The storm blow the clouds away and it grow clear over in the east. A stillness in the air at last.

A clump of snow fall from the bare branches of the bushes, a crow flap up from the opposite bank. He aint been expecting me as I creep out, my breath like smoke on the chill morning air.

It's strange being down at the bottom of this great empty canal. The tall gray walls curve away before and behind. Dirty brick rising high above me. I got to go west. Toward the sea. Out of the city and then find a horse. Take a horse and get back to the Rhinogs. To Geraint's farm.

I can see our track through the drifts where we come last night and I follow it. I'm gonna head on down this canal. Don't look like too many people gonna be down here to bother me.

A ray of sun crack over the city behind me. A low orange light catch along the top of the bricks. The shadows on the drifted ridges of snow turn purple and blue like a frozen river heading out through the city. And the city coming awake with this new day you can hear it.

Soon Mary gonna wake up.

I got to hurry on.

Soon she's gonna be calling out.

Cos I aint told her nothing.

• • •

Don't need that sickly pup running at your heels. You're Number One, remember. Got to find your pack. An eye for an eye. Remember.

• • •

Good dog come back!

• • •

Remember, Willo?

• • •

Good dog run down from the mountain in the night. Good dog sniff me out in this cold dark city. He aint forgot me. No way. Dog gonna help me.

I got a feeling full with hope in my footsteps now. It's a good feeling, with the dog back and all. All I'm gonna need is a bit of food to keep me on my way. And a bit of luck, and a bit of cunning.

23

The old rat catcher got a good idea making himself a place down here. Better than those ragged tents in the settlements. I get along the bottom of the canal in the shadows under the cold brick walls. Picking through the drifts and dirty snow.

Sometimes I pass under buildings that run either side of the canal. Great dead-looking buildings high up on the path. Must be hundreds of windows in them, black holes in the gray walls. And a couple of dogs trotting along up there—one look down over the edge at me. Look like they know where they been going. Don't slow their pace.

The sun getting higher. Way down under the snow I can hear water trickling. Don't reckon that old river dried up yet. In the distance a bridge cut high over the canal.

Then I see the ship.

Past the bridge. Long way off. Leaning, rusted against the wall of the canal. A great ship dumped on the canal bed.

It must be a pretty big ship come right up to the top of the canal walls far as I can see from here. Rusting windows and doors and rails sticking up all around the top and some kind of chimney poking out the middle. Big round chimney, bit of paint still clinging on.

It look like the dead whale I seen by the sea a couple of years back. That ship look the same way wrong, tilting over to one side, flat on its underbelly, deep in the snow. Like it been forgotten. There's something about it aint too friendly somehow.

A truck pass over the bridge.

Got to think what to do.

Dug out of the drifts by the side of the path, I come on a hollow. The hollow look just like the camps the little kids dig in the snow when they should be collecting wood or water.

People been in this dugout. Seats beaten down, snow all dirty. Proper good glass bottles just lying on the ground. I pick one up. It's empty. ERGUOTOU written on the bottle. ERGUOTOU. I smell it. Grog.

I look back where I come. Aint seen no dwellings. Nothing except that old ship in the distance. I got a bad feeling stuck down in the bottom of this canal, like it's a ravine with no way out.

I get to thinking about Mary. Get to thinking of her cold hand falling on my face. Trusting me in her sleep.

Someone shouting high up from the path for a second. I crouch low. The noise die away. I hope Mary gonna be all right with that old graybeard back under the arches. I wonder what she's gonna do when she wake up and find I aint there.

Hope that old rat catcher gonna be kind. Mary aint much younger than Alice when Alice got pregnant with Geraint. Aint gonna trust an old graybeard in some things.

But Mary aint stupid. I seen that.

Just a bit further along, there's an opening under the wall. Pitch-black inside. Another truck rumble over the bridge. I duck into the archway.

The tunnel seem to disappear into the earth. Can't see nothing cos my eyes aint used to the darkness. Maybe I got to go back for her. Mary I mean. I squat on the cold ground. Take out Patrick's traveling pouch with the last of the oatcakes in it. Patrick make the pouch real nice and even put a new pattern on the leather. He's a dreamer really. Instead of talking he's got to be fiddling with things. I hear my dad tell Magda it's cos he aint got a woman.

Magda get really interested in that kind of thing. She been planning to get Patrick to go downriver in the summer when we all go for a Meet with the others at Barmuth. I feel sorry for Patrick cos when Magda starts thinking of putting a boy with a girl at the Barmuth Meet, she's like a fox in cunning. I watch Patrick make that pouch cos I want to see how he do the pattern. That's number one for learning stuff if you aint got a book.

I got a low feeling thinking of Magda and the others. The city aint so ordered like I think it gonna be. The way my dad always talk about it, I been reckoning that there's gonna be police everywhere and all the people stuck in cold boxes who got to work in the coal mines or get sent off to Wylfa for no good reason. Like Patrick. But the city don't feel like that. It feel like a craggy bit of rock rising up out of the mountain that you aint never gonna know roundside about, aint never gonna climb up it the same way twice. Feel like the city don't care about nothing. Just got people scurrying about scared, trying to get on. Aint got much order to it far as I can see. I feel like a worm, a tiny worm lost in a huge nothing.

Mary pulling me back like a magnet.

I seen a magnet when I been a kid. I don't know where my dad got it but he show us all the tricks you can do with a magic thing like that. Make other bits of metal stick to it and stuff. Dad say you can make electricity with a magnet, and it aint magic, *it's science.* Well, if that aint magic, I don't know what is cos even the magic tricks they do at the Barmuth Meet sometimes, they just tricks done by one of the dads with mud on his face for the little ones, and you know it. But the magnet been real, pulling everything toward it.

Something make me turn. In the dark at the back of the tunnel.

I strain my eyes, heart beating hard in my chest. I aint expecting it. Aint expecting nothing to be in here scratching in the dark.

Just a whimper.

I stand up now, looking into the blackness.

Another whimper.

I get my tinder out quick and strike a light to that stubby bit of candle in my pouch. I hold it up, shielding the flame with my hand, and step forward into the tunnel.

A glint.

Something at the very back.

Something back there in the dark.

Aint moving.

Something hanging from the ceiling.

Got limbs.

I look down.

Dark patch on the snow.

Blood.

My guts freeze.

A carcass. Flayed. Hanging by its back legs with no skin. Skull a mass of sinews and eyeballs bulging out glassy. Frozen blood trampled into the snow all about. The flesh hacked at.

Everything about it bad.

A dog. A butchered dog. Something daubed on the bricks.

There is no law beyond Do what thou wilt.

I hear the whimpering again. In the farthest corner, another dog, this one alive, tied to the wall by a rope. This dog only been a puppy. Mangy brown puppy cowering in the corner, tail tucked under it, ears back, shaking.

"Shhh. Little pup. I aint gonna hurt you."

I crouch down. Feel along the rope. The puppy pulling away from me, whimpering and scrabbling in the dirt.

"Come here, little one. No one gonna get you now."

I put my hand on its soft head. Run my hand over its shaking back. It been pretty thin. I untie the fraying rope around its neck. The frightened pup back away from me.

"I aint gonna hurt you."

But the pup scuttle along the wall and scrabble out the tunnel into the snow with its stubby tail between its legs. Just want to be free.

I got a scared feeling in my guts then thinking who tied it up in here. That butchered dog hanging from the ceiling and everything. Reckon I got to get out of this dirty old canal.

But that thought been a thought too late.

159

"Oy!"

Shadows fall across the entrance.

People, dark against the light outside. Kids. Tall ones and small ones. There's a rush of noise as they fill the tunnel.

A little girl come dancing in front of me, can't be more than about eight years old. Skin drawn taut across her face. Red-rimmed eyes. Hands and feet wrapped in rags. She's got a stick and she start poking it hard under my ribs.

Someone pull me, grab my arms behind me.

"Hang him up with the dog!"

An older girl push the kid with the stick out the way. She got one white eye, all milky like old Roger who been building the boat at Barmuth last summer. It's the last thing I see. Dead white eye. Unblinking.

"Hood him."

Someone pull a sack over my head. Rough dirty-smelling sack.

Everything dark.

Something smack against my head.

I hear my head crack like a splitting branch.

The world slip away.

Hands pluck at me.

Dark now.

Sinking down.

Dog. *Help me.*

24

My hands are cold. So cold I can't feel them. Gloves gone. And my coat.

I make those gloves from a good big hare I trap up on the Farngod. After I trap him, I say my words and run home to Dad. We aint gonna be hungry that night for sure. And Dad say, *This skin's not for Geraint.* So I skin the hare and scrape the bloody fur of fat and flesh. Soak the pelt til the fur is as soft as if it been alive. And then Magda show me how to cut the gloves to a pattern from my hands and make the fine cuts in the pieces and restitch them so that the fur falls soft and loose. And then I grease the leather and tool it with a pattern of my own on the gauntlet sleeves that come up your arm and keep the snow out and I brush and pick out the fur from the stitching, so you can't see the seam, double stitched with gut, that's gonna swell in the damp and keep your hands dry and warm in the winter storms.

They been a good pair of gloves.

But I aint got them no more.

Worse still is my coat. Feel like I'm gonna freeze to death on this frozen ground.

It been so cold. I need to be sick with the pain in my head, and it comes out of me the vomit, inside the hood, warm against my face. My feet feel like they been at the end of a cold river—and I'm the river. Blood beating behind my eyes. I been drifting far off, away from the pain in my head, dancing like leaves in the wind.

And I think of Mary.

I got a dream dragging me away. I hear my dad. Calling me. Got to run. *Men aint men sometimes,* he say.

Run!

They gonna catch me and stretch me over their fire, scrape me, scrape my skin, and make a tent with it, boil my bones, but it aint cos of the leveret. The leveret sitting under its still-warm mother, so flat and scared, but I aint killed it.

In this dream I see the dog sitting up on the crest of the hill. I can see him, just bending down and licking his flank like he aint got a care in the world. *I told you, leave the sickly pups, look out for Number One.* Behind him the sky turn blue. Bright blue and the sun shining down on me in the snow. Like in summer but warmer, and I get up and Dad take my hand like I remember from some time long ago. I forgot why, but he's taking us somewhere special. I done something good I guess, can't remember what. But Dad take me to some trees. It been a long walk and the sun been so warm. Down in the valley a last stand of oak trees. Leaves all come out fresh like chubby green baby hands.

Dad lift me up into one of the trees. The bark all deep and hard and my fingers fall in and out of the cracks and Magda say, *Climb up, Willo, see how high you can get.* And I climb up the tree cos my dad's down there watching and I'm gonna show him that I *am* a

162

Spartan or an Eskimo or one of the things he tells me when I been clever.

Dad and Magda down on the ground collecting acorns. He gonna put one of the acorns in the ground and show me over the years how it grow. *We've got to plant trees for the next ones,* he say. Then one year when the snow melts in summer the little tree just dead. Aint survived all the cold and snow.

But these trees, these trees grown big before the snows come. Just think, Magda say, in the old days the forest was green and warm all summer and sometimes snow coming at Christmas but everyone all happy and kids get sledges out and people skating on the lakes. Imagine that. No one making bread from dried acorns then. And Magda start crying in great big sobs and she lean against my dad's shoulder saying, *I'm sorry, Robin, I'm sorry, it's just my whole life—* and Dad's stroking her hair, and I catch him look up to me in the tree and he whisper to Magda and she look up too, trying to smile but her eyes all wet, I can see. *Look at you all clever up there,* she say, wiping her face. *Look at you, Willo, like Robin Hood.*

And I feel like a king.

A bird flit past with grass in its beak, making a warm nest high in the tree, and when I look down my dad aint there no more, nor Magda, just a big black hole all around, and the sky aint blue no more. Far off wolves howling and the wind blowing and the snow coming down. I been so cold. And the branches shaking and I been hanging on and calling, "Dad! Dad!"

In the darkness I see wolves shuffling around under the tree, and I hear them snarling, snapping at my feet, hear Dad shouting and fighting, and the wind buffer against me but I'm holding on tight. My dad scream out but I can't see him now. Just got to get higher up in the branches. *Look at you all clever up there.*

I scramble up and the branches scratch at my face and catch on my legs, but I get to the top and push through the leaves.

I can smell the sweet air now. Full with the scent of grass. When I push my head through the canopy, the sun blind my eyes, the darkness disappear below me and up above the sky brim full of light and the wind suck me out of the branches, and I'm floating high above it all. Down below the shouting so faint. Fainter and fainter and I can see a dog, my dog, sitting on the top of the mountain, ears pricked in my direction, all around him long grass ripple in the wind. Dog get up lazy then like dogs do and trot back over the ridge, but I don't need the dog no more, just floating up here in the sky, higher and higher. I can see the earth below me, snowy hilltops covered in hares. The valleys green. I can see the seas blowing and stormy with great whales spouting. I got so high now, I been among the stars. The sky growing dark again, but aint black like before, just deep green like the bottom of a pool, and the stars so bright like specks of dust catching in the light all around.

You can see everything, can't you? It's Mary, she been right beside me, holding my hand, floating up toward the moon. Or maybe it's the sun. "It's all right, we can wake up now," she say.

"But where's Dad?" I ask.

"We've got to wake up now, Willo. Wake up!"

• • •

"Wake up!"

I feel a hand on my shoulder, turning me.

Someone pulling the sack across my cheek. On the floor in front of my face is a candle, little candle stuck on a tin plate, flame so bright and orange, fluttering in the cold air.

And my coat bundled up on the floor.

I'm awake. Everything in the dark spinning soft about me.

A hand on my shoulder. A girl's voice speaking.

"Mary?" I say.

"You've got to get up. Quick. They'll come soon."

A face comes down by the candle, hidden in a hood. It aint Mary. It's the girl with the white eye. From the gang of kids.

"How long I been lying here?"

"You've got to get up." She pull me up by my shoulders.

"Where am I?"

"Barton Lock. Come on, can you stand?"

I rub my wrists and push myself off the floor. "Yes, I can."

"I've got your coat. Here. Follow me."

I pull that good coat smelling of home over my frozen shoulders.

"How long have I been here?" I whisper.

She turn with a finger to her mouth.

"All night. Come on. Shhh."

I can feel the cold air from outside drafting up the dark icy tunnel. Hear the girl ahead of me.

And then the light brighten, the dim morning grayness reflecting off the white snow.

"Wait," I call to the girl.

She turn. Looking at me.

"They'll be out after us soon," she say. "There's no time."

"Who?"

"The gang."

"Why did you help me?"

She shrug her shoulders. "Maybe you can help me. Aint no good being alone if we get inside the city. And your coat, it's worth something—" She turn and look away up the canal bed. "It isn't safe anywhere down here. Why did you come down in the canal? You want to die?"

"I come down with an old man, further up. He live further up under the arches."

"The old rat catcher?" say the one-eyed girl.

"Yes. Reckon it's the same."

"But where do you come from with your gloves and coat made from fur?"

"I come from the hills." I don't understand. "Far away from here."

She stare. "You can't come down to Barton Lock in the winter. People are gonna kill you for something warm to wear. Or maybe just for fun."

"I don't understand," I say.

"You got caught by our gang—they live in that ship there. That's all. It was stupid to come down in the canal. No one comes down here. But you're going to help me. That's why I got your coat back. It's worth a lot."

"I don't remember what happen much."

"You got hit pretty bad on your head," she say.

Far off towers rise up into the sky. Behind us been the empty canal and people like wolves and the smoking tents of the settlement like an illness.

The girl clamber up a great drift blown across the path.

"But I got to go back. Look for my friend," I say.

"You can't go back down there. They'll come along soon. We're close to the city. If we get past the checkpoints . . . look, I aint helped you just so you can run off."

The girl turn toward the hard cold buildings jagged on the distant skyline. "It isn't far. But we've got to move. Now."

And I wonder if all the things the grown-ups tell me been true. If the old days gonna come back like before. If this just been a time when men forgot to be good.

Cos I don't know. Maybe my dad and the graybeards just been telling us lies around the fire. Talking about beacons of hope and teaching us lessons. What Patrick call "moralizing."

That's all well and good, Patrick tell me when we been felling the dead rowan, down by the river last spring, *but sometimes you got to follow your guts.* He hit himself in the stomach then. His muscles tense under the scratchy woolen tunic Magda knit him. *Your killer instinct,* he say, lifting the axe above his head, *sometimes that's the thing to follow.*

The girl turn and look at me proper. Scratch at her head.

"You've never seen the city before, have you. You really are from the hills."

"Well I aint lying, if that's what you think."

"I didn't say you were lying," she say.

"Look, I got to go back. I aint coming with you. Mary. My friend."

"If they catch you again they'll kill you."

Then off in the distance we hear the shouts. Sticks banging on the brick walls. Echoing up the canal. Screaming and baying like the angry noises I hear in the settlement. The girl start up.

"I told you! Quick!"

In the dimness way back a torch flare up—I see it bobbing in the distance. Aint no dream.

"They're coming," she shout. "Run!"

• • •

The canal been far behind us now. The girl slip through some tents and crawl under a broken wall. We come up onto a road. Blackened buildings loom up all around. The streets full with people. I just been following, cos I aint got no clue where I am.

"We're going to need to find us food." Girl look at me with her milky eye. Rub on the inside of her arm, moving uneasy on her feet. "Come on. Got to get to Saint Ann's before the queue gets too long. We can beg up the Arndale after."

I been tired and hurting proper from the run. Hunger stirring like an angry dog in my guts now.

Big truck come honking down the road, everyone pulling over. Soldiers in thick gray felt coats and fur hats staring down at all the people, wet in the slushy dirty snow, holding their guns tight as the truck bump along.

"Why they got guns?"

She don't answer. Pull me away.

168

"Why they got guns?"

"I don't know. They're soldiers, that's why." Across the street, over on the corner, I see a tall brick building, big square windows, ledges high up and thick with snow. Queue of ragged men and women hanging around the door. People come and go like tired horses except it don't look like they got much to show for all their coming and going. Women dragging little kids and old men shuffling in saggy canvas coats.

The girl push me along, in among the crowd of people. Through the doors. I aint never been in a room so tall. Big long room. Either side dark wooden benches all facing to the front and the ceiling high up like a barn. The shouting and talking echoing up into the roof and all around.

Down each side of the room are tables. Women stand behind piles of rags and boots, handing out clothes to people crowding around.

"One at a time! One at a time!"

A short man, his face hot and sweaty, struggle across the floor with a large bucket of soup. Put it down on a table. The people close around him.

A baby squawk loud in this din, a shrill cry rising above the wall of sounds, rising up into the rafters. Baby shrieking out to someone. Even these starving people understand that sound. The sea of legs part and hands push the mother to the front of the queue, the mass of legs closing tight behind her.

"Got to wash a bit," the girl say. "I know the woman."

She go to a door in the wall. Bang on it.

The door open up. A round-faced woman stick out her head in a cloud of steam.

"It's me Cath," the girl say.

The woman let us in. I duck under her arm.

"This a friend of yours?"

I don't say nothing. I aint gonna tell the smiling round-faced woman that I don't really know this girl with her milky eye. Just making the most of the warmth in the long windowless room. Look like a proper wash day, with vats of boiling water on the stove, vats full up with rags and the smell of hot soap in the air.

No I don't say nothing cos I still been thinking about what happen to Mary and how I got to get back to the hills and find my dad and get Geraint and stuff like that. And the woman aint interested in me really. She got that helpless look on her face people got who been kind and doing some good thing.

Come shining right out.

"You look like you could do with a wash up, Cath. Take that basin and get yourself a bowl of hot water. Over there."

In the corner there's a steaming urn full of hot water, and the girl fill a metal basin from the shelf. Take off her coat. I can see her red scrawny hands dipping in that bowl of good hot water.

"You too, young man. You've got blood all over your face." So I got to go over and wash my face. It been good to feel it warm on my skin, on my hands. I put my face right in. Wash away the blood and dirt. It been a good feeling.

"You've got yourself in a wee spot of bother laddy, haven't you?" The woman talking to me.

170

I wipe the water off my face with my sleeve.

"Don't say much for a boy who's obviously old enough to get his own baby and who's got himself a nice fur coat from somewhere," she say.

"He's shy," say the girl, giving me a stare.

"Aye, well that's no crime. That's no crime right enough. And get yourselves down to the shelter. No place out on the streets in this cold. No place at all." Then she look about like someone watching even though there aint no one here except us. "Here, take this." She take a sliver of soap out of a cup and wrap it in a rag. "Don't go telling anyone or I'll have half the women from the shelter around here. And that's where you should be, down at the shelter. Come on, you've got to leave now before someone finds you here." She push us toward the door. "Off you go now and God bless you. God bless you."

Sound like Magda—thinking soap so precious and spouting on about God like that.

The girl pocket the soap. The woman hustle us out of that good warm room and the noise from the crowds of people in the church—the noise and the smell and the cold of it—hit me straightaway.

"That blind old cow in there. Look, she didn't even notice I got a whole bar of soap." The girl pull a big square block of soap out her pocket. "I can sell this down the Arndale and get some grog for us both."

"Why do you want grog?"

"Something to do."

"Aint it better to get something to eat?"

"You don't want any grog? That's all right by me." She pocket the soap. "I'll have it for myself." She laugh then, rubbing her arm and shifting around on her feet. She got a proper nervous look about her all of a sudden but kind of excited, which I aint seen before. Looking around all the time.

"I don't think you shoulda take that soap," I say.

"Yeah, I know. But you want to eat don't you? Give me your coat—we'll get good money for it up the Arndale."

"I aint gonna sell my coat. It's all I got to keep out the cold."

She look at me.

"I risked a lot to get that coat away. Why do you think I helped you? You think you're better than me cos you've got a home up in the hills where everyone's got fur coats and plenty to eat?"

"No. It aint that."

"Some people say aint no stragglers left"—her voice turn mean—"just stealers who take their old people to die up on the mountains in the snow. That's what they say."

"Well we aint eating each other or chasing after hungry kids."

"Well it's just what they say."

"No straggler been half as wild as the people I seen in this city."

But the girl aint listening really, rubbing her arm and shifting on her feet.

"Why do you think I helped you?" She grab at me. "You should give me your coat to buy grog."

I push her back. "I aint selling it!"

She get a proper mean look in her thin face then.

"Suit yourself. You won't last a day."

She spit it out. Turn into the crowd.

Then she's gone. Between the dirty stiff sea of legs and canvas and rags in that great tall building.

Seem like you aint gonna get nothing for free here. Not even a friend.

25

The girl don't come back.

I slink about that building trying to find her among the people scrabbling over scraps of blankets and old shoes.

But she aint there.

I get myself wedged down against the wall where no one gonna notice me. I can keep a lookout too. No one gonna see me down here.

I fall asleep.

Someone knock into me and I wake up. Don't know where I been for a moment. But it don't take long to remember.

There aint so many people about no more. Evening come on already and hunger burning inside me. Someone shouting.

"Come on, everyone out!"

But I aint got nowhere to go. Girl aint come back. I'm glad I aint given her my coat at least.

A sound behind make me turn. It's the wash woman with the round face. She come bustling out the door, big coat covering up her pink arms. She got a key and been locking the door. I come up close. Tugging on her sleeve.

"What am I gonna do?"

For a minute she aint understanding me. Then I see her face remembering.

"You're still here? I told you to get down to the shelter before it's full."

But I aint got no clue where the shelter is.

Her face look blank. But I know she got a good heart if only she gonna take off that great canvas coat she been wearing like a shield.

"Well, I don't know why you're telling me. What am I supposed to do about it now? You aren't the only hungry child on the streets. God knows I've got my own problems right enough. You've got to go now. We're shutting up."

She's right. A big man standing at the door shouting how it's time for the service. A few old men hobble toward the door.

The woman's about to turn, but then she look down. She put her bag down.

"Look, this is all I've got, and God help me for giving it to you. Here."

She got a little jar out of her bag. It been filled with milk.

"You can have this. Are you on the opium too?"

"Opium?"

"The madak. Like the girl, Cath."

"No. I aint."

She look right in my face then. "I'll buy your coat from you, give you a good price. If you want."

"I aint selling it."

The woman look down. "No, right enough. And I wouldn't sell it for all the money in China if it were mine either."

"Where can I go?"

175

"I don't know, lad. If I knew where we all should go I'd go there myself. The shelter will take you. I'm sure of it. I can't help you more."

I slip into the shadows and crouch down with the milk.

All the people who been handing out clothes and ladling soup all day, all those people come out from the dark corners now. They got tired faces too, those men and women, but they come out silent and sit on the benches, looking down the hall. And a man get up and climb some stairs around a pillar. He stand up on a little platform.

"Friends," he say.

I gulp the milk down. Good and creamy.

"'The Lord is my light and my salvation—whom shall I fear? The Lord is the stronghold of my life—of whom shall I be afraid?'"

The man on the platform look about at those sorry tired people.

"'When evil men advance against me to devour my flesh, when my enemies and my foes attack me, they will stumble and fall. Though an army besiege me, my heart will not fear; though war break out against me, even then will I be confident....'"

Someone cough.

"Remember those words, my friends. In these bleak times. Of whom are we all afraid? Just as it is winter now, the summer will come. It may not be long, but the sun will shine a little and wash away our cares as it washes away the dirty snow and ice.... 'The merciful man doeth good to his own soul, but he that is cruel troubleth his own flesh!'"

Sound like he gonna give those tired people a lesson from the way he talk. But they murmur like sheep together in a barn. He spout on about a man helping someone out on the road where he been riding. I mean it been the kind of thing anyone gonna do really but his voice drag on about being what he call *a good Samaritan,* about snow and ice and forgiveness. It been a good story right enough. But all I been thinking of is my empty belly and what I'm gonna do this cold night and how it been funny that some people got jobs feeding other people and some people got to take their charity and others just take things from others without asking. And me, I don't know what I am.

The people hang their heads down, saying words under their breath.... *Give us this day our daily bread.... forgive us this day our daily trespasses....* Just like Magda. She say the same words every night, with my dad, shuffling under the bedclothes, saying, "You need a coat not a prayer, so get in, woman. You'll freeze if you don't get in."

But I know why Magda say her words. Same reason as me. I say my words up on the Farngod cos sometimes you get to want someone to listen to you, want something to be out there in the cold windswept valley with death crunching about in the crisp snow. Something more than wind and snow. Reckon it aint much different for all these people, just they aint got no hares to catch and no dog to talk to. Just that man standing up in front of them trying to get them less frightened of all the gruesome things they probably got on their minds.

I finish the milk now.

The round-faced woman look back over her shoulder at me and sort of smile.

The lesson been over. I got to get out of the church I guess.

26

Being out of the wind all day make me forget the weather. Make me forget that everyone on the street probably want to knock me on the head just for my coat. I been pretty thankful for sleeping in that church all day for sure.

The big doors close behind me. The snow all trampled down outside where the people been standing about. A kind of smog over everything still hanging down in the cold air in between the tall dark buildings. And the smell of the city bad and deep, burning my nostrils with its foulness even in the cold dark. All the shutters closed and snowflakes starting to fall, big flakes, dropping down slow.

The wash woman tell me how to get to the shelter. Don't reckon I'm gonna remember it all. She say it been *a long walk*. "Up to Corporation Road," she say. "Ask someone if you get lost." Don't reckon I'm gonna be too keen on asking anyone anything.

Wish Mary was here.

Aint too many people out on the street this time of night, just an old man hunched over carrying a bag. Shuffling along.

He don't look too dangerous. Don't look strong enough to rob me. I aint really got no clue where I been heading. Cos there aint no trees or rocks or valleys to tell you where you been. Just those tall dark buildings every side all look the same to me.

I walk a bit faster. The old man turn a corner up ahead and I jog along trying not to slip. All of a sudden out of a pathway between the houses a gang of boys rush out—just as that old graybeard shuffle past. They get all about him shouting. Something hit him in the back and he fall down. I been scared and pull myself flat against the wall. But they aint seen me. The old man shouting out scared. *Get away. Get away with you!* He put his hands up to cover his head. His bag spill out and a few potatoes roll onto the snow.

But the kids aint interested in the potatoes, they just having fun. Laughing, cuffing at his head. I hope they don't see me in my good warm coat.

The gang run on. They got other things on their mind for now.

The man scrabble about in the snow for his potatoes. When he see me come over he cower down.

"Take them. Take them. Yes, yes. Just take the food. Take the food."

"I aint gonna hurt you."

The old man look up from the ground. His eyes scared. I see he don't trust me. Not one bit.

I bend down, find his potatoes, put them back in his sack.

He got up on his feet now. I hand him the bag.

"Here. See, I aint gonna hurt you. Just want to know the way to the shelter."

He hold the bag. Pausing. Waiting to see what I'm gonna do.

"You've got to get back on Corporation Road. Yes. Got to go back and up to Redbank. If you want the shelter you've got to get to Redbank." His face is thin, a wispy bit of gray stubble covering his lined cheeks.

"Is it far?" I say.

"Is that a dog-skin coat there?" he say, reaching out.

The man's glove rest on my sleeve.

He look down at the stitching.

"A real old-time coat, isn't it. Isn't made for show. But a good skin. Where did you get it, boy like you out on the streets?"

He look into my face.

"I make it," I say.

The old man glance up and down the street. Mutter to himself. Chin pressed into his chest.

"Mmm. You can come back with me and share a few potatoes around my fire. If you want. Nearer than the shelter. Much nearer. Just me and my wife at home. Just the wife. What do you say to that?"

I don't know what I think to that. Old graybeard looking at me from under his hood. Eyes don't look at me hungry—but it been hard to tell.

I feel the dog spirit. Running through the snow with his pack. Back up into the hills. The dog sleek, his fur shining, his nose wet. He stop. Look back at me over his shoulder.

Seem like the dog slipping in and out of the dark corners of this city. Never know when he's gonna be nipping at my heels. He aint been too keen on that girl Mary. No. He aint been to keen on being here at all.

Out in the cold dark, you've got to follow your guts, Willo.

Further off the rest of the pack stop and howl. *If you don't come now, you're on your own.*

The old graybeard look at me. Waiting.

"You come with me. Come with me. Have something to eat around a warm fire. Mmm?"

The old man's voice sound good.

Follow your guts, Willo!

But that good warm fire sound too much like home.

"I aint gonna sell my coat," I tell him.

"No! No! You wouldn't want to do that in this cold. Come on. Yes, yes, a nice warm bit of stew."

Old man looking at me kind of reading inside my head. "Quick though. It won't do to stand around on the streets for too long. It isn't far. Mmm, not far at all."

He start off down the road, beckon me with his hand: "This way, not far, not far."

• • •

That old graybeard say it aint far but it been a long walk with his feet shuffling slow along the icy streets.

"Here we are. Yes yes."

A great tower stretching up into the sky. The sharp smell of smoke heavy in the air. Outside a group of kids hang around a pile of burning rubbish. They don't pay us no mind though.

The old man lead me past them, up some steps. Into the great dark hole that been the doorway. There's a smell of cat piss and a stench of things decaying under that mountain of brick and con-crete towering above us. Just dark steps rising up inside, our feet echoing up them as we fumble along, hands feeling the way on the wall.

"Be careful now. Mmm, careful on the stairs now."

Far above us in the guts of this old-time building a door slam shut. Footsteps echo on the stairs. Every now and then we come to a landing. The smell come right out of buckets of slop standing outside every door.

He see me stop. "Never mind that, never mind."

I aint too keen on coming in this damp smelling building. That's for sure.

A cat come hissing out from some dark corner and shoot down the steps in the darkness. A woman snoring on the stairway and we pick around her. Filthy-smelling woman got grog on her breath. And then the feeble light go out. We been in the dark good and proper now. The old man stop. I can hear him breathing ahead of me.

"Are you all right?"

"Yes."

"Yes yes, just be careful. Got to be careful on the dark stairs. But it isn't far now. No, not far now."

Careful not to trip on one of those slop buckets I follow the sound of him struggling up the steps, stooping over, huffin' and puffin'. Finally he stop and pull a key from his coat and fiddle in the darkness at a door. He open it up with a click.

"It's only me, dear," he say into the darkness.

The room smell of breath and onions. A huge window along the far wall. Aint got no boards on it or nothing. The night sky look like a picture so bright in the darkness of the room through that window. Cos when your eyes get used to the dark you see the night aint so black like you think it is.

Up here you can see the whole city spreading out down below. Snow-topped roofs and smoke smudging the buildings and houses that melt out all around til the skyline and the city disappear in the shadows of the clouds with the moon glowing out behind them. Same old moon gets up over the barn on a clear night.

The old man fiddling around in the corner. I can hear him trying to get a strike on something. He been muttering to himself. From the back of the room come a voice.

"Jacob. Is that you back already?"

"Yes yes, my dear. It's me."

"Did you get the potatoes?"

"Oh, yes, got the potatoes, won't be long, dearest. Just getting the stove going. Got a boy too. Mmm, a boy."

The old man place the candle in front of a cracked bit of mirror and the flame struggle to life. In the corner of the room is a bed piled up with blankets and pillows and in it an old woman, just her head and hands poking over the blankets. Staring at us. Her eyes glinting in the candlelight.

"A boy, Jacob?"

"Yes yes. Very kind boy, helped me but with nowhere to stay on this cold night. Cold thin boy. Mmm, very cold night."

"Why have you brought him back? He's going to rob us for sure."

"No, no. Not going to rob us, are you?"

"No," I say.

Above the bed is a shelf of books and an old clock ticking.

The old man Jacob stir up a little fire in a stove by the window. Fishing lumps of coal out of a bucket.

Every spare inch of wall got basins and buckets hanging off it and bags and bits of rope and old metal wire and all manner of things. Above the fire been a rail, hanging from ropes in the ceiling, a woolen sweater draped over it, just like at home. Jacob take off his gloves and coat all stiff and damp and let down the rail above the fire. He hang up the coat and put on the sweater.

"Come a bit closer, boy. I can't see you over there," the old woman croak from the bed.

Jacob shuffle over. Push me toward his woman.

"Look at his coat. Look at it," he say, holding the candle up.

The old woman sit up against the pillows. "What are we going to do with a boy?" Her hands all thin, just skin and bones.

"Now don't pester him, my dear. He's hungry as a dog. Aren't you? Hungry as a dog." The old man light a candle by her bed and shuffle back to the fire, clanging at pots.

The old woman look at me. "What's your name?"

"Willo."

"The coat, Elizabeth. Look at his coat. He says he made it himself."

The smell of the stew cooking up on the stove torturing my hungry guts but I pull my coat over my head and pass it to the old woman reaching out with a gnarled hand and I sit down in the warmth of the fire.

Those two old people got my coat between them. For some reason they been mighty interested in it. Peering close at the stitchwork and turning it inside and out.

I been looking about their room. Hard to see much in the tatty light of that tiny candle. There's a door beside the bed. In the corner a chair. A basin hanging on the wall. A little table bashed together from some boards with a scrap of material hanging over it. Same sort of thing Magda do at home. She got to be making any useful place so you can't go putting a cup or plate on it without a warning that it's *gonna get dirty* and she *aint got all day for washing*.

"You say you made this coat yourself?" say the old man.

"Most of it. Got a bit of help with the pattern."

"It looks like a hare lining and—dog on the outer layer?"

"Aint gonna get cold in that coat," I say.

"Mmm, I don't doubt it. Don't doubt it."

He ladle out some food onto tin plates.

"Perhaps you can tell us what you're doing here?" say the old woman. "With a fine coat you say you made yourself."

I can't speak cos my mouth been full with hot potato stew.

"Mmm, straggler coat for sure, my dear, for sure," say Jacob.

I swallow. The fire warm my back and my belly been full with hot food, and I feel that my eyes gonna fall shut even if I don't want them to.

Don't reckon these old people gonna hurt me. I hear the old man fussing to his wife.

"He's too tired to talk now, dear." A cushion been put under my head and a heavy blanket over my body. I hear them talking,

186

Jacob moving about the room quietly, but my eyes stay heavy and closed whether I like it or not. Sleep crawling up my body. And it feel good. The floor against my shoulder. Been the first night I been full and warm since I left the mountain.

"We'll ask him tomorrow...."

It's the last thing I hear Jacob say. I breathe down deep and heavy with a picture of Mary in my head. A picture of Mary with her tangled hair, pulling the covers up on that old rat catcher with her crooked finger, lips parted, smiling down at me.

The city been stranger and crueler than the fairy stories Magda tell where Jack climbs up a bean stalk and witches make houses out of bread. Really. And I reckon I fall asleep right then cos I don't remember nothing more, just wake up with the blanket over me and the fire rustled up new as the light come flooding in through that great big window the next morning.

27

The room look tired and broke and dusty in the light. The old woman still snoring a bit. On the stove's a good pot of last night's stew and I get a plateful.

There's a sound from the other room. Old man Jacob sitting at a workbench under the window. The cuffs of his sweater fraying over his wrists. The weak morning light fall across his thinning hair and strong gnarled hands. He got himself bent over. A soft white fur in his hands, his square fingers disappearing in it.

The shelves on the wall been crammed with tools and rolls of leather and sheets of metal all covered in dust and boxes of nails and bits of wire and pipes and old boots and jars of fruit and pickled vegetables. Just like at home. It aint too cold in here cos the stovepipe come through the wall. Jacob got it tied to the ceiling with bits of wire. There's a door half boarded over and through the door a small balcony deep in snow, a pigeon making a little dance with its feet on the ice.

Jacob look up.

"Look!" I point quiet as can be to the bird.

"Very good. But, no no, we don't eat him now, boy. In the spring he'll build a nest out there and we'll have lots of pigeons. Not just one. No no, patience is a virtue. A virtue."

"What you making?" I say. Still got my eye on the pigeon though.

"A coat. Mmm. Coat for Dorothy Bek-Murzin."

"Can I see?"

"Certainly, certainly."

I come over. Outside the pigeon flap into the air. I get the skins off the table and have a look at the seam. It's a soft white fur, well-cured. It aint too big, two pieces together look like the pattern for a sleeve.

"I thought you might like to earn your breakfast. Lend me a hand," he say.

"I'll help stitch it up if that's what you want. I need a needle. And a sharp knife too."

"Yes yes. Got one somewhere." Jacob start poking about in a small wooden box. I got to lean over and find them for him. He's gonna be looking all morning.

I got his work in my hands. Turn it over.

"See this aint the way I'm gonna stitch a sleeve," I say. "You aint stitched it close enough."

"No, no—it's my eyes. Bad eyes now."

I lay out the pieces, feeling the good fur in my hands like I been sitting at home with Dad.

First I cut the seams fresh. Stitch them up careful. When I done that, I brush out the fur on the other side and pick it through the threads. It look alright. Won't be able to see where the two skins been put together when I finish it up. It's good to be working quiet. I hold it up to him.

"See? Can't see the join now."

"Yes yes, mmm very good indeed."

"But this sleeve gonna be stiff as a board if you don't slash it," I say.

"Slash it?"

I take the knife. "You got to know where to do it."

Jacob grab my arm. "You'll ruin it. I'll never afford fur like this again."

"No I won't. I done this before. Watch."

I make the cuts careful where they got to be. Then I stitch them up neat in my softest stitch, brushing the fur and teasing it through the threads again.

"See?"

Jacob hold it up. The fur fall soft and supple. He play it through his old hands.

"Yes yes. I see now."

I can hear stirrings from the other room.

"How about you stay here with me and Elizabeth awhile, mmm? Just awhile. You finish this coat and you can sleep here and we'll feed you. Yes food and a warm fire. Mmm? What do you say to that. You just finish the stitching and you can stay."

I look out the window at the cold day and the gray smoking city. My guts filled with food. Warm fire burning in the other room. Good piece of fur in my hands.

I can hear the old woman awake. Jacob get up. "You think about it, Willo." He shuffle off into the other room. I hear him fussing about, scraping some of the stew onto a plate for his wife.

"Bring me a spoon, Jacob."

"Yes, my dear, a spoon." Jacob riddle the fire. The pots clang. "Willo, bring that sleeve in here. Look what the boy did with Bek-Murzin's coat, my dear. Mmm, as soft as if it was still alive."

I come to the door, hand her the sleeve. The old lady feel it and hold it up.

"Oh yes, very good."

Jacob turn and look at me.

"So, what is it to be, mmm? You stay and finish this coat, and I'll give you a hundred yuan when it's finished and food and lodging too. That's all right, Elizabeth, isn't it, dear?"

"How long will it take you, boy?" she ask.

"If you got the skins cured already and the pattern fixed I reckon a few weeks."

"A few weeks, my dear. Did you hear that? A few weeks."

Jacob bend down. Get down on his knees slowly, kneel on the floor and pull a wooden chest out from under the bed. I help him get it out. Inside the chest wrapped in oiled paper are the cured skins. All soft and white, small skins, some of them with a black leg or streak of brown I reckon got to be cut out if he want this coat all white. I aint never seen this sort before.

"What are they?" I say.

"Cat. Fine white cat for the most part, mmm. You've nearly finished the embroidery on the collar, haven't you, my dear? Mmm, yes, Willo. My wife still makes fine embroidery."

There's a little parcel tucked down the side of the chest. Jacob lay it open. It's a scrap of stuff, soft and fine, like nothing I seen before—the color of the sky on a clear day. And all over it that old woman stitched a sea of snowdrops. I can't believe her old hands gonna be so able. The snowdrops been done so clever they look like they just stuck their heads out of the snow. Better stitching even than Magda do. Flower heads and blades of grass bending and twisting as they catch in the light. Threads so fine they shine out.

"This is the lining for the collar. Snowdrops are Bek-Murzin's favorite. Oh, yes, her favorite. She'll pay a fortune for this coat if you can make the furs fall softly without a seam in sight. We won't go hungry this winter. Not hungry this winter, my dears. What do you say, Willo? Eat some stew, stitch up this coat for a week. It won't hurt you to stay a bit."

"What else is he going to do?" say the old woman. "Have you got papers?"

"No. I just come off the hill then I got a truck ride here. I aint got no papers."

"You just came down from the hills. How did that happen?"

"They took my dad away."

"Who?"

"Government trucks. Up on the mountain."

"Well, I don't know how you got into the city with no papers. It's been such a cold winter, hasn't it, Jacob? You won't get out in a hurry, boy."

"That's what I been worrying about," I tell her.

"Worrying won't help you much," she say. "Everyone's got something to worry about. You're not the only one."

She's got a point. There aint nowhere else for me to go. Don't know no one in this city except Mary. And I don't know where Mary is.

The old man pull out the skins from his trunk. Carry them into the workroom and lay them out on the table, muttering to himself. "Now. I'll cut the pattern. Yes yes. I can cut a good pattern. Come on, boy. I'll show you."

I look at the old woman sitting up in the bed.

"Help him. It won't hurt you, will it?" She put out her weathered little hand. Hold it out. "Please."

. . .

So I get to stay with that old couple. It's good to get my hands deep in some work with Jacob spouting on like the grown-ups around the fire giving a Tell back home. It been hard to think that those two old people aint been old people all their life.

They show me a picture they got of themselves. Jacob standing in a garden of flowers and it must be the old woman beside him—just she got lots of dark hair then and look pretty happy. So I know they been young once.

The way I understand it, when Jacob get all fired up rattling on to me, is that in the old days, people been too busy to know how lucky they been. He sound a bit like my dad when he go on like that about how people just got to *get back to making things with their own hands* and *thinking with their brains*.

I don't say much, same as when my dad spout on. And working on the coat stop me thinking too hard on all the bad things rattling in my head—the snow and wind blowing cold outside and the words of my dog. Can't forget them either. *You're on your own now, Willo.*

. . .

Slowly over the weeks that coat come together. Jacob cut the pattern out of old paper first. He say he know what he been doing, but I tell him, it aint practical what he been cutting out. Aint gonna keep the snow out. Jacob say Dorothy Bek-Murzin aint so worried about practical—it's just got to look good. He say I got to go with him when he brings it to her. Says she's gonna give me money to make her lots of things when she sees how fine my stitching been.

Jacob keep forgetting that I got to get back to the mountain. I aint staying here to make coats forever, I say. "Well, you aren't going to be going anywhere soon, are you?"

. . .

Jacob come back from the market one evening with a worried look on his face.

"There's trouble in the settlements. Gangs barricading the roads. They've blown the lock gate at the quays. Dear oh dear. Flooded the canal. Soldiers everywhere. Very bad. Mmm, very bad this winter."

"What do you mean?" I say.

"Can't get in or out of the city. No one can now. There won't be much power this winter. Very bad."

I think of Mary.

Think of Dad.

"I got to find my family."

"You won't be able to get into the settlements until they lift the roadblocks," Jacob say.

"How long's that gonna be?"

"Well. Not until the melt. No no, not until then. And you wouldn't want to be there, Willo. There are things you wouldn't want to see."

My heart beat fast. I just gone and left Mary down in that dread place. Down in the canal with the old rat catcher. With the bad and the hungry and the stench and the smog and she aint got me and aint got no da or no Tommy either.

I go to the window. Look out over the city. Down below huddled figures trudge along the roads. A truck rumble around the tower block. The air been so cold and still these last days. Smoke twisting from every gray chimney hanging heavy over the bricks and stone and snow and ice. The smog thick in the air. Somewhere out there been my dad and Magda and the others. They can't just disappear. Just got to be out there somewhere. Maybe far off across the hills.

"You're lucky you're here with us, boy," say Elizabeth from the bed.

I turn away from the window. I don't feel lucky. Not one bit.

Magda always say sadness and love and pain, they're easy to feel—but not luck.

28

We got the coat wrapped up in oiled paper tied tight, and rolled in a canvas pack. Ready to take to Dorothy Bek-Murzin. The old man fussing over it getting creased or wet.

"You mustn't talk to her unless she asks. No no, let me do the talking. You stay quiet. Mmm, can you do that?"

I nod.

It been the most fantastic coat I ever see after I got it finished to his pattern. Over fifty skins I got cut up and stitched together. The body tight and close flaring out from the waist in a wide skirt. All white fur from head to toe, and the collar lined with stiff cow hide so that it stand up tall—gonna come up as high as the lady's head and keep the wind out, with that pale-blue silk embroidered with snowdrops fanning out behind her hair. Gonna look mighty fine if the lady been as beautiful as Jacob say.

The rest of the coat Elizabeth line inside with soft white wool. Jacob sit at the table for two days hammering and tooling the brass buttons. He spend the last bit of money he got buying all the brass and the wool and the satin thread that come all the way from China. It probably been the most beautiful bit of clothing anyone ever saw.

Jacob tell me he been making coats and gloves since the troubles and he aint never made anything so good as the way I done this one cos his eyes aint good no more. He say we gonna get a big heap of money for this coat. I feel pretty good inside when he say that even though I been tired from sitting in that room stitching for weeks worrying about how I'm gonna get back to the mountain.

Jacob say Dorothy Bek-Murzin know all the government people and everyone, cos they all come and *see* her.

"Why?" I say.

"Because she's beautiful," say the old woman.

"She grew up in the settlements," say Jacob, "and sometime she helps the little people—if you've done something good for her, mmm."

"Like this coat," I say.

"Yes," say Jacob, "maybe this coat's going to get her to notice you. Just got to be patient. Let me do the talking. That's how you'll get money for your papers, boy."

• • •

The stink of slop been hanging about the stairwell. A fat brown rat just sitting on the stairs. Jacob shout at it, and it slink off along the wall. The gray light of the day come filtering through the broken windows. Below us, someone come out of their door too, great coat pulled over their head, trudging down the dirty stairs below us, carrying their slop bucket.

"Where are we going?"

"It's not far. Chinatown. Yes yes, that's where her house is. Mmm, now don't get dirty boots. Oh no, she won't like that. We'll take a cart today. Yes yes, too dangerous for walking with this valuable package, eh?" Jacob got a smile on his old face.

I follow him as he hobble down the thousand steps and out onto the road. Shadow from the tower fall over us. All along the street women in shapeless coats shovel the snow into dirty piles. Jacob find a gap in the banks and shout out at a cart. The limping horse pull up.

"Where to?" say the driver, looking down.

"Chinatown."

"Three quid."

Jacob count out some coins from his pocket and hand them over.

"Each," say the driver.

Jacob sigh but count out three more coins and we climb up onto the old wooden cart. Two women huddled under a blanket been sitting all glum up there with a basket of eggs at their feet.

"Heeyup," say the driver, and the horse lurch out into the road among the handcarts and people and snow and ice, the snow shovelers shouting out all angry as we pass by splattering them in dirty slush, the driver slashing down on that poor old horse with a long whip even though it been plain to see that horse doing his best already.

It aint a quick journey but it been good not to have wet feet. Good to sit up above the people haggling over a sack of wool or a bucket of coal down on the road. Most of them dressed head to toe in canvas with rags against the cold around their hands. From every building wisps of dirty smoke feed up into the gray sky. The cart trundle on, the blackened buildings closer and taller at each turn of the road.

City aint like the mountain one bit. It aint good and clean here. You can feel it. It fill my head looking at all the people and things and buildings like I aint never seen before. It got something about it make you want to know where all those people going to and coming from and what they all doing. Aint like back home where you never gonna see a stranger one year to the next and got to get over to Barmuth just to smoke some fish and have a dance and a big Meet.

"Look!" I say to Jacob.

Up ahead, above the street, all red and gold and shining with carved dragons glinting and bells chiming. A great shining archway towering over the road.

The street seem to glow behind that archway. Windows lit up either side of the road, colored cloth flutter outside the shops, drums of burning coals smoke into the air and everywhere a sea of people, strange-looking people dressed in fur and silk and the smell of food on the air.

"Chinatown," say the driver.

"Come on, Willo. We're here. Yes yes, we're here." Slowly Jacob climb down from the cart.

"I aint got all day, old man," the driver grunt. We hardly got our feet on the ground, and he raise his whip and that poor old horse got to jolt up and move on.

"Stay close," Jacob say.

"What is it, this place? And all the people so strange-looking."

"Heart of the city, Willo. Oh yes, the heart of the city. They're Chinese."

He seem to know where we got to go. I follow close. The street been scraped clear of snow and covered in sand. We pass a shop that sell knives. Every kind of knife you gonna dream of. Long ones, short ones, ones got sharp points on the blade for sawing, slim ones with painted handles. I stop and look at them.

"Come on, Willo. No time, no time for looking. We're nearly there."

In the open doorways, dark-haired men hold out cabbages and squawking chickens and silken scarves and dainty slippers. Old women walk through the crowd selling bunches of tiny paper flowers. "Hua, hua," they shout.

On the other side of the street, I see a bright building. CHEUNGS KINO painted in red and gold letters above the doors. A queue of people waiting along the front of the building. NEWSREELS FROM AFRICA it say on a wooden stand outside.

Jacob turn around. "You should see it all at night, Willo. Lights burning in every window. Electric lights and music. But come on, we're here."

We stop beside a door. Jacob pull on a chain in the wall. Far off a bell jangle.

The girl who open the door got dark hair and strange eyes pretty like a doll.

"I'm the furrier. Come to bring a coat," Jacob say to her.

The girl smile with a little nod of the head and let us into a big room with stairs sweeping up on one side. Jacob take off his boots, and I got to do the same. The girl give us a pair of felt slippers to wear.

The floor been covered in rugs, deep-red patterned rugs and animal skins all mixed up together. It been warm underfoot. A small fire burning in the corner.

"Madame has just finished breakfast. You can come up," the girl say.

Padding in our slippers, we follow her up the great tall staircase. Up to a pair of carved wooden doors. The girl knock. Open the doors.

The warmth of a well-kept fire hit my face. Jacob come in with a low bow.

"Jacob! My dear. You have come at last. You promised me a coat six months ago, you naughty man. You've left poor Dorothy with nothing warm to wear all winter. You should be punished. But come, come in by the fire, and let's see what you have for me this time. Oh but you've brought a boy! Let me see him."

Jacob push me forward. "He stitched your coat. Very skilled, yes yes. A very skilled boy."

"It's been such a cold winter. When will it ever end? I haven't even been hunting in the Peaks this year. None of them will go. The roads are too deep in snow."

"Yes yes. Very cold this winter. Mmm."

"Come closer, boy," she say. "What's your name?"

But I been staring all around at the room. Two tall windows look down over the street outside. Aint boarded or nothing. Just sparkling glass panes. Thick goatskin curtains falling down to the floor. A great fire glowing in a large fireplace. On the dark red walls, heavy cloths hang down on chains. All about been soft-looking chairs covered in colored cushions and little tables piled high with books and bottles and bowls. Candles burning on every surface. She musta spent near all summer making candles if she gonna burn so many. And in the middle of the day too. I aint never seen such a place of comfort and warmth filled with so many things. But the thing that catch my eyes the most been the person lying all lazy on a seat beside the fire.

She been looking at me through sleepy gray eyes.

Hair dark and shiny as a deep pool of water. Piled up high on top of her head. Face as smooth as an egg, lips touched with red, cheeks pink like a baby. Body soft and round and womanly.

She probably been the most beautiful thing I ever seen.

All I can do is stare.

A little laugh been growing at her mouth. My face feel like burning cos she been laughing at me I reckon. All dirty and wrapped in ragged old sweaters. I pull my hat off. Hold it in my hands.

"Is he a mute Jacob?" she say.

A glinting nest of stones been tied around her neck on a ribbon. Her dress been tight to the waist, then it spread out around her in folds of soft green cloth. Tiny pale hands stick out like mice from the end of her long sleeves. Hands covered in shining rings.

"I'm Willo." I stare at my feet.

"Well, Willo. Let's see what you've made."

Jacob kneel down onto the carpeted floor and start unwrapping the package with his fumbling shaking hands.

The coat fall out as Jacob untie the strings on the oiled paper. He brush it out and hold it up. The white fur fall soft down to the floor.

"Please. You must try it on. Feel how soft it is. Look at the collar."

Dorothy Bek-Murzin drop her slippered feet down off the seat and reach out for the coat.

She stroke the fur with her delicate fingers. Turn it over in her hands.

"It's a fine piece of work. The seams are good. Oh! The collar! Snowdrops—my favorite." With a lively step, she's up. Jacob hold the coat over her back, and she slip her arms into the close-fitting sleeves.

"See how the collar stands up behind your hair. If you do up the buttons you will see the fit. You look exquisite. Yes, yes, exquisite."

She step over to a long mirror and brush her delicate hands down the front of the soft white fur, arranging the folds and buttoning the buttons around her neat waist. Admiring herself.

"But you can hardly feel you've got it on. It hangs so—so perfectly." She turn around then with a smile across her face. "It is a beautiful coat, Jacob. And you say this boy here stitched it?"

"Yes, yes. He is very skilled."

She been staring at me now. Jacob standing awkward in the room like a stalk of grass. Wringing his hat in his hands.

Dorothy Bek-Murzin turn to the girl waiting by the door. "Mei-Li, bring us some warmed chocolate. We'll drink it by the fire. Now, Willo. Can you make other things as well as this coat?"

"Well, I . . . I reckon I can make a good pair of gloves and some hareskin socks if you want to keep the cold out," I say.

"Hareskin socks! Wonderful. What about a pair of lined boots? Can you do that?"

"Reckon I can do most things with fur and leather," I say. "If Jacob cut the pattern for me."

I look at Dorothy Bek-Murzin standing by the mirror like a

painting. She aint big but she fill up that room with dreams. Her body soft and round under her dress. Underneath all the clothes and the paint on her face I guess she just been a person like anyone else. But it been hard to imagine. She been like a flame glowing in the hearth. Can't take your eyes off her.

I seen Magda sometimes, tying her hair in the little bit of mirror we got by the fire. "What do you want with that?" my dad gonna say. "You aint a girl anymore." He turn to me. "Women always wanting to dress themselves up, Willo—vain like butterflies." Magda elbow him in the ribs. "And men are like moths, beating themselves against every flame, Robin." She laugh. "And that til the day they die!"

The girl Mei-Li come back in the room carrying three cups on a little tray.

She hand them out. They smell sweet.

"So where did you find this boy, Jacob?"

"The thing is, Dorothy mmm, the thing is . . . the boy has *no papers*. He's from the hills."

"Is he really?" Dorothy move back to her seat. "You can go now, Mei-Li." The girl leave the room.

"Yes. Yes he came down from the hills."

"Well, he'll have to be careful. With no papers. They're clearing the peaks. And the mountain." She look up over her cup. "So I've been told."

"Yes. Yes, needs to be very careful." Jacob speak softly. "He isn't really—"

"They take my father away," I blurt out. "And my family—"

"He isn't legal, Dorothy," say Jacob. "He's trying to find out where his father is. The police took his family."

"What is your father's name, Willo?"

"Robin. Robin Blake," I say. "They . . ." But Jacob raise his hand a little.

"We'll have to think what to do about that if I'm to have the finest boots in Chinatown this winter." Dorothy Bek-Murzin raise her dark eyebrows. "Yes, we'll see what we can do. But there's trouble in the settlements. They'll barricade them so tight that no one will be able to get in or out, papers or not. And papers will be harder to get, Jacob. There are few in the city who will make them anymore."

"I just want to know where they take my dad—"

"Willo. You can wait downstairs," Jacob say, giving me a look.

"But—"

"Wait downstairs, boy."

I hear Dorothy Bek-Murzin's voice get pretty firm as I inch down the stairs.

"Now, Jacob, let's discuss the *price*."

29

"One thousand yuan. That's over three thousand pounds. Do you hear that, Willo? Three thousand pounds! We can buy you papers with this money."

Jacob bend over getting his old boots on. He nod to Dorothy's girl, and we been out in the cold street again. Jacob pull his hat low down over his ears.

"What she say about my dad?"

"Patience, Willo. Mmm, patience. She wants you to make her more clothes. Boots and gloves. Yes, yes. But one thousand yuan!"

"What she tell you about finding out where my dad is?"

"Come come, Willo. She will try and find out. But it's going to take time. She knows a lot of important people. Mmm, very important people. But she can't just ask them straight. She's got to feel her way. Yes yes, you'll have to be a little patient. Make her some fine clothes."

"I aint got time for patience."

Jacob turn around and see me. Look right in my eyes. Put his old hands on my shoulders. "Time is a funny beast, my boy. Yes, a funny beast. What if they've taken them ... away?" He look down. "What will you do then?"

"Get them back."

"How?"

"After the melt. I'll go after the melt."

"Listen. You're lucky you're here. Alive. Yes. You're here alive. Got to make the most of it."

"But they aint done nothing wrong!"

"Yes, yes, but who knows where they are now."

"I aint gonna just forget them. Got to find out where they gone—"

"Yes I know. But maybe get yourself a little stronger. Eat some good food. Make some money. That'll help. Yes, you can make some money here. She likes you. Bek-Murzin. Taken a liking to you. She'll do her best to find out about your family. Just need a bit of patience. Yes yes, patience . . . You aren't going to do anything about it now, are you?"

Feel like everything falling down around me. Cold hands stealing around my heart. Got that lowdown feeling like a stone tossed into Trawsfinnid Lake again. Know that feeling roundside about by now. Down into the dark black water. I guess I been lucky having the old couple needing me. Lucky I aint strung up down in that empty canal, that empty canal breeding bad out of every brick. Lucky I aint starving in the settlement. Or caught by the government and sent to some freezing place.

There aint nothing I can do. The old man say I been lucky. But it aint luck. Aint no luck at all. Just chance. Wish I just come running down the mountain when I hear them all taken away. Magda shouting out like that. Wish I aint been sitting up on the hill with the spirit of the dog inside me, keeping me still and quiet hiding in the rocks. Wish I been taken away with them. All of us together.

Seem like the dog been teaching me good things and bad

things all mixed up together. But the dog just looking out for me. Aint his fault. He just been a dog. Looking out for number one.

Everything go past. Pictures of my dad and Magda and Mary trailing behind me like logs on a string. It aint an easy life up on the mountain, but you been free up there. If you aint too stupid and been good with a snare and a trap you gonna be all right.

Mary. Feel like she been the only person I got to look out for now. She got to be here in the city somewhere. Maybe if I find Mary I can take her back to the house. To the place low down in the hollow where the river pools out. Maybe Dad and the others gonna come back and we can turn over the little flat field by the stream and sow some oats after the melt. On the longdays of summer cut grass up on the Farngod. Mary can hunt eggs on the moor. We'll hew a tree. Stack the sheaths of hay in the barn. Aint nothing gonna bring a smile to your face better than a barn smelling fat and sweet with bundles of fresh hay and dry logs stacked to the eaves at the end of summer.

My dad tell me that he's gonna die before someone take us down to the shanties and put us in some freezing tent. Reckon he been right about that cos this aint no place to live. Even Dorothy Bek-Murzin with her thousand candles and fires piled high with coal and food more than you need. I aint gonna want to be her no more than any of the people climbing in and out of trucks taking them off to the power plants and coal mines a long way under the pylons.

But the old man been right. Don't need no dog to tell me there aint nothing I'm gonna do about it right now. Dog run off back to the hills with his tail between his legs.

Like I said. It aint his fault.

That's what dogs do.

30

After we get back home, Jacob and his wife talk all quiet together but I know it's about me. He put the money in a place under the bed.

Then his wife want to know why I got to get back to the mountains and the whys and wherefores of it all. I aint too bothered about them knowing. So I tell them most of the things which happen to me and why I got to be washed up in this city. About Mary and how I been trapped down in the canal.

"You came into the city along the old canal?"

Then they been mighty interested to know all about Geraint and my dad and Magda and our house up on the Rhinogs too. Those two old people ask me a lot of questions about how we live up on the mountain, what we gonna do for food in the winter and how we make rules and keep warm and get clothes and what we trap and how we cure skins and all the kind of stuff that seem pretty obvious if you ask me.

"And you can read?" the woman ask.

"We all got to do our reading. Graybeards decide that at the Meet."

They look at each other. "And you have books?"

"We got books we find in the house and ones we find in other old houses up on the mountain. We got enough I reckon. To learn on I mean."

"But no permits, no papers?"

"We aint got no papers. My dad want a license to farm. So we can sell stuff in the city. But we aint got one and Geraint got to sell the skins for us—"

"Wait a minute, Willo." Jacob take a knife from the table. He kneel down under the doorway, holding himself steady against the wall. Push the knife in between the floorboards, ease up a plank. He reach down into the hole and pull something out.

"You've seen this before?" he say, holding out a book.

He hand it to me.

It's big and heavy. I wipe the dirt and dust off the front. On the cover it say, *IN SEARCH OF AN ARK* by John Blovyn.

"Open it up. Yes yes, open up the book."

I open it up. Turn the first page.

"'Now is the tenth winter.

Our children are hungry.

We have begun to fear our neighbors.

Fellow men and women—the age of excuses is over. The time is made for action! You look for a sign, but it will not be given. Step up! Death stalks the streets.'"

• • •

It been my dad's book. The one he got in his box. Same words and everything.

I turn the pages some more.

It been the same book. Got the pictures of Eskimos and Scott

of the Antarctic and all the stuff about making snares and curing skins and how you gonna help a baby into the world and all
the other useful things you gonna need to know out on the
mountain.

But my dad's book all tied together with string. Aint never
known what it been called or who write it, cos Dad's book aint
got a cover no more. It been battered and all the pages thin and
he aint gonna just let you turn them on your own. He keep it
wrapped up safe, locked in his box.

"You've seen the book before?" ask the old woman again.

"We got one with the same words and everything."

"I knew it! Knew it from the moment I saw that coat."

"Know what?"

"You're a proper straggler."

"Yes, but how come you got the same book as my dad?" I ask.
"How come you keep it all hidden up?"

Jacob lean over and take the book gentle from my hands. He
run his fingers over it. "We had dreams once." He look up at me. "For
some people this book is like a bible, Willo. But there are some—
There are some who see this book as a *call to arms*. I'm too old for
all that. But if they find this book in here we'll all end up chipping
stones at Ravenscar for sure."

"'They'? Who are 'they'?"

"The ministry, the security police. You don't want to meet *them*.
No no."

The old woman lean forward in the bed. "Have you heard of
the Island, Willo? Does it exist?"

"No. I aint never heard of no island before."

The old lady lean forward even more. "So you stragglers don't know anything?"

"No. I don't know nothing about no island."

"Have you read Blovyn's book?"

"Well. I . . . I aint read it all, just the bits my dad teach me. Like what I tell you. Interesting bits about how we got to be like Eskimos now and how to tie a snare good for catching hares. Those bits he show me."

Jacob turn the pages with his thin fingers. "Here. Mmm. Read this then. Yes, read this."

He hand it back to me.

· · ·

"Optimism! We must all share it. Around the fire. When we Meet. When we Tell. We must pass this gift to our children.

They must become our Beacons of Hope. Our future. Their hands will be worn and rough, but their minds will be ready.

Heed your own spirit. You will be weak if you follow where you are led. Remember this, a society that is unable to foresee its future is bound to perish.

You must find sanctuary.

My survivors. You the Disenchanted. My men and women and children of tomorrow. My sons and daughters. You listened when I said, 'Come to the hills.'

The biggest challenges are still to come.

You must find your Ark. Build it strong. The Island has been abandoned. When moths are on the wing, reclaim it for yourselves.

Make it yours. Come and build your shining Beacons of Hope for all to see. For all our tomorrows."

. . .

That old couple looking at me like those words got some kind of magic in them.

"I don't understand what it mean," I say.

"It's simple. Anyone who has that book has read those words. They have read those words and are waiting. Yes, waiting for the time. Time to leave for the Island, Willo. The stragglers will leave for the Island. That's what they say."

"Well, I aint never heard of no island. My dad never tell me about that. The man who write this book, is he still alive?"

"I don't know, Willo. He could be. But if he is he'll be hiding."

"Hiding? It's just a book."

"John Blovyn said a lot of very controversial things. Mmm. He said truth was better than fear. Truth was better than fear. He told the people to think for themselves."

"Was he right? Do you think he been right?"

"I don't know, Willo. But it was the Chinese who built the nuclear reactors while we were putting up wind farms and solar panels that stopped working during the very first winter. Mmm. While we were shoveling snow and trying to keep warm. We need a new way. That's what Blovyn said. Oh, yes. People listened to begin with."

"My dad say the snows gonna come anyway. No matter what we do. And he say they gonna go away again too. And we got to be hunters in the snow and beacons of hope til then."

"Well, he was a follower of John Blovyn then. That's for certain."

"But why we got all the snow? You know that?"

"Some people said it was all the cars, others said it was the planes. Some said it was the sun, others said it was nature's way. But whatever they said—it did get warmer, mmm. The ice at the poles began to melt. And all that cold fresh water flowing into the sea slowed the warm currents in the Atlantic. And when that happened, when there was no more warm water flowing around, mmm? That's when the snow started to fall and didn't stop. At first it was just a few bad winters. Yes yes I remember that. But the snows kept coming. And the summers got colder. And shorter. All over Europe."

"It all came so quickly," say the old woman.

"Yes yes. And people began to panic. The roads covered in snow for most of the year. No one had planned for it, you see. No trucks or cars and no food in the shops and the power supply cutting off every day. The water freezing in the pipes. Mmm. Very bad times, Willo. And it hasn't got any better." Jacob get up, riddle the fire. He get that book wrapped up again, crouch down and hide it back under the floorboards.

"We're lucky to have survived," say the old woman, clutching at the blanket.

"Yes yes. They were very bad times. You're lucky you weren't alive then Willo. Mmm, very lucky." Jacob got himself up from the floor, hand on his knee, pulling himself up on the door.

"But what been so good about this Island? Where is it? Aint there gonna be people there already? And government making all the rules, same as here?"

"Who knows?"

"How are people gonna get there?"

"I don't know, Willo. Boats, I suppose."

"Where is this Island?"

"We don't know that."

"But why are you still here?" I say. "Why didn't you go to the hills? You got the book, aint you?"

Jacob's wife look around the little room. Her eyes glance from the shelves to the cracked jars and the tin basin hanging from the door and the pots and pans by the fire.

"We're old now. This is our home, Willo. Where we belong. For better or for worse."

"Do you think we like it here, mmm?" Jacob get up from his chair. "Do you think anyone likes being cold and hungry and scared of the gangs and the dogs and the soldiers? Their children dying of cold and hunger in their arms—never knowing what's around the next corner? Mmm? Do you think we want to live like this? But we're lucky. We aren't in the settlements. I have work still. People dream of going to China, Russia—anywhere. It's a dream that keeps their noses to the ground. But some of us want a better world right here!" He hit the table with his hand. He got a proper fire inside him, sound like what Patrick call *someone who gonna die for an idea* the way he's spouting on.

"And the reason your family have been taken away is because the hills are being cleared. Yes, cleared. ANPEC are buying the land and the ministry don't want people like you up there. Do you understand? Mmm?"

"ANPEC?" I say.

"They built all the reactors and own all the coal mines. They grow all the food. They don't want stealers or stragglers up in the hills causing them trouble."

"We don't cause no trouble."

"They don't see a difference, Willo. You're all the same to them. Stealers, stragglers, settlement dwellers. All the same to them. They're scared of all this talk. Scared of that book. Scared of any resistance. They've got the money and they want the land. Mmm? And the government is going to give it to them. They don't want people talking about free islands. They want people buying their coal and electricity and food."

"But ANPEC aint the government. How come the government aint saying something?"

"Pah! The government are in the East's pocket so deep they can't get out. When ANPEC come along wanting something, the government, they say, 'Let's see what they'll bring to the table.' What table? Mmm, what table? Yes yes, the table we'll be sacrificed on one day. They smoke Hongtashan and drink Chinese whiskey, they give away our land, and all this in the name of seeing what will be brought to that proverbial table. They will discover too late that we are the lunch. Mmmm. Oh, yes, we will be the lunch."

"Calm down, Jacob." The old woman reach out from the bed.

But Jacob aint calming down. He sound like my dad when he been banging on about beacons of hope and government people and all that stuff.

And like Patrick say, *The trees around the door aint gonna help you then.*

216

But I don't believe they gonna take away a few stragglers just cos what it say in some old book. And anyway, how they gonna know my dad got the book? It don't make sense somehow.

And Patrick. Patrick aint gonna sit by while they take him away off the mountain. He been big and strong now after cutting wood all winter. He got out from the camp at the Wylfa reactor. He gonna fight for sure. Dad and Patrick gonna be thinking of some way to escape. Maybe they all got away somehow.

Jacob slump back in his chair. "Mmm, so you see, you'll have to be patient, boy. Maybe Dorothy Bek-Murzin will help you. But don't get your hopes up."

PART III

THE MELT

For winter's rains and ruins are over,
And all the season of snows and sins;
The days dividing lover and lover,
The light that loses, the night that wins;
And time remembered is grief forgotten,
And frosts are slain and flowers begotten,
And in green underwood and cover
Blossom by blossom the spring begins.

—Algernon Charles Swinburne

31

May come. All over the drip drip drip of the melt. Start early this year.

Jacob give me a tin of money. He say, "You earned it, Willo."

We been stuck inside most of the winter. Trouble on the streets. Flames from the shanties. Gangs in the settlements come roaring out at night. I watch it from up here in the tower block. See it pretty good through that great big window. Down below the trucks bristling with soldiers. No one go out after dark no more. Jacob say they barricade the whole settlement now. Aint no way in or out. The streets get quieter. I want to go back and look for Mary. "You won't get near," he say. "Can't get through the streets for a foot of mud. You don't want to see what they're doing out there."

Even in the city the streets turn to muddy slush after the rains. Worse than the snow. Sheets of water washing ice from the roofs. Running in gullies down every road. The stink even worse. Out of every drain putrid slop come bubbling up and everywhere damp and musty. Rats get bold as dogs. Whispering in my ear at night. *Slip through the cracks, Willo, slip through the cracks.* Sometimes I listen out for the dog. But I guess he been running on the hill.

You watch a pack of dogs in the melt and they look like they got a pretty good thing going. Playing and jumping about licking each other. And they get proper excited when a bitch bring her pups out the ground in spring. I tell you, it gonna make you smile when you see dogs leaping around all over the place like that. And they look out for each other sure as snow gonna fall. Just got to watch out if you been the runt that's all. But I reckon that been the same for people too. People always looking to find the runt in you and needle it out if they can. I hate that.

But now it's just those hissing rats. Dog got free back to the hills for sure.

Still, the few weeks of the coming summer in everyone's mind now. Just like Patrick always say: "Everyone waiting to feel the sun on their shoulders."

The old woman get out of bed for the first time. Jacob got her propped up in a chair by the window. She busy herself stitching and stirring the pot.

But still I feel like I been trapped in a cage. Trapped in this bad-smelling tower. Feel just like those rats stuck in here.

Now the melt come, old feelings flood back. Wake me up in the night with panic in my heart. In my dreams I see Mary pressed against the barricades, the people crying out for food. She been calling for me, the twins hanging around her legs. Make me sit up pretty sharp. I been here too long. Getting soft. Bad feelings jumping about in my head. Like hares leaping and fighting on the Farn-god in the spring.

We been luckier than most though. We got coal enough and food enough with the money we get for the coat. I got papers now. Dorothy Bek-Murzin been true to her word.

"You can come and see me, come and go as you please inside the city now, Willo," she say. I smile to her, but it don't feel much like "coming and going as I please" to me.

Sometimes I walk through the dirty streets. I got to know the city now. Got to know the different buildings and corners like they been rocks and crags on the mountain. All the time I been looking at the faces of the people passing in the smog and rain. Maybe I'm gonna see Mary one day.

The first time I come alone to Dorothy Bek-Murzin I been shaking inside. Up the stairs with my hat in my hand, back into that warm room.

Mei-Li pin Dorothy Bek-Murzin's skirt up so I can do the measuring. Her legs are white and smooth. I get down on the floor with the tape. Fold the leather around her ankles and shins. My hands trembling. She got a warm-smelling perfume about her; I got the smell of it on my hands when I finish.

"Come back next week and take me to the bathhouse, Willo," she say. "I need someone to carry my trunk."

• • •

With the money we got for the coat, Jacob buy an old sewing machine. He say we gonna need it to make the boots cos the leather gonna be thick and hard to stitch by hand. "They've got to fit like a glove, Willo," he say.

The machine's a solid black lump. You got to turn the wheel by hand and fight the heavy needle to get it to punch down through the leather. But it make a pretty neat job after I got to know it roundside about and fiddle with the knobs and threads and bobbins so it aint pulling the thread too tight or too loose or not at all.

"Where does she get all her money?" I ask Jacob one day when we been cutting the soles out of a thick piece of hide.

"She has friends."

"And they just give her money?"

"They're very important friends. Mmm. Hand me the scissors."

"She aint married, is she?"

Jacob got the awl between his teeth. "Nnn, nuh sher issn marri."

"But she got men who come and see her?"

Jacob take the haft out his mouth. Look up from the table.

"Yes, Willo. But why all this interest? Mmm? Rich men want a beautiful woman to look at. To touch. That's how she gets her money and fine things and candles burning all over the house. Mmm, and these clothes too. Pass me the scriver."

"But she always been so happy and laughing."

"Well, she's as tough as leather under that smiling pretty face, my boy, yes yes." He pull the scriver down across the leather. "Tough as this leather. And probably not as happy as she looks. No no. Not as happy as she looks. Now stop asking questions and hold this skin flat for me."

The rain stop that day so I sneak out and wander on the streets. The piles of snow on the sides of the road near all melted away now. People walking through the mud, their boots wrapped in canvas. Little girls sell snowdrops.

I feel different inside.

It been five months I been here now. Seem like forever.

224

Trapped in the city. The fight in me gonna smoulder away if I don't get a plan. The Farngod seem a thousand miles away. I don't say my words no more. Cos it don't seem they gonna help me with the dog so far away and all. Aint got no news of Dad or Magda or the others. Even Mary getting to be a memory. But it been the bad memories that stick—like the mud.

The graybeards always say there aint no point trying to burn a log when it's green. Got to let it season. Grow hard and dry.

That's how I feel.

Like I been drying and hardening.

• • •

When it aint raining Jacob open up the windows and let the fresh air wash away the stink of smoke clinging onto every bit of clothing and blanket in our little rooms. We wash the soot off the walls. Scrub the floor. We rent a tinbath from the soap seller. I help Jacob collect rainwater in buckets and heat it on the stove. Aint no use waiting for the power to come on. Jacob hang a curtain around the fire.

It been good to sit in the bath. Soak away my worry in the steaming water. Fire warming my face. Take me right back home. Magda hauling water over the stove, shouting out, "Willo, come down and get in!" The twins all laughing and steaming, standing by the hearth, dripping wet with the sheet wrapped around them both, Magda rubbing their hair so that it stick up like new-grown grass. Me got to get in the tub, filled to the brim. Covering myself. And Magda telling me, "Don't be silly, Willo, it's only me," but I'm still gonna cover myself up til she go out. Then I can pour the water over my head and feel it running down my shoulders, tickling the skin on my back. Bath day always better than you think it gonna be.

Sometimes at night the tears feel like they gonna come. And I turn to the wall then. Try to breathe still. That lowdown feeling make me want to blub like a kid. It really do.

But blubbing like a baby aint gonna bring my dad back, nor Magda nor the twins. Aint gonna help me find Mary. And now the melt come I know I got to find them. Even if I die in the trying. Got to get into the settlement, go back to the canal, the beerhouse. Maybe Vince gonna know something. It aint the dog telling me what to do. It been in my heart.

I got to get a pony.

Got to be soon.

Sneak out one night and head west.

I feel the sap rising up in me.

• • •

Then the weather turn cold again. All the meltwater and mud frozen on the streets. It kind of freeze the smell up so it aint all bad. The streets get like a frozen pond. I see a horse scrabbling on the ice, falling down on its knees between the shafts of a cart. Horse screaming out. Driver shout, trying to pull that horse up. It bellow out more. He whip it and push it and pull it until it just give up. Fall over on its side exhausted. Nostrils wide. Breath steam in the frozen air. The people from the cart crowd around. Horse look pretty scared. Someone got to come and shoot it cos it been broken in the legs. Army truck come and do it. Drag the horse away. Make a pretty big crowd come out to see what all the fuss about. But they get off pretty soon when the soldiers come out with their guns. Driver shouting that it been his only horse. They aint got no right to take all the dead horses, he shout. He got mouths to feed. But the soldiers push him away. I get away too. I got papers but I aint in a hurry to show them to no one.

"Why Bek-Murzin want me to take her to the bathhouse? She got a girl for that, aint she?" I ask Jacob.

"She likes you, Willo. Remember. Patience."

"But I aint never been before. What she want me for?"

"You aren't going in the bath with her. No no." He laugh. "Just carrying her trunk."

"Why she got to take a trunk to the baths?"

"She's hardly going to come out with wet hair and no rouge on her cheeks, is she, you silly boy?" say Elizabeth. "She'll have a new set of clothes and all her potions and perfumes in that trunk. Too heavy for her girl. So be sure not to drop it."

Before I go the old woman reach out to me.

"Take care, Willo. Take care."

Reckon she's getting soft in the head.

I sharpen up the remains of the studs on the soles of my boots. Aint much left of them with walking on the icy roads. But I don't want to slip carrying Bek-Murzin's trunk.

Today I'm gonna ask her. I'm gonna say, "What about my dad— you hear anything about my dad?" I aint told Jacob. It get him wringing his hands and whining, "Now don't pester her, Willo. Patience, patience, patience."

But I aint got no more room inside for patience. I been storing so much of it, it gonna come bursting out like beer that ferment too quick and blow out the bottle. I been patient enough when I been sitting out on the Farngod waiting for hare. That kind of patience got an end. A good big stewpot of an end. But this kind of patience aint got nothing good in it. It's just like waiting for bad really.

So I been cursing the street and the ice and the carts and the grog sellers and the flurries of snow that whip down from the peaks and the shitty smells and the choking smog and the man whipping his lame horse and the beggars sitting in the gutter and the cold burning my nostrils. I been cursing it all on that walk across the city to Chinatown.

Mei-Li waiting at the bottom of the stairs. The trunk is open and she wrap a hairbrush and comb in a square of silk, fold a linen towel and place it on top.

"I pack it all for her good. But keep it upright. No tip. No tip the trunk. Everything fall out. Madame get angry. No tip."

"I aint gonna tip it up, Mei-Li."

"No no. You no tip it, Willo."

"Did you remember the powder, Mei-Li?" Dorothy say at the top of the stairs.

"Yes, Madame."

Dorothy, wearing a loose cotton shift tied at the waist, coming down the steps. Over her dress, a soft wool coat. Mei-Li fetch a hooded fur cape—lay it over her shoulders and tie it at the neck.

"Such a fuss to be clean," Dorothy say through her soft red lips.

Mei-Li bend down with a pair of clogs, the flat wooden sole

raised off the ground on tall wedges. Dorothy Bek-Murzin climb up onto them—hold my shoulder to steady herself. Mei-Li tie them tight with ribbons, and towering above me Dorothy clop out into the street. Slow and careful like she's crossing a stream. Her feet and hems high off the dirty ground.

"Stay close, Willo."

The trunk bite into my legs. But I tell you, people move out the way quick when something pretty as that come walking down the road.

She start talking all soft under her breath. "Now don't speak. Look straight ahead."

"Why?"

"You'll find out. I have some news for you, Willo. It is about your father. I want you to meet someone. A friend of mine. He is coming to my house later. That is why I asked you to come with me to the bathhouse. To tell you this. I don't trust anyone anymore. They watch me. Mei-Li especially."

The studs on my boots crunch down in the ice. My arms ache with holding the trunk out.

I have some news for you, Willo.

32

"Put the trunk down, Willo. Come upstairs."

Mei-Li take off Dorothy's cape and the wooden clogs and she step down to the ground on her clean slippered feet.

"Empty the trunk, Mei-Li, and wash the linen. Willo is measuring me for a new pair of gloves. We are waiting for a furrier who's bringing some skins. Be sure and listen for him at the door."

Mei-Li nod. Her face is still, can't see nothing on it. Some people you can tell right off what they been thinking. Not this girl.

"There's no need to come up. You can have the afternoon off after you've shown the furrier in. I'm not hungry."

The girl make a little bow and take the trunk.

When we get upstairs Dorothy close the doors and put her finger to her mouth. Beckon me over to another door. She take a key from a chain around her neck and put it in the lock.

We been in her bedroom I guess cos there's a great big bed hanging with curtains. The windows been shuttered. She light a candle on a table. Open the drawer underneath. Draw out a small box. Out of the box she take some money. A bundle of paper yuan. She hand it to me.

I aint got a clue what she want.

"Take it," she whisper. "You're going away. It's all I have. Give it to Callum. You can leave after Mei-Li has gone. He's going to take you."

"I don't understand. Who is Callum?"

"Keep your voice down. He's coming soon. He knows about your father."

"My father?"

"Listen, Willo. Bad times are coming. There aren't many who are ready. Everyone is needed. You are needed. Especially you."

"But my dad. What about him?"

"Callum will tell you."

"I don't understand."

"Listen. Your father, Robin Blake . . ."

A knock on the door in the other room. Dorothy push the box back in the drawer.

"Quick—"

"But—"

She dip across out of the bedroom, close the door, pull me over to a chair by the fire. Hold out a hand. "Come in."

Mei-Li step silently onto the carpet.

"—and I want the gloves to widen at the cuffs, Willo. Oh, Mei-Li, has the furrier arrived?"

"Yes, Madame, he's here."

"Well show him in. Then you may leave."

Mei-Li back out of the room, and a large man wearing a pony-skin coat step inside. He got a small pack on his back. Mud on his boots. Thick stubble on his face. Look like he been walking long without much sleep.

"I've come with some fine hareskins, Madame. Fine hareskins. I believe you're wanting them for gloves now." He look back over his shoulder.

The door clicks shut behind him. Dorothy is up. Drawing the curtains at the windows. She poke the fire. It been the only light in the room now. She step gentle to the keyhole, bend down with her ear pressed against it. "She's gone."

The man take his hat off. His head is big and square and solid. The hair cropped short. His cheeks thin and dark beneath the stubble. His skin been bit by the frost some time for sure.

"You made it. How did you get out of the settlement, Callum?"

"It was difficult. Roadblocks everywhere. Soldiers everywhere. Betham gangs rampaging every night because there's no madak getting in. You can only come in and out with a work permit. And even then—and the rains. The mud. I came along the flooded canal."

"What about the children?"

"I was caught. In a blizzard. I lost the boy. I—"

Dorothy come close. Take his arm.

"I'm sorry. I'm so sorry."

He wipe his face. "There's nothing anyone could have done. . . . But I got back. Found the girl. Spent all winter in the settlement. It's terrible. Terrible. No one can get in or out without papers. Hardly any food—"

Dorothy run her hand over his arm. "Maybe you'll find the boy."

The man look at her with sad eyes. Shake his head. He take off his pack. "And you, Dorothy?"

"They came. Asked questions."

"About what?"

"If I'd heard things. You know, who I'm seeing."

"Do they know?"

"They—they know more than they say. They were tough, but I told them nothing. They know I have contacts—friends in the settlement."

"You must be careful. You're alone here. And this is the boy?" He look at me.

"Like a bird in a cage . . ." she whisper. "Yes, Robin Blake's son."

"Dorothy says you came from the hills, Willo. Alone." He got his tired eyes on me, Dorothy at his side.

"I've given him all the money I have," Dorothy say.

The man look down at that pretty face looking up at him. He take her hand. "Won't you come, Dorothy?"

"Across the mountain? Look at me. Look at my hands, Callum. Look at them."

He turn her pale ringed fingers over in his gloved hand. Hold them at the wrist.

"Can these hands dig down in the snow for potatoes or haul wood, lift heavy buckets of water?" she say.

Callum smile. "We'll make you gloves—"

She pull away from him. "Listen to me, Callum. I can't come."

"But what will you do, Dorothy?"

"What I have always done. Look after myself."

"They're watching everyone. It isn't safe for you here."

"I can look after myself, Callum. You know that. I was born in a tent like you but I've grown soft. I remember the feel of rags on my feet but I found chinks in the walls. You're like a dog but I am a cat, always seeking the warmth of the fire. I cannot come where you are going. But the boy. He will go."

Callum turn to me. "So you're Robin's son."

"How do you know my dad?"

"Dorothy told me about you. That's why I came."

"Why? What about my dad?"

"They took him away and his wife. Anyone up on the hills."

"I know my dad been taken away. But where did they take him? Why did you come here for me?" Anger building up inside me with this big graybeard talking to me like he know something that I don't.

"You don't understand, Willo. But you have to trust me. Have to come with me. Tonight. We haven't got much time. It's what your father would have wanted, Willo. He would have wanted you to come."

"You don't know. You don't know what my dad gonna want!"

"But I do. It's because of him that I'm here. Because of him we're going."

"Going? Where?"

"They've built the boat. It's time. We're going to the Island. Moths are on the wing."

"What island? What moths? Tell me how you know my dad."

"Because I read his words every day, Willo. We all know him."

"What do you mean? What do you mean you read his words? Where is he?"

"He doesn't know, Callum," say Dorothy, turning to the fire. Leaning her head on the mantel.

There's a hot wind. Rushing in my head. "It's the reading make you human, Willo." Dad's showing me how to scrape a skin clean— his hands tight round the scraper. "We've got to be beacons of hope." Dad leading the graybeards cutting hay up on the Farngod. "This is just a time when men forgot to be human—see?" I see a picture of Dad in my head, striding toward the river. "Step up, Willo. Death stalks the streets. The bad things—the animal bit in everyone's head." Reading to me from his book.

The boat at Barmuth. Old Roger and the fishermen who stay there all winter, even after the Meet been and gone. I hear the grown-ups talk about it. Everyone bring food and caulk and timber to Roger cos he stay all winter.

"Willo."

They both looking at me.

"You have to tell him, Callum," Dorothy say.

But I'm sinking into Trawsfinnid Lake. Down into the blackness like a stone. Dad standing on the grass naked. "You got to learn to swim, Willo."

No. He aint told me everything.

"Willo"—Callum take me by the shoulder—"look at me!"

• • •

"Step up, Willo. Death stalks the streets. The bad things—the animal bit in everyone's head."

And the wind is thrashing and blowing and whipping the air, and I sink into the blackness. Arms reach down for me. But I'm falling and twisting.

Dorothy screaming out.

Downstairs the crack of splintering wood.

"Willo!" Callum grab my arm. "The window. In the bedroom."

But boots are on the stairs.

Thud

Thud

Thud

THUD.

"Dorothy! Quick!"

And the telling screaming and spitting.

The doors fling open. A rush of faces.

The room fill with men in long coats and hard gloves and guns and the smell of cold leather. The gentle flames from the fire lick up the chimney but dark shadows fall across the doorway. The wind still rush in my head. The river inside me rage in the melt.

"There! It's him."

The strange-smelling men shout and stomp in their boots. Tables fall. Glass smash to the ground. They got Callum. Pull him back from the window.

Dorothy leap at them screeching. They grab her arm and push her aside as they fall on Callum. Dragging him by his legs. Smash his head with the gun. Someone got me down on the floor. Everything in that dark room broken and altered like a whirlwind ripping the trees from the ground.

And in the eye of the storm, a figure stride across the wreckage. Soldiers parting. He drag Dorothy up by the hair. Twisting it in his big hand. Lifting her up on her delicate feet. Callum just groaning on the floor. Just see the glint of the big man's shining boots. The broad muscles on his back tense under his coat.

"You think this is a way to repay us?"

"No! Please!"

Big man yank Dorothy's head back. She grab at his hands.

He pull back his hand. Raise it high.

"You want to talk? Whore! You want to talk now?"

The back of his hand smash across her face. Blood come gushing out her nose. She sag down under him.

"How long? Huh? I knew you were rotten inside. I'll get every last drop of rottenness you've got up in that pretty head of yours. We have plenty of time for that."

He pull her up again. Pull her face up close to his. "Come come, you aren't looking your best, my dear." He wipe the blood off her lip with his thumb. Hold his hand against her face.

"You're getting older, Dorothy. An old settlement whore. With no guts."

Pthth! The spit land on his cheek.

Slowly he wipe the spittle away with his hand. "I thought you'd be reasonable, Dorothy." He hit her again. The force of it crack on her jaw. Break a moan from deep inside her body.

Dorothy sink to the floor like a crumpled rag. A rough hand push me down. The soldiers hoist her up by the arms. Tie her. Roll her onto the ground.

"Get some fucking light in here!"

Someone rip the curtain from the window.

The man with shiny leather boots and blood on his hand turn around then.

He turn around in the cold gray light falling over the upturned table by the window. The light catch the broken glass on the carpet, the toecaps of his boots. It glint on the shiny buttons of his long coat. Right up to his face. Clean shaven now but still the same square chin. Scar above his left eye. He push a strand of hair off his forehead. His middle finger a stub at the knuckle. He look down at me. Those cold blue eyes got a look of surprise seeing me there.

The wind raging in my head can only whisper a memory, whisper it low. *"I'll tell you a secret, Willo. Men are bad and all their ideas too."*

Mei-Li standing quiet in the doorway. Her face a blank page.

• • •

Patrick. Patrick. Patrick. Patrick.

33

It's dark. So dark I can't see. But I sense the walls close around me. The sound of my breath on the floor. The rope tied so tight about my wrists I can't feel my hands. The floor hard against my head. Hard and cold and smell bad.

A grille in the wall clang open. A rectangle of light on the wall. A shadow behind it.

Light come on then. Flip on like a shot. Blind me for a second. I hear bolts snapping open.

Across the bare stained floor I see the polished leather of his boots in the doorway.

He step inside.

"Willo," he say as if he been sad to see me somehow. "Oh, Willo."

Slowly Patrick take off his gloves, hand them to the guard at the door. The door swings shut. The grille scraping back.

We been alone.

He drop down onto his haunches. His boots creak. I see the seam of his trousers tight inside his thigh.

"Hello, Willo."

But he aint my friend no more.

"It's a big wide world out here isn't it?"

"I thought you been our friend. I thought you—"

"I listened to enough moralizing up on that freezing mountain for half a year, boy. I don't want to listen to it anymore. But you're right. I'm not really your friend"—his eyes stare down cold—"but I like you, Willo. I like people who see things as they are."

"What you done with Dorothy? What you done with her? She aint done nothing wrong."

"The person here asking questions is me. You better learn that quick if you want to make this easy." He stand up. Look about the dank walls of the cell. "But for the moment I find I still like you, Willo. Remember." He stand up. Wave a hand down at me. "Just for the moment."

"You aint who you say you are—you're just a lowdown rat like Geraint."

"Geraint?" he laugh. "What have you got against poor old Geraint now? At least he knows which side his bread is buttered. But you don't like him fiddling with your sister? That it? Don't like him playing around with Alice? Rolling her in the hay like a goat. At least he was good enough to take the girl and her brat."

He crouch down again, look close into my face. "At least she had the sense to breed with someone who could take her away from that freezing sty you lived in. You should be pleased for her. Proud of her. Geraint saved her life."

"What do you mean?"

He reach down and grab the back of my coat. He pull me up off the ground, my arms tight behind me. "The best thing she ever did—getting on heat and letting old Geraint stick it in her behind the barn."

"Don't talk about her like that. You aint been there. You——"

"But I know where she is now, Willo. Safe with Geraint and the brat on a convoy to the promised land. To China, Willo. Somewhere the sun might shine one day. I told you—that old farmer saved her life."

"You're lying!"

"I'm not. And I know where your dad is too and Magda and those screeching brats and all the rest of them."

"Where? Where you take them?"

"First things first." He get up. Bash on the door. Shout to the guard, "Get me a chair!"

Patrick take the chair in one hand, swing it into the room. Bang it down hard on the floor. I see a chain hanging down from the ceiling then. Big rusty chain with a hook on the end. Stomach come up in my throat. Patrick drag me up. Patrick who been sleeping in my dad's house all winter haul me up onto the chair. Lift my arms behind me and over the back. I scream out—but his rough hands aint listening.

"Where have you been hiding, Willo? Who have you been with? We've got Callum Gourty and that whore. But who else is there, Willo? Who's been feeding you all this winter?"

"I aint telling you nothing!"

"If I was you, I'd have curled up on the mountain and had a good long sleep in the snow."

"You aint caught me cos I hid up on the hill!"

"Has it occurred to you that I might have known where you were? I told you, Willo—I like you. I'd rather you had died up there in the snow. But I guess you've got a bit of your father in you. And you've got to be meddling in things you don't understand. Is that it?"

"I aint telling you."

Patrick kick the chair over with the sole of his boot. My face fall smack onto the floor. All I can see are his boots again. And the pain throbbing hard through my skull. Helpless as a stoat in a trap.

"Don't fuck with me, straggler brat! You're going to tell me, so don't fuck with me!" I see him turn. Just the back of his boots. And the pain and the fear fluttering about inside me so bad I want to be sick but there aint no way out—nowhere to hide. I close my eyes. Cos I don't want to tell him about that old man Jacob and his wife. Or Mary. Not Mary.

"I had hopes for you, Willo. I hoped this was going to be easy. But I'm beginning to lose patience. Who have you been with? Give me the names!"

"I aint been with no one. No one—"

His foot press down on my cheek. Big, rough, damp-smelling leather sole grinding my face into the floor.

"I promise . . . aint . . . been with . . . no one."

He lift his foot up. A low sigh come from his head high up above me. And he kick me hard in the guts. The blow stop my breath. Pain shoot around my head like it's gonna burst out of me somewhere but don't, and I can't breathe. I been trying but the breath won't come. I'm gonna die on this floor. Then I suck it in. The air fill my lungs and the vomit spew out hot on the floor.

But he aint finished.

"Don't. Fucking. Lie to me!" He kick me in the guts again. My legs jerk up with the pain. I call out for Magda then cos it been the only word gonna come. But aint no Magda here. Aint no mothering in this room. And I wonder if Patrick got a mother. What she gonna say if she see him now. I hear myself moaning and blubbing and puking on the floor. Look up at his face. Same face. Same Patrick I seen stitching up his pouch all careful. Same Patrick chopping logs with my dad. Same Patrick leaning over his bowl of yewd at the kitchen table.

"Something to say, Willo?"

"Why?" It croak out of me. And I wait for the blow.

"Why what? Why are you here? Why do I want to know? Lot of why's, Willo."

"We aint done nothing wrong."

A mean laugh snort out his snout then. He grab the chair, hoist it up with me on it. The vomit smelling bad on my chest. Pain dancing all about like a storm.

Patrick lean against the wall. From the pocket of his coat he take a packet of baccy. Roll a smoke up slow. "I longed for some decent tobacco up there on the mountain, Willo. But I had patience. Reckon I used up all my patience. And every time I find some troublemaker, I find that book. You know the one. *In Search of an Ark*. They've all got that book—"

He strike a match.

"Have you ever felt a good hot sun on your back, Willo? So hot it makes you want to take your shirt off. Swim in the sea. Ever felt that?" He draw on the smoke. "No. I didn't think so. It's a powerful thing the sun. I've been to Africa. I've seen the desert covered in shining solar panels. Hundreds and thousands stretching out as far as the eye can see. So hot you can't bear it almost.

And all of them soaking up that beautiful sun and turning it into energy. Amazing thing, Willo. A solar farm is a wonder of modern technology. And what were we doing?" He drag on the last of the smoke and throw it down onto the floor, grind it with his boot.

"What were we doing while the Chinese bought up that good hot desert? Putting up wind farms and sorting our fucking rubbish. That's what we were doing. And fighting for the last few drops of oil." He point down at me. "That's what we were doing. And I'm not going to choose the runt of the litter to be my guard dog, why has everyone got a problem with the East? I don't. But everyone who does has got that book. Looking over their shoulders to the West. We've got to look East, Willo—"

He get down low, grab my face. I can feel his fingers digging into my cheeks. He's close to me. I can smell the stale smoke on his breath he's so close. "East. The future. That's where I'm going to when I've worked my ticket. Land of the rising sun, Willo. So you're going to tell me who's been feeding you and I'll find that book there too. And then I'll find the next link in the pathetic chain of your so-called Resistance. What do you all think this is? The fucking second world war! Think the Americans are going to come and rescue you this time?"

"I don't know what you're talking about. I aint been with ... no one. Just ... getting by ... on my own."

His head drop. The hand grabbing my face relax for a second.

"You fool, Willo. Same as your father."

"What have you done with him? With Magda? The twins?"

Patrick's fingers tighten again, dig painfully into my face. "Want to know something about your father? Want to know what he told me?"

I got to look at him then.

"He told me how disappointed he was in having a simpleton like you for a son. How he couldn't love you."

"You're lying. You don't know my father!"

"I do, Willo. I know him very well. Better than you think. You know who your father is?"

"Robin Blake. Robin Blake is my father."

He laugh. "Your father was the great John Blovyn. Do you hear? Your father wasn't Robin Blake. And he didn't love you."

The wind howl around my ears. Spinning and blowing and beating at me.

"Did you hear that?" Patrick shout. "John Blovyn. He wrote every word in that book. That's your father. He lied to you, Willo. Hiding up on the mountain all this time. He didn't even tell you. He wrote that book that I find in every rat's nest I go to. But he didn't tell *you*, Willo. Because he didn't care about you. Do you know how long it took me to find him? How many long nights like this? Long nights in these freezing cells. Squeezing out names. And then I spend half a year eating his gritty oat yewd that stuck in my guts like lead. Half a year sleeping on a lumpy straw-filled mattress. Half a year I had to feel wool scratching at my back. Half a year I had to spend listening to him moralizing at me with his crackpot ideas. About change and human fucking nature. And he told me nothing. Nearly drove me mad, Willo. Nearly drove me mad.

"But you. You never answered his stupid questions. 'No, Willo,

245

MY FATHER IS NOT ROBIN BLAKE

MY FATHER IS JOHN BLOVYN

guns are bad.' 'No, Willo, reading's good.' 'Put the scraper down and listen to me, Willo.' You just put your stupid dog skull on and hove off to the hills. I envied you then. Because I had to listen to him night and day."

"He aint done nothing wrong. What you done with him? With Magda—the others?"

It choke out of me cos the black hole of his words been growing like a storm inside. I can feel the tears spring hot behind my eyes like burning pain. And there aint nowhere to hide from it. Everything fall away and I'm nothing. Just like that stone sinking in the lake. Gonna be better if he just kill me.

My head fall forward. And then Patrick hit me again. I don't know why. The full force of him. Back of his hand smash across my jaw. So hard it throw me to the floor.

I can taste the blood now. The blood and the vomit and the pain. And I know this just been the beginning.

"Your father was foolish til the end, Willo. Shall I tell you about *the end*, Willo?"

I aint doing nothing but moaning on the floor in a pool of my own blood and vomit and fear.

"Maybe you're telling me the truth. You never were very clever. Just a simple boy. I can see why he was so very disappointed in you. You. Son of the great John Blovyn. Running about the hills like a wild dog. And he never told me. Never told me which islands. Never told me who it was they were in contact with. Nothing. He was the same in here. Even with the others dead in front of him. Even when he was screaming out to God, Willo. They all find God in the end."

I see Patrick through my swollen eye. He go to the door—
bash on it. Then turn.

"I told you once, Willo, that I'm not the sort of man who's going
to die for an idea. It sickens me. They used to burn men. Torture and
burn them for the ideas in their heads. Nothing's changed. I never
understand why men are prepared to die for the shapeless thoughts
in their heads. And your father was one of those men. So maybe.
Maybe he decided to tell you nothing. His wolf boy simpleton son.
Who he could never love."

"He never said that—" I shout it out then to stop the voices
pounding in my head. And Patrick weaving and slipping like a snake
inside my mind. "He never said that!"

"Oh, Willo. I already know more than you think. Dorothy was
very forthcoming. So I don't need you to talk. But I need you all
the same. And Bek-Murzin gave me plenty of names."

"She didn't. You're lying."

"You really don't understand people, do you? That whore was
as easy as peeling a rotten apple. A pretty skin for certain. But
underneath it all, a squirming mass of flesh and maggots."

"You're lying!"

"I remember, Willo, how you wanted a gun. How it made you
feel to hold one. And you're right. A gun is just the thing for shooting dogs."

He stoop down and drag me up off the floor. I aint got nothing left in me. Nothing to say. No fight in my body.

My father is John Blovyn.

Thoughts crashing about in my head like waves.

Patrick push me out of the cell into a dim corridor. Single light hanging from the ceiling. Metal doors either side. I wonder if there been people in those dark rooms. People like me.

A guard open the door—faceless man underneath his hard boots.

The bolts pull back. It's a cell like mine. Same bare stained floor. Dark patches on the concrete. The stain of human blood. Of tears and vomit and pain. Same dim light. Same smell of fear and sweat and cruelty.

And everything inside me die when I see her. Aint got nothing more to empty from my guts. All that been left is the blood in my veins. Pumping through my heart. Quivering still in my flesh.

Her head slumped forward on her chest. Her hair hanging down in dark sheets over her face. That face that had all the softness and beauty and delicate womanness in it black and blue now. Her lips swollen. Her cheeks bruised. Blood smeared across her broken mouth and vomit staining her remaining clothing. Pale feet dangling above that awful floor. Hands high behind her. Hanging from the chain.

I fall down on my knees. I aint got nothing left. No fiber to hold myself up.

But Patrick pull me up.

"Look at her. Just a piece of settlement scum. Like I said. Underneath that pretty skin is the squirming flesh. She told me everything in the end, Willo."

Dorothy moan. And she raise her broken face.

"Now, Willo. You see the world as it is," he say.

Through the swollen slits of her eyes Dorothy look at me.

She just look at me. And I forgive her the world.

"She's worse than a dog, Willo. Hearing me, whore? Dogs don't bite the hand that feeds them."

Dorothy move but no words come from her mouth.

Patrick got the back of my neck. Holding it to look at her. He pull back his coat with his free hand. Slide his hand into his belt. Take out a gun.

"Now, Willo. What do you do with an injured dog? You put it out of its misery. That's the kind thing to do, isn't it?"

"No!"

"Put it out of its misery." He push me closer. "You want to be put out of your misery, don't you, Dorothy?"

She twitch. A broken sound escape her lips.

Patrick take the gun and press it against her head. "This is how you shoot a dog, Willo."

34

Maybe this been the time for my dying. And I don't want it to be now. Maybe it been the end. And the end coming up proper slow with the taste of fear in your mouth. It aint quick like you think.

It been like your whole life floating about you, and every sight and sound and person you ever know gonna come knocking and telling and laughing and crying and you gonna be thinking on every thing you said and didn't do and the things you did do too and all the bad and the good muddled up together like there aint no end or no beginning neither.

Like the stars stretching up in the neverending sky.

They throw me like a sack. Into the back of the truck. I can smell the truck. Hear the truck. Taste it in the dark. My hands tied tight at my back. Another body tossed in beside me.

Maybe it's Dorothy.

The truck shudder. Engine jump into life. Dad tell me about engines. But he didn't tell me about the smell. The smell of it. The smoke that come coughing out. Reckon that aint the only thing he aint told me. My dad aint been the man I think he been. But he aint been the man Patrick say.

Got to try and forget the bad things Patrick tell me. Cos everyone gone now. Just me and this body beside me. And it gonna be the bad memories that stick. Patrick been tunneling inside my head like a maggot when it get in a potato. Aint gonna see much change on the outside but inside there aint gonna be nothing left. *It only been the things inside your head that count, Willo. Aint nothing can get inside if you don't let it. You can carry the good around in your head like a ship on the sea. Carry it around in your head where no one gonna touch it.*

The truck bump along fast, lurching left and right as it goes. The body roll against me in the dark.

The body trying to talk. Spluttering like it got a mouth full of blood. Talking like talking aint easy.

"Who are you?"

"Willo Blake," I whisper.

"Willo? It's me."

"Callum!" I turn over on my bruised body.

"What did they do with Dorothy?" he say, his voice hoarse.

"They . . . She's dead."

"You know . . . for sure?"

"I seen her."

I can hear his breath in my ear. Our heads rattling together on the floor of the truck.

"You need to know something. I didn't tell you. Your father—"

"I know. Know who he is."

The truck turn hard to the right. I can feel Callum Gourty's taut body beside me.

"Where are they taking us?" I say.

"They'll kill you, Willo. . . . You're important to them. . . . You've got to—" He gurgle deep in his throat. The cough come up and I hear it. The blood spluttering out of him.

"You've got to get out. Got to—" The coughs wrack his body again. "Got to get to the boat," he whisper.

"Boat?"

"Inside my shoes there's a blade."

I got to get my face close just to hear him. Lying on the cold floor of the truck with my face close to this hurting man.

"What?"

"My shoe. There's a blade."

"But what is the boat?"

"The boat. To the Island."

"What island?"

"Away, Willo—"

"Dorothy talked," I say.

"Dorothy didn't know . . . much."

"You mean about the boat?"

"Nothing important."

"What about Jacob?"

"I don't know anyone called Jacob." The pain croak out of Callum Gourty with each mouthful of words. "Never heard of Jacob."

"Where is the boat?"

He cry out. His breath rasping deep and hard.

"The beach under Harlech Castle. They'll leave before the melt's over. Something you must do for me. Someone who's waiting for me . . . Someone very important to me. You must get to them."

"But what about you?"

"The boat, Willo. Like your father wanted."

"I aint got a clue what he wanted."

"Listen, Willo—"

I got to get nearer cos Callum been talking in tiny whispers now.

"He couldn't tell you because it was too dangerous. But the boat. It's ready. You must try and get away. And help her. Please. We need you."

"Who? Who is it?"

"My daughter. She's waiting for me. . . ."

The truck slow down. Outside I hear voices.

We come to a stop.

I can hear boots on the ground. I lie still. Footsteps at the back of the truck.

Is it gonna be now? Is it now—the end? I close my eyes.

"Two prisoners."

"Where to?"

"Wylfa camp."

"Move on."

The footsteps move away.

The truck move off.

"Callum? Callum?"

"Make sure—" The blood bubbling up inside him. I hear it. He cough. His body retching.

"Callum," I say. "My father—"

His legs scrabble against the floor of the truck. Strange high-pitched sound coming out of him. I try to pull myself upright. Try to sit. The truck take a bend in the road and I fall back.

A sigh come out from his mouth. "Get my daughter on the boat—"

"Wait!" I sit up. Shuffle around. I can feel his body behind me. Feel the rough fabric of his trouser leg. I feel down his leg with my fingers. Feel the damp blood on his knee. The hardness of his shins. I lean back. I got my hands on his feet now. I got to the laces on his shoe. Feel the knots with my swollen fingers. Got to unpick the strings. Like tying a snare in the dark.

His legs stiffen and jerk up. I pull my hands away. The breath gurgle out of him and he's limp like a rag.

It been his last moment. I hear it. In the dark. I aint never lain so close to someone dead. Like when you snuff out a candle. And the whisping smoke get in your nose. It got a bad smell the last burn of the wax.

I wonder where the last smoke of this big man gone. I can't see it or feel it.

There been a time before when I been thinking I'm gonna die. Up on the Farngod. In the cave. I got lost in that cave with no light. Lost in the dark tunnels burrowing into the mountain. And no one know where I been. And the mountain breathe so slow and quiet like it only take one breath every thousand years. And there aint no stars. No sky in that blackness. You aint never gonna know how long you been down there. Aint no point in calling out.

But I do call. I call out to the mountain. And the fear got so strong I lose myself. Just like a dead cold stone lying there alone.

And when I wake up, I still been alive and the mountain sighing and whispering to me. *I'm only a mountain. I'm only a lump of rock. It's your thoughts you been scared of.*

And the voice of the mountain and the hare and the dog and the people who been in that cave a thousand years before whispering in the dark. And then I aint been scared. And I feel it. Smell the mountain behind me and the living air before me. And I crawl out from the tunnels.

And I aint never been scared of the dark after that. Just the things in my head.

So I got to do it.

Got to get out of here. They're gonna kill me or make me talk otherwise. That's what I know in my head. I seen what they do. That picture of Dorothy—broken—hanging down in that cell. That picture burned behind my eyes.

I got to get his shoe off. Find the blade.

Got to get the shoe off this dead man I don't know. Don't know except his name.

I close my eyes. Feel the strings. Follow them. Make a picture in my head of the knot. Tease it out.

I undo it. Loosen the lace. Pull the shoe off his foot. And when I get my hand inside it's still warm. Still warm and damp. I scuffle about inside it with my fingers and pull up the sole.

Feel a hard piece of metal.

I can hardly feel my fingers. But the blade bite into the fibers of the rope. One cut. One cut at a time. Just got to be patient. Cos I don't want today to be the day when I get tossed into the blackness like a stone.

I get myself free and blow into my palms. Get the blood back, hack at the rope around my ankles. I put my face down against

Callum Gourty and feel his stubble rough against my cheek. There aint no more blood running about his veins cos I put my finger on his neck. It aint pulsing *paam paam paam*. It been strange feeling that face so close. Can't remember what it look like even.

I put the shoe back on his foot. Don't seem right to leave him with no shoes on. I push his eyelids closed in the dark like I seen Magda do before when that woman from the city got dead. "Push them closed so the dead don't take you with them."

And every second I think the truck gonna stop. Some faceless man gonna come around and drag me out. Throw me into that pit of bodies in the plantation.

My body been racing so hard it stop the pain. Stop the telling racing through my head. Just got to get out.

I got the blade between my fingers and draw it down across the canvas at the back of the truck. Like scoring leather.

The fabric scratch with every cut. I feel the air on my hand. And I start again. Scratching at the canvas. Scratch, scratch, scratch. Cutting across it.

I can see the roadside flashing past in the dark. The cold wind snatch my breath away. Under the wheels the hardpack of ice still solid and white. The wheels big and fast and the roar from the truck loud. We been among trees. Dark either side of the road.

Aint no time to let the fear shake in my legs. The truck veering to the right. I see the whiteness of a bank of snow in the black night.

And I jump.

I land in the last bit of a drift. Probably save my life cos that truck move along so fast. My body hit the snow. Crashing and tumbling on my back. Down the bank. Down onto the road. Ahead of me the truck clanking and grumbling and roaring away. But I lie still. Flat on my back on the cold ice, watching the lights disappear into the darkness.

I crawl to the bank. Get in among the trees and slump on the cold hard ground. My body feel like it been beaten by a thousand fists. Sleep calling my name. But I got to get up.

The man's shoe. Warm in my hands. Warm and damp. And the man ask me to do something before he die.

A telling beating behind my eyes.

And I got a choice.

Cos there's someone I left behind. In the city.

Mary.

Above me the great legs of a pylon straddle the road. The wires humming. I can feel them. Tingling on my skin.

The night sky been so clear and black and the stars twinkling beyond—all those thousands of miles away. Far off.

You. Son of the great John Blovyn. Running about the hills like a wild dog. He never loved you, Willo.

Patrick's words squirming in my head.

He never loved you, Willo.

• • •

The ditch is frozen. Filled with snow. Bare thorny branches rearing up over it. I can smell fox.

I don't know how far I come after I jump from the truck. But I got myself back from the road. Into the trees.

There aint nothing to cover my tracks. No new snow. The melt coming good and strong. And I know they're gonna come soon.

I fight through the trees til my body scream out for rest.

It aint sleep come to me though lying in the ditch. Just dreams that been so real they aint dreams. I can feel them. I can hear them and taste them.

I got myself back in that tree with Magda and Dad gathering acorns down below. And I been shouting down to them. "The wolves! The wolves are coming, Dad!" I see them all about under the trees. "Get up!" I shout. "Get up!"

And the wolves come creeping and growling all around with their low-slung heads and sharp teeth and slathering drool. But Dad aint seen them. Magda putting acorns into her bag. "They're coming! Get up!" I shout so loud, but I can't hear my voice however hard I try.

Everything fading but the snarling snapping jaws. Then I can't see Dad no more. And I can't see Magda. Just hear her screaming out.

And I got to jump down and help them.

A bird call out a warning.

Whit, whit, whit, whit!

I got to help them. "Dad!"

I sit up like a shot.

• • •

It only been my dream.

The sky grown light. A blackbird flit off in fright above me in the branches of the hedge.

Whit, whit, whit!

• • •

I crawl out and look over the field. Across the hill patches of ice lie on the ground in heaps. The grass flat and dark in little islands where it start to thaw.

Every bit of my body aching. The damp cold biting. Teeth chattering like they never gonna stop.

Down below the pylons march off to the west.

But I'm still alive.

Over across the fields, high up behind a copse of oak I see the broken roof of an old building.

I get up by the hedge. Duck along beside it. Run along the ditch, across the fields to a stand of trees. I fall down in a patch of grass. I tear it up and stuff it in my mouth like a sick dog.

It feel better in the trees. They're good trees. Big strong oaks, bare branches spreading up. Ash and sycamore growing tall. Good smell of the earth coming out from the ground. The woods run down over the other side of the rise to the fields and hedges spreading out to the east.

From the edge of the woods a low stone wall snake off across the fields to the house. The low morning light cast long shadows from the trees. I can see the house good now. Made of big stones dug up from the hill and placed one on top of another, proper square around the windows just like home. But the roof fallen in one end. Elder and ash growing right up inside it. Windows boarded and dead. Great pile of snow almost reach the eaves at the back. A broken-down barn and low shed run along two sides making a yard. Maybe find something to eat down there. Somewhere to hide up a while.

A flash of brown from the shed catch my eye. It's only a small she-fox running toward the hillside. But what's she running from?

I see them then. Far off like specks in the distance. Coming out of the trees down below. Men with dogs. The dogs straining on ropes, noses to the ground. They got my scent.

They're coming for me.

Now I got to run. Run like I aint never run before. Stumble along the wall. Back through the trees. Up above the house.

I come out of the woods to the south. A small brook running down the hillside above me. Meltwater coursing over the black rocks. I jump in. Follow it upstream. Got to lose my scent. The water is cold as ice. Soaks through my boots. Freezes my toes so they burn with pain.

But I got to keep running. Running for my life like a hare cos the dogs and men gonna come up the hill soon. Higher up I fall down in the tussocky grass. Just fall on the ground beside the water. Drink like an animal. Breath heaving out of me. My legs hurting. My back hurting. Everything hurting. But the wind carry the sound of the dogs. High-pitched baying as they pick up my trail and the fear jump up in my chest.

I pull myself off the ground. Dripping and freezing. Up away from the stream. Up toward the moors.

The heather is tall as my thighs. Thick like a hedge. I pick up a deer track weaving among it. I got to get higher still. Where I can see. Onto the flats where the bald rocks push up out of the ground. Where the cold dead rock been worn by the wind and the snow and the ice and the rain, pushing up out of the ground saying, *This is what I am, boy, cold dead rock mighty beneath your feet. Make no mistake.*

That's where I got to get to.

· · ·

Why do they want me? Why aint my dad told me who he been? The way people talk about him make him sound like he been Robin Hood.

But he aint. He been my dad.

And he aint never told me about no boat. Or where it's going. Or none of that stuff.

And he aint here to answer me now.

I push on until the heather get thin, then I crouch down inside it, breathing hard.

I look back down the hill.

I can hear the dogs again. Their baying scare me right down in my guts.

I look up the hillside. The crusting snow lying thin on the ground above the heather. I got to get up somewhere I can see.

There's a rocky crag on the western shoulder of the rise. In one hard run I been up there. On the edge of the hill. The slopes falling steep below me.

The wind buffeting against my face.

And I can see. Far off across the pale misting of the Afon Eden Valley I see it all.

It grab my heart with both hands.

Trawsfinnid Lake—the flat waters catching the sky like a mirror. The dark green of the plantation around the northern shore so far away it look like moss spreading out onto the plain. And rising like giants. Fach and Fawr. The Rhinog Peaks white with snow. Mountains rolling off behind them to the south. To the north the

Farngod crouching bald and bare. All of it rising up gray and purple and mighty and magnificent across the plain, the sky big and blue all about and the banks of clouds playing great shadows across the earth.

I see it all from up here. My home. And over the mountains, the sea.

But down below, the road running back to the city.

• • •

I scramble down the slope. The wind bite my ears and the thin snow is cold underfoot. Further down I can see the green and brown of the heather.

I hear the dogs again. They still got my scent. Slathering dogs and big faceless men coming fast.

I got to find a track. Get myself thick inside the scrub. My feet fall down the hillside. I look up to the top of the hill. Dark shapes on the snowline moving among the rocks.

I gain cover under some scrubby hawthorn. Little spring running down in among them. The men with dogs picking up my scent on the hillside. I can hear them.

I thrash through the trees, splashing in the waters. Down to the flats of the Afon Eden Valley, thankful for the firm grass springing up fresh and strong under my wet boots.

The sun come up strong now. It's a good warm sun. The stone chats and blackbirds twitter in the bushes. Insects come alive in the long grasses, hovering over the damp ground.

An old stone wall worm its way west, disappearing behind overgrown hedgerows.

And then I feel a shudder in the earth. A great noise coming up under my feet.

The noise grow louder. Thundering on the ground. A pair of gray heron flap their wide wings into the air from the slow waters winding across the plain. There's a beating like a thousand feet stamping in the valley. The thuddering shuddering sound building like a quake from the north.

My legs feel like blocks of stone. Hurting hurting hurting. The dogs howl. They still got a strong smell of me. I scramble down to the flats. Toward the wall of noise and the earth shaking like some terrible storm coming hard across the valley.

Along the wall. Into the bushes. I look through the twisted trunks of the scrub onto the grassland.

A horse gallop past. Then another.

Great herd of horses galloping onto the pastures of the Afon Eden. Like the pictures in the cave. The plain alive with animals. Ponymen bringing their herds from the city to graze the rich melt pastures of the valley.

"Heeyup!"

A rider skirting the herd, his sheepskin saddle hanging with bags, his bedding rolled up behind him. He's standing in the stirrups, ponyskin coat flapping in the wind, one arm in the air cracking a leather whip, concentration on his dark weathered face.

"Heeyup! Heeyup!"

The calling of the horsemen ringing out over the plain, the sound of hooves beating the earth.

In front of me a small group of ponies break free into the

clearing and drop their noses to the ground, tearing at the grass, drinking from the stream.

I get up and come in among them. They start up. Eyes wide. Their bodies rising and falling with the run. The sweat foaming and white on their necks. I can smell them. Good smell of pony.

I push ahead to a stand of hawthorn. Crouch down. Ponymen still wheeling and shouting and cracking their whips. And the horses fly past, mud spraying from their hooves, mud coated on their flanks. Thousands of horses and the young foals galloping across the valley, and that stamping, sweating-smelling herd of animals gonna be just what I need.

Gonna cover my tracks and hide my scent for sure.

35

The moon is full. Glancing icy on the rocks. The good warm day turn into a frosty night with that big clear sky up above. Down below I can see the light of a fire.

I can smell meat roasting on it.

A group of ponymen got their camp set up beside an old stone shed sitting lonesome in a stand of trees. All about the plain the horses and cattle from the city make a gentle bellowing and whinnying in the dark.

I been lying up in the rocks since I cross the valley. Run right in with the animals—limping from hedge to ditch—right to the foothills of the Rhinogs. Too washed out to think. The herd trampling my tracks, masking my scent. I aint heard no more dogs then and rest up a bit.

The smell of cooking food drift up from the fire. I been so hungry and deadbeat it aint true. My body don't want to go no more. I been so stiff that even breathing hurts. And the night frost aint helping much.

. . .

I been on this side of the Rhinogs with my dad and Magda once. He take us down the mountain to show us the valley and hunt for eggs. I been pretty small then. It been summer. A cold summer. We still got the pony. I ride on it clinging around Alice all the way. Dad leading the pony by the head. "Look at that, children," he say, pointing out at the Afon Eden. "One day it will be green and warm and the sun will shine all summer long. Remember that. One day we'll be able to come off the mountain and have a farm down there."

"Don't fill their heads with dreams, Robin," Magda say.

"They're not dreams. They're hopes—"

But I get down off the pony when he been talking cos I see a nest in the heather. A grouse whir up as I come close. It glide across the moorland scrieking.

"Dad, look! Eggs!" Alice shout from the pony.

It been a good nestful.

• • •

But Dad aint here now. If he been standing next to me he gonna be good and pleased seeing all those horses grazing down on the plain so early in the year and the grass so green already. He gonna talk on it til it bore you half to death I reckon.

But now all I got in my head is getting across the mountain safe. Getting to the boat that people been talking on so keen. The boat my dad aint told me about. Seem to me like the mountain just the same as it always been. It's me who's different. And change coming. I seen it up close. I seen the dirt and the smoke and the trucks and the fear of it. Dad just been sitting up on the mountain like that bird on its nest all these years. Aint seen things coming til they been right on top of him.

And everyone thinking he been some sort of Robin Hood with

his book. Patrick talking about the people who all got Dad's book. People looking west not east. People plotting and planning.

Plotting and planning what? Dad aint never told me about no plotting and planning. He just show me how to tie snares and plant oats and give me lessons about everything. And all the time I been thinking these mountains been my home.

Maybe Dad did know. He musta known. Musta known about the boat. He musta known he been in trouble if the government find him cos he change his name and hide up on the hill. It start to make a kind of sense in my head. The Meet with all the graybeards quiet and serious every summer at Barmuth. The way he always talk like he been preparing you for something. Always talking about how things gonna change. How the snow gonna melt and everything gonna go back like it was before.

But why is he gonna want to sail away on some boat if the snow gonna melt? Where's that boat gonna sail anyway?

Patrick say everyone looking west when they should be looking east. But west is just that great big sea. Dad draw me a map once. Big sea and he draw whales spouting water and squirly lines to show the waves. Thinking on that big empty sea make me want to plant my feet deep down in the earth, it really do.

• • •

I watch the woman and children come slow across the plain. They got their ponies loaded up with pots and pans and canvas tents and all the children squished up or slung on their backs. Peeling off in small groups—they must know the places where their man camp cos they find them bit by bit. Little fires start burning across the valley. The ponymen slump by the fire. Their hard ride over for the day.

Down in the camp I watch the woman unsaddle the ponies and rub their sweaty flanks with twists of grass. Laying blankets over their backs to keep off with the cold night air. Their ragged kids sit on the ground squabbling and playing with sticks.

I see it all from the rocks. And no one following me yet.

Mary's dad been a ponyman. That's what she tell me. Guess he just got the idea one day to head off into the hills at the end of the summer 'stead of back to the tents of the shanties. It seem like Mary been a thousand miles away though. It seem like everything I ever know been trailing so far behind me I can't see it no more. Like I just been cut loose from it all somehow. And the pain and the fear and the hunger filling up my head with their noises. Aint no room for much else.

I got to eat. I want to sit among people. Hear their talk. Feel the warmth of a good fire.

I guess I been creeping down the bank with it all cos I lose my footing on the scree. Tumble and slide on the icy rocks. The loose stones roll and bounce down the hillside.

"Da! Da! Dogs!" a kid shout out.

The men jump up around the fire. A woman shriek.

"I aint a dog." I shout it out. Lie still on the ground. My body hurting. "Aint a dog."

Dark-haired man with a gun cocked at his side come up the slope toward me.

"Da. Da. Is it a stealer?"

The bearded ponyman peer down at me.

"I lost my way. Can't find my camp," I say.

"Lost your camp?"

"I been looking for eggs. With my sister. Up on the hill. And now it's dark I can't find my way. I aint a stealer."

A stout woman come forward with a child on her hip. "It's just a boy, for heaven's sake. Not a stealer. He's hurt himself. Look at his face all black and blue. You'd better come and lie with us tonight, child. You'll freeze out here otherwise. Get him a blanket, Huw, and put that gun down."

"Is it a stealer, Ma?"

"No it isn't. Just a boy. Now pipe down and fetch a blanket."

The woman come to me. Help me down to the fire. She put a good hunk of hot roasted meat in my hands.

"Eat if you're hungry," she say.

The meat taste good. The children sit back staring and whispering with open mouths.

I see the men looking at me in the flickering light of the fire.

"Pretty big bird you had to fight off the nest by the look of it." It's the man with the gun. "Where's your sister then?"

"I . . . she run off before me. I—"

"Hungry, aint you? Good coat you got there too. Straggler work by the looks of it. Find that up on the mountain?"

"Let him be, Huw."

I stop tearing at the meat. Men staring at me around the fire.

"Don't worry. You're all right here, boyo," the man say. "Just don't steal anything and be gone by the morning. Better get back and find your sister, eh?" He throw the remains of his drink on the fire. The logs hiss. "No trouble. That's all." He put his gun across his knees. He gesture over the fire to the children. "Get the boy a drink, Talf."

A dirty-faced boy come over and hand me a cup of grog. I can smell it strong and bitter.

"Drink that and you'll sleep quiet. No trouble, look you."

I nod. Mouth full with hot food. I tip back the cup.

• • •

I musta fallen asleep right off with the grog cos when the cold dawn scrabble at my back, I see my boots upturned on sticks by the embers of the fire. Mud cleaned off and a bundle of food tied up beside them. I sit up. All around the whisping fire, the men snore in their blankets. The women and children too, huddled up close under the rugs. A little girl open her eyes, smile sleepily, turn back to her mother. Their hobbled ponies stand about with heads hung low. I look back behind me up the slopes of the Rhinogs.

A bearded ponyman keeping silent lookout sitting up on a rock with a gun in his hands.

I put on my boots. Good and warm and dry. I pick up the bundle of food. The man beckon me up.

I clamber up the shale where he been sitting.

"I saw soldiers and dogs sniffing up the valley in the night, boyo," he say. "I'd get back up into the mountains if I was you." He pass me a leather water sack. "Keep it. You'll need it."

He point up to the flat pass between the peaks.

"That's the best way. Up the pack trail, the old Roman Steps.

Hope you find what you're looking for, straggler boy." He pick at his teeth with a stick. "Better get a move on though. They'll be back."

• • •

I make my way slow from the camp up into the pass. Away from the fires smoking across the plain. The sun coming up clear and strong again this morning. A mist hovering low over the wet grassland. The animals like dots on the patchwork green of the valley.

It feel good to have that parcel of food and water pouch over my shoulder. But I can smell the mountain now. The mountain calling me.

I pick my way up through the low heather and damp bracken. The pass lead to the old pack trail. Broken slabs of stone winding up the mountain like an ancient staircase. Leading down to the lake at Cym Bachan on the western side. From there I'm gonna pick up the gullies and woods tumbling to the sea.

A buzzard wheel overhead in the wind. I look up. The great crags towering to my left. Heaps of unmelted snow in the cold shadows. I rest a while by the side of the pathway. Take a drink of water. Wriggle my toes in my good dry boots. Thinking on it all I guess.

On the ground I see a hoofprint. I glance up the pass. Look like more than one horse. Tracks tumbled together. Heading up into the hills. But there aint no pastures up there.

One thing I aint seen is small hoofprints. Aint no foals with these horses. Must be men on horseback. Men coming up the mountain on horses. Ponymen maybe. What they gonna be doing up here?

I follow the hoof marks. The tracks lead to the start of the old stone steps, falling in the mud here and there either side of the path. The steps ford a running stream, a small stone bridge arching over it. Lonely thorn tree growing up gnarled and windswept on the other side. Seem like old-time people always getting busy building things, even up here on the Rhinogs.

I follow the tracks. A mean wind cut over the flat icy stones. The higher I go, the colder it get. Thin drifts of snow still lying on the ground. The melt never come to the top of the mountains.

It's always winter up here.

· · ·

It been a long cold walk up into the hills. I lose the hoof marks in the bracken and heather. They just disappear. Reckon I musta got myself over the pass by now though.

I stand up on a crag of rocks. I can see the waters of Cym Bachan still below me. Just a thin layer of soft-looking ice on the surface.

It's all down now. Down down. Far below, far off, is the sea. The Barmuth estuary away off south and the abandoned houses of Harlech to the north. Only that big old castle standing over the beach like a squat toad at the water's edge. That's where I got to get to.

I aint seen no horses yet. But it don't feel bad being up here with the wind and the rock and the mountain roundside about. Feel like the good clean mountain gonna wash me clean if I let it. It's just I aint too keen on being all alone and Number One no more. Time like this you're gonna want to say your words. Time like this the words start singing to you. Even if the bad been swirling like a whirlpool trying to suck you under.

I get down off the rocks. At the far end of the waters the trees grow thick in the gully at the head of the dam.

Down at the water's edge, I wash my face. Fill the water pouch. Everything feel tired and beaten. I pull up my coat and see the blackblue bruises seep across my ribs. Wish I been close to my place on the Farngod. Gonna crawl up in the tunnels and light a candle up there. Say my words. Hear the spirit of the mountain. Rest a bit.

Cos there been a great big bank of black clouds gathering inside me. All the things that happen. Dad and Magda and Mary and the twins. Dorothy swinging in that room. The storm inside those black clouds gonna break like a fury if I let it.

I pick up the water sack and make my way toward the shaded gully. It aint my spirit putting one foot in front of the other. Aint no dog telling me what to do. Just a great big emptiness that drive me on.

I clamber down the boulders at the mouth of the lake. The river a trickle below, seeping out from the frozen stones.

It's gloomy under the mossy trees. But the weak sun that shine through the branches play on the banks of frosted ferns and catch the wet black rocks of the riverbed. Time been I woulda seen something magic in it all.

But a feeling of panic grab at my throat like a stealer in the night. What am I gonna do if the boat been gone before I get to the sea? What am I gonna do then?

The still bare branches arch up over the riverbed. The drip of the melt starting good and proper. Little yellow holes in the few patches of snow where the water been dripping down like rain on the forest floor.

A dipper swoop low along the water and land on a rock, bobbing, his tail flashing. He see me and whir and dip down the river in fright. I slide down the bank on the soggy brown leaves and patches of snow. Down to the water's edge, where I can pick along the riverbed at the bottom of the gully.

I see it then. A movement under the shadows of the branches. Far up ahead. A pony and rider.

Hand on the pony's rump, the rider look about a bit, nudge the pony on. They disappear round a bend in the riverbed.

I get back up the bank. Follow them quiet. My heart thump hard as I climb the steep bank and scrabble along the top of the ridge.

I stop. Breathing fast. Catch a movement down in the gully again. Stout gray pony slipping between the trees. But they're alone. The rider hunched over ducking under branches.

I stumble above them quiet as I can. Up ahead the trees thin out. I can see the rider is a girl. Something in the way she sit. In the way she look about. I see hair coming out from underneath her hood. She dig her heels in and the pony trot up through the patchy snow and come into a clearing by a small pool.

My heart beat faster.

She's looking back through the trees. Wiping a hand across her face. Fiddling with the packs hanging at the pony's neck.

I creep closer. A twig snap underfoot. The pony hear me. Its ears prick forward. The girl sit up. Look about. I been close enough to call out.

"Hello."

Girl start up scared. The pale oval of a face under the hood turn in my direction.

"Who is it? Where are you?" She gather the reins in her hands.

I slip down the bank. Through the trees. Toward the clearing.

"Who's there?" She got fear in her voice. "Who are you?"

That good little pony stomp on the ground.

"I can't see you. Is it you, Da? Who is it?"

I can see *her* face good and clear though.

I pull down my hood. Step out of the trees.

The whole world and everything in it shining in the weak sun like it just been born.

"Mary," I say. "Mary. It's me."

36

Mary slide off the pony. Mary coming to me.

"Willo?" she say, eyes wide.

Mary putting her good warm hand up to my face.

"I didn't think I'd see you again, Willo."

But Mary pull her hand away then. Her eyes get dark. "You left me. Why did you go without telling me?"

"I'm sorry."

"I thought you were my friend."

"I am. Mary. Please."

"So why did you go?"

"It's a long story but you. You got out of the settlement?"

"I left with the others."

"Others? Why?"

"The boat. We're going to the boat. I'm waiting. Waiting for Da."

"Your dad?"

"Da's going to come. He promised."

"Your dad's dead, Mary. Remember? He been dead up on the mountain. He aint coming back."

"No he's not. He's alive. He didn't die—he made it back."

"He come back?"

"Yes. That day when he went out to look for food, he got

caught in a blizzard and lost his way. When you found me in the house on the mountain."

She step up quiet. "I never thought I'd see you again, Willo."

A hot wind blow in my head. We been standing close. Mary holding the reins of her pony.

"When he came back to that little house all he found was Tommy. Dogs had got him. He thought the dogs had got me too. So he made his way back to the settlement."

"How did you get by?"

"I stayed wi' Piper for a while. I waited for you. But I thought you'd gone forever. Then Vince gave me work at the beerhouse. Enough to get by on. Somewhere to stay. That's how I found Da again. He knew everything. When the boat was going. All that. And he got the pony and I came up wi' the ponymen. To the pastures. Da was supposed to meet me. But I know he'll come. He promised...."

"Where do you think he been now?"

"I don't know. He had to go back to the city. To get someone."

"Who?"

"John Blovyn's son. He had to get Blovyn's son."

• • •

"*—the boat. It's ready. You must try and get away. And help her. Please. My daughter. She's waiting for me....*"

• • •

I think Mary see something in my face then. Cos a look pass across her mouth like the shadow of those clouds growing in my head.

"Callum Gourty?"

"Yes. Callum Gourty. How do you know, Willo?"

Time stand still in that shady clearing by the pool. It got to be me telling her. That man been Mary's dad. He aint been no stealer. She tell me that up on the Farngod. But I aint been listening then.

"He's dead, Mary."

"No, Willo, he isn't dead he's alive, he..." The shadow rest on her face good and proper now.

"Callum Gourty. Your dad. He aint coming."

She turn away from me. Walk to the edge of the water. Her hands to her face. I see it and look away. The pony drop its head, snuffling in the leaves.

"How do you know?" Her words are quiet like the murmur of the water.

"Mary." I step toward her. "He told me to find you—"

"How do you know?" She look at me. Her eyes red.

"I—"

"How do you know, Willo!"

I go to her.

"I'm sorry. I am." I put out my hand. "Believe me, we aint got time for talking, Mary. There aint much time." She aint hearing me though. "We got to hurry, Mary."

"How do you know he's dead?" Mary swaying like a sapling.

"Your dad come for *me*. I aint got a clue he been your dad. Not til now."

"On the mountain?"

"No, Mary. In the city."

"Why?"

"He come to find me and then we got taken. They gonna come looking for us too. We got to get to the boat. We got to go."

The clouds break. Mary got that storm inside her now. Look like the rain coming down like an ocean. She fall down on the wet rocks. Great sobs and calling out for her dad. I pull her up.

"Who took him? Willo! What happened? I can't go without him. I—"

"I aint got a clue why it happen, Mary." I get her up, hold her tight. "So many things aint no one told me all my life—"

"But why you?"

"Because . . . I—"

"Because what?"

"Because of my dad, Mary. He's dead too. My dad's dead too. It's just you and me."

"But why did Da go back for *you*, Willo?"

"My dad be John Blovyn, Mary. That's why he came for me. Aint my fault."

Through her wet eyes she look into my face. "John Blovyn? You? You're his son?"

"Yes."

"But *you*?"

• • •

"I can see why your father was so disappointed in you, Willo. You. Son of the great John Blovyn. Running about the hills like a wild dog. His simpleton son."

• • •

"Now aint the time for talking on it, Mary. We got to go. Get to the boat before it's too late."

"I can't, Willo—not without Da."

"You got me."

There's so much I want to say but talking don't help when you been swallowed up in grief. We got to keep going. It aint over yet. When the weather turn, you just got to bury yourself in your collar and bend with the wind.

I get her up on the saddle. Lead the pony on, snorting as it pick its way along the rocky riverbed. There's a kind of rhythm to it lost inside our dark clouds.

The pony feel warm. It's a good little pony. Strong and keen. Its wiry mane long and thick, falling over its neck this way and that. Mary got her hands buried in it. And Mary feel warm too. My arm holding her up.

• • •

You're on your own now, Willo.

• • •

I look quick behind us. Aint nothing there.

But the dog telling me I got to be Number One.

For Mary.

"We got to hurry. What we gonna do if the boat go without us." I say it quiet. "We got our whole lives for crying. But that boat aint gonna wait for two kids no one know about."

Mary pull the pony up.

"I don't want to go on, Willo. There's nothing left."

"But, Mary, you got to. What you gonna do? Lie down under these trees? It aint gonna go away."

She start crying again in great sobs. I get her down off the saddle.

281

She's like a bird fallen from the nest. I remember her thin frozen body when I get her warm in that broken wincone on the mountain. Her hands tight round my neck when I carry her up through the snow. It been a miracle she aint died right then. But she's strong under her skin. I know it.

"Mary. You aint the sort to just lie down and give up. We got to get to the boat. Wherever it's gonna take us."

I can't bear to see her face so wet and broken.

"Far away," she say, her eyes all distant. "The Island. The boat's going to take us somewhere far away. Somewhere safe. Away from here. That's what Da said. He said it was going to be a new beginning. New everything—"

"Yes, it's what your da wanted Mary. He wanted you to get on the boat. He told me."

"He said that to you?"

"He was right Mary. Aint nothing much left here for us, is there?"

"No."

That picture of Dorothy burning in my head. Patrick. His foot against my face. The things he say. The things he done. To my dad. And Magda. All of them gone.

I feel her close then. Our bodies together. The pony standing quiet beside us.

"I aint never thought people gonna be so bad, Willo."

"They aint all bad."

"I know. But it's hard to forget." She put her face in my neck. "Why do they want to hurt us?"

"They don't like people like us because they got scared. Scared we're gonna make it. That's why we got to go."

She's still crying soft in my ear. Arms all around me. The trees around look sharp like I never seen them before. The world is under those trees with the water running gentle and Mary in my arms.

"I been thinking about you all the time, Mary . . . thinking about taking you to the house on the mountain—"

"So why did you leave me? . . . I don't understand."

"I don't know. Dog got up inside me. He come down from the hills. Calling me. And then it been too late. I know I got to come back to you, but it been too late. Things happen. I got stuck in the city. But I aint stopped thinking on you. I—"

The pony shy up in fright.

Rocks on the riverbed tumble in the shallow water.

"What's that sound, Willo?"

The water lap at our feet. The horse whinny.

Strange sound coming down the gorge.

"Quick! Mary! Get up the bank."

"Willo! What is it?"

The sound get louder, the ground shaking. And I know what's coming. Can't believe I been so stupid.

"The meltwaters, Mary!"

The pony break free and leap up the bank.

Water rush across the rocks. And that sound. Like a monstrous beast. Coming from behind the bend in the river.

"Mary!"

I grab her hand. Pull her. Pull her toward the higher ground. Scramble up grabbing at branches. The rumbling booming meltwater breaking down from the lake.

Mary slip on the wet leaves, hanging on to me with her hand, grabbing at a tree trunk. I cry out but my voice get lost in the roar of the wave. A great wall of water from the lake above. Rumbling and thundering and filling the gorge. Swelling and crashing through the trees. Aint nothing gonna stop it. Nothing gonna get in its way.

I see it now and it take my breath away. Crashing and pummeling and grinding, a mountain of water. Towering over the riverbed. Filled with rocks and ice—crashing down the gully, engulfing the trees, uprooting them from the ground. Splitting them like matches. Washing down the gorge like an almighty storm. Scouring the banks. I can feel the mist of it spraying on my face. Ripping and roaring and unstoppable.

"Willo!" Mary mouth a scream.

I haul her up with all my strength. Pull her up the slope. The pony scream out. Stamping beside me. Nostrils flared. I grab the loose stirrup hanging at its side. Just in time as the icy waters of Cym Bachan shudder against the banks. Crashing just below us.

The pony drag us up neighing and foaming. We been breathless on the wet ground. A huge tree swirling in the waters below our feet. Thudding against the bank. Huge tree ripped from the ground like a stick. The waters muddy and icy and angry emptying themselves into the valley.

I should have known. I should have known not to be down on the riverbed this time of year. When the melt come you aint gonna stand in its way.

We lie on the bank breathing hard.

And a laugh like a storm got up inside me good and proper. The black clouds break open. I can feel the rains come. It come up from deep inside. I been laughing in great bursts with tears in my eyes. Lying safe on the bank with Mary at my side. All the fear and the hurt and the pain and the joy just bursting out of me in that laugh. From deep in my guts. Laugh ringing out above the sound of the swirling waters below us. Everything flood out in that laugh.

"What? What, Willo?"

I say nothing just turn to face her. Put my hand up to that good pale face. Then I see the hare. Running from the river.

"Shh! Look. Over there."

I grab Mary's hand. Like it been the most natural thing in the world. "There! The hare."

Big brown hare racing into the bare hawthorn. Young leveret at its side.

"Come on, Mary." I crouch down. "Look. The leveret."

The hares disappear under a hedge. We get down and crawl through the bushes. Push out from under the branches into the light.

And we been up on a high flat rock looking across the flats down to the sea.

"Look, Willo!"

It all stretch away as far as the eye can see. The sky wrapping around us. The horizon bending around all about. Bending *"cos the earth is round, Willo."* And you can see it from up here. The great wholeness of it and the sky clear and the thin wispy clouds floating on the edge of the world. The great wide world. My world.

"There! On the beach. Look!" she cry.

I can just make it out. The telltale wisps of smoke from camp-fires. And people. Huddled in groups on the shore. Out across the sea in the glimmering light, boats sitting on the waters of the bay. I can see their wide sails flapping in the wind. Like silver wings. Dinghies pulled onto the sand.

"Willo. The boats."

She's talking all quiet.

She still got her hand in mine. Sweet and soft and warm.

"We're not too late," she say.

But that fire blow hot in my head. Blowing with the smell of the coming spring. I hear the voices. Maybe the dog come down off the mountain for me after all. The voices ripping and tugging and tumbling inside me.

I turn to her. The sun catching on the heathery peaks behind us. Soft greens and russet on the hillside. The sound of the swirling water filling the river on the other side of the trees. And Mary. Lying right beside me.

"Come on. We can make it, Willo. The boat. We've got to get down there!"

I roll onto my back. The sun on my face.

"Willo! Come on."

Yes, soon the russet heather gonna be humming with insects. The grass gonna be tall and soft and sweet. Dogs gonna be bringing pups out of the ground. Birds laying eggs in the bracken. Time to turn over the ground and plant a few oats for the winter. Time to wash the soot out of blankets and beat the rugs. Time to mend the roof. Let the goats out of the barn. Smell the earth under the snow.

"Willo?"

"Look, Mary. The whole world. It's right here."

"We've got to get down there, Willo. Before they leave."

"Is it gonna be better than this Mary? Wherever it is that boat's gonna go?"

"I don't understand. It's the boat that's going to take us away. To the Island. New beginning and everything. Somewhere safe."

"But don't you see? It's all here. This is where we belong. In the trees and the mountains. Across the valleys. In this great big sky all about. The ice is only frozen water Mary. Got to shout it out loud and clear. This is the Island. You. Me. This place. The Island is right here. *In us.* I see it now. Cos you can carry the good around in your head. Like that ship on the sea. Aint nothing gonna touch the things in your head if you don't let them. I know it."

Mary look across the bay. She's close, so close I can feel her breathing. Her hand still in mine. "I don't know what you mean."

"Maybe what's on that boat aint gonna be any different in the end. If we get on that boat it's the same as if they killed us. They won then."

There's a big silence between us. Just the sound of the wind in the sky and the trees moving. But those things aint shouting now. Just rustling soft.

"We could go south," she say in a whisper.

I turn and look at her. Wipe the hair from her damp forehead.

I can feel the fear. But it's strong. Good and strong inside us like the sun cracking through the stormclouds blowing in my head. Nothing aint certain but the new day ahead.

"Yes, Mary. You see? We got the pony. We can go south. Find a house down there. Plant some oats. Cut some wood. Start fresh. Got to be beacons of hope. If it aint us, who's it gonna be?"

It's in that moment. Just looking out at the world all about. Saying and believing.

"And you won't leave me?"

I look into her eyes.

"No, Mary. No. I won't."

She pull back and look at me.

"You promise?"

The wind blow inside me. The voices Tell.

• • •

"Heed your own spirit, Willo. Optimism! We must all share it. Around the fire. When we Meet. When we Tell. We must pass this gift to our children."

• • •

"Yes, Mary," I tell her, "I promise."

• • •

And it been my voice. It always been my voice. Not the hare. Not the dog. Not Dad. Not anyone. Just me.

Thanks and Acknowledgments

Timothy Shepard, Julia Churchill, Emma Young, Gordon Stevens, Daniel Crockett, Tony Lawrence, Claude and Therese Mesmin, Michelle and Francis Domps, and Debi Squirrell.

Et enfin (but not least) Louise Bacou.

Thank you all.

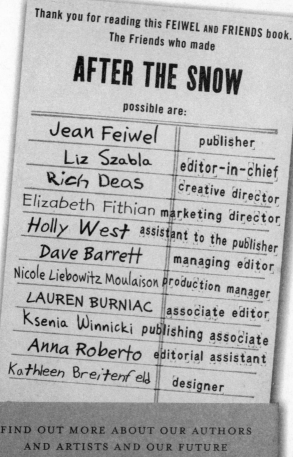

Thank you for reading this FEIWEL AND FRIENDS book.
The Friends who made

AFTER THE SNOW

possible are:

Jean Feiwel	publisher
Liz Szabla	editor-in-chief
Rich Deas	creative director
Elizabeth Fithian	marketing director
Holly West	assistant to the publisher
Dave Barrett	managing editor
Nicole Liebowitz Moulaison	production manager
LAUREN BURNIAC	associate editor
Ksenia Winnicki	publishing associate
Anna Roberto	editorial assistant
Kathleen Breitenfeld	designer

FIND OUT MORE ABOUT OUR AUTHORS
AND ARTISTS AND OUR FUTURE
PUBLISHING AT
MACTEENBOOKS.COM.

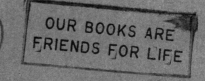

OUR BOOKS ARE
FRIENDS FOR LIFE